I ate up most of the trip thinking about all the dirty little secrets people spend their lives hiding. Years earlier, when I was a cop, a Frenchman came into the precinct and admitted to poisoning his wife thirty years earlier. He couldn't stand it anymore.

Dirty little secrets . . . Me, I was already worried I'd get knocked unconscious in a car wreck and somebody'd find the photo of the naked kid on me. That was why I'd shown it to Kathy. I had a witness that *this* dirty little secret belonged to somebody else. . . .

EARL W. EMERSON
Winner of The Private Eye Writers of America
Shamus Award

FAT TUESDAY

Earl W. Emerson

BALLANTINE BOOKS · NEW YORK

Copyright © 1987 by Earl W. Emerson
Excerpt from *The Million-Dollar Tattoo* copyright © 1996 by Earl W. Emerson

http://www.randomhouse.com

Library of Congress Catalog Card Number: 86-23468

ISBN 0-345-35223-8

This edition published by arrangement with William Morrow and Company, Inc.

Printed in Canada

First Ballantine Books Edition: July 1988

To SANDY,
with love

I believe a man is as big as what will make him mad.
—Line delivered by Robert Ryan in
Bad Day at Black Rock

"So long, guy," he said gently. "You were a louse—
but you sure had music in you."
—Raymond Chandler, *The King in Yellow*

I WAS TRAPPED IN A HOUSE WITH A LAWYER, a bare-breasted woman, and a dead man. The rattlesnake in the paper sack only complicated matters.

It started early that morning, when the grinning lawyer, Kathy Birchfield, skulked into my house and dumped me out of bed, cackling and waggling the dead pit viper in front of me until it did S's in the air. "A case, Cisco. A case. Maybe you can get enough money to resole your shoes, eh!"

"Oh, Pancho," I groaned. But a rattlesnake carcass swinging in my face was just intriguing enough to hook me. I called her bluff and told her I'd take it—maybe. Easily the prettiest attorney in Seattle, she was my best friend, male or female, and could bamboozle me into scaling Rainier on stilts.

For several years Fred Pugsley had been a client of the firm where Kathy worked, though Birchfield had been assigned to him only two days earlier, after Fred had burst into the offices toting a shoe box that concealed a dead rattlesnake. Cursing, he announced angrily that he wanted to know who had mailed it so he could sue their pants off. Kathy got the assignment partially because the stodgy partners thought Fred was a

1

pain in the behind and partially because it was going to involve working with a detective. At Leech, Bemis, and Ott detectives were déclassé.

As we drove to the Pugsley home that Wednesday morning, Kathy said, "Fred's cantankerous. I'm the only one in the office he hasn't totally alienated, and I think that's because he wants to date me."

"Funny. You're the only one in the office I haven't totally alienated. Date? I thought you said he was married."

"Married? Not to worry. Fred's what I would call a man's man. About a year ago the firm paid off the parents of a girl who was fifteen. Fred knocked her up."

"Sounds like he's a pig."

"I'm glad you said it."

"You were thinking it so hard I could hear the words."

"He works for Micro Darlings."

"The Micro Darlings?" Every stockbroker in the country had gone scrambling last spring when they'd hinted their stock might go public. "They get an article splashed across the front page of the *Wall Street Journal* about once a month."

"To hear him tell it, Fred was one of the founders. You'll find him interesting."

"Don't you think it's time to tell me where that snake came from?"

"Four dwarfs delivered it to his door."

"Damn it, Kathy. You want me on this case or not?"

"Somebody mailed it to him. At least that's what he told me. A handwritten note said, 'Watch it, Freddie.' "

"He have any idea who?"

"Said he did, but he was so belligerent the other day at the office we couldn't get it out of him. He'd been boozing. Was standing on his lips."

"I got a snake in the mail, I might take a drink, too."

"You don't drink, buster."

"Got a snake in the mail, I might start. Sounds as if somebody were trying to tell him something."

"He got it Saturday. He came to the office Monday. I would have called you then, but you were in Walla Walla, watching that triple murderer get his neck stretched. That's where you were, wasn't it?"

"That was where."

"Thomas? What was that like?"

"Give me the house number again. We're almost there." It was in Laurelhurst, a ritzy, old-money section of town near the University of Washington, overlooking the lake and the floating bridge and beyond that, the Cascade mountain range. The streets were narrow, and the houses were tall and stately, and any one of them would have made a nice spread in the Sunday magazine section. It was the sort of place crafty middle-class mothers staked out as prime trick-or-treating territory on Halloween.

The roads were quiet, and I hadn't seen a weed in ten blocks. My '68 Ford pickup was the only truck within hooting distance as well as one of the oldest vehicles inside a square mile.

It was February, not yet eight in the morning, and the air bit your cheeks. We could see a rowing crew below, plowing through the glaucous chop and the whitecaps, batting at the waves. The Cascade Mountains were obscured by a wispy haze stretching along the eastern horizon. Sunshine scorched the lowest clouds into a striated tangerine.

The last house on a private lane, the place overlooked the beach, the lake, and the East Side. The dead end narrowed to a makeshift concrete alley, and we had to drive past another house, where a middle-aged woman screened us from her kitchen window.

At the side of the house under a carport I spotted a four-wheel-drive Bronco, a new Porsche, a BMW sedan, and a Kawasaki 900 motorcycle in the back. Also a snowmobile on a small trailer. Not one of the vehicles had been free of the factory longer than two years. A

reasonable guess pegged the resale value of the house
at eight hundred grand, a big chunk of money for a
home in this part of the country. The architecture was
Georgian, large white pillars acting as rigid sentries on
either side of the front door. The back lot could have
been a city park, but it was private, a gazebo, a view
of the pimpled whitecaps on the lake, dormant fruit
trees standing like storm-stripped umbrellas. After
Kathy had nudged the bell and we had cooled our heels
for a while, I touched her arm.

"What is it?" she asked, then noticed the knob,
which was smeared with something resembling dark
brown finger paint.

Using my fingertips, I shoved on the door panel. It
was unlatched. When I bumped it with my palm, the
door popped open and creaked. The mansion was worth
megabucks, but they couldn't afford a thirty-nine-cent
can of oil for the door hinges. The entranceway was
empty and silent. Not even the ticking of a clock. I
turned around to see how many of the neighbors were
rubbernecking, but in this domain people didn't stare.

"Hello," I shouted. Kathy did the same, announcing
her name, and when nobody returned our salutations,
we stepped inside and peered around. We were standing
on a slate floor that had cost a bundle. The smooth rock
was spattered with a dried brownish pigment, thick,
goopy stuff. I dropped to my knees and found some of
the large curds were moist enough to rub off on my
fingertips. It wasn't paint.

"Fresh," I said.

"Fresh what?"

"Blood, sister."

"God, you're kidding. There's so much of it. Somebody must be injured . . . bad."

I grunted. It had the look of something a trifle worse.
Something a trifle final.

Kathy began dancing a little jig, lifting one foot and
then the other, not traveling anywhere, just dancing.
"Pooey phooey," she whispered.

"You talk to this dude yesterday?" I asked.

"No."

"Take it easy," I said, laying a hand on her bobbing shoulder until she calmed. "Mr. Pugsley?" I shouted, then began tracking the droplets across the rocks. On the floor in the first room beside an antique dining set I found a tangled chalk-colored brassiere. Spattered with cinnamon brown, it looked as if it had been discarded in a great hurry.

"What the hell?" I muttered, and strode through the dining room into the modern kitchen, passing a rack burdened with knickknacks.

I almost skied across the half-dried tiles. When I wasn't sliding, my footsteps made candy-wrapper-in-the-theater crinkling noises, my feet sticking at each step.

The man on the floor was pale and large and out of shape. He had mouse-colored hair, sloppy arms that had been muscular once, and a fleshy face, what was left of it. Beside him, sopping up blood, lay a woman's blouse. Only one silken corner was still ivory. The rest was crimson and purple and blackish, a sponge. The back door off the kitchen was ajar.

Kathy followed me in, gasped loudly, vacated the battle zone, and, skirting the gore, pinned herself into a corner. I could hear the wallboard protesting behind her shoulders as she wedged herself in and sucked air.

He was dead, one eye glowering at the spattered ceiling. The other eye was a hand grenade that had gone off onto the tiles somewhere. The bottom of his pajamas was speckled with new ugly color, the top shredded and unrecognizable. Wielding some sort of metallic whip, somebody who had a strong stomach and kept his conscience in his pocket had flogged him until he was snug up against the peephole of hell.

"This Fred Pugsley?" I asked. "Your client?"

I had to wrench around and establish eye contact with Kathy before she gathered the fortitude to speak. Her movements had rumpled her gray suit. In her tight fists she clutched the sack containing the rattlesnake. Before she could lubricate her mouth enough to form a sentence, she swallowed twice, and even then she choked on a tongue of wool. I should have hugged her, but I had other things on my mind.

"I don't know."

"Yeah," I said, noticing the woman in the next room for the first time. Tears skated down the slope of the woman's unclad breasts and dangled for a split second before plopping onto the floor. Her hair, the color of a bread crust, was tucked up into a frizzy bun, and her face was done as if for a day at the office. Fifteen years ago as a girl she might have been pretty, before nerves began eroding her zest, injecting drudgery and doubt into her cocoa brown eyes. "Sort of hard to recognize anything, isn't it?"

Kathy shuddered, and I prayed she wasn't going to be sick.

A pair of misshapen empty slippers—old favorites— sat by the door as if the victim had been knocked right out of them.

2 THE WAY I SAW IT, FRED—IF FRED THIS be—had opened the back door to greet somebody he knew, or somebody who looked harmless enough to confront in pajamas, and then got whacked for his trouble. A charnel house. Blood dappled the walls, cupboards, toaster, even the clock fifteen feet away. A pot of java had tumbled into the fray so that the floor was a swamp of drying plasma and Starbucks coffee.

I tracked naked, bloody footprints out of the room, retracing our path, my feet singing like adhesive tape being peeled off a window, followed them through the dining room, past the empty brassiere, and around the corner, through another passage and, from the back side, into the room adjoining the kitchen where the weepy woman huddled. I took that route because a more direct path would have been too slippery. Besides, the cops weren't going to appreciate more footprints. The bloody spoor grew fainter and fainter until I was standing in front of the crouching, glassy-eyed woman.

"Mrs. Pugsley?"

From the kitchen Kathy spoke. "Margaret. Her name is Margaret."

I squatted beside the woman and spoke softly. "Margaret?"

Tears dripped off her cheeks. She was the number one suspect, and I had never seen her before, assumed she was the dead man's wife; mistress perhaps, though she was a mite plain-looking for my idea of a rich man's mistress.

She didn't reply, had the look of a woman who would have no replies for a long while. Weeks. The next presidential election perhaps. She was almost catatonic. Hell, she was petrified. A swipe of blood crisscrossed one eyebrow, as if she had inadvertently rubbed an itch. Another streak matted her hair at a temple. Her pale shoulders, arms, breasts, and stomach were entirely clean, but her forearms—both forearms—were soiled to the elbows. She had shucked her blouse and bra, both lousy with blood.

A steel rod with a twelve-inch length of bicycle chain attached to it was clutched in her right fist. If I hadn't known better, I would have thought it was a street fighter's diabolic weapon. On the haft of the thing was etched a lopsided star.

"Mrs. Pugsley? Margaret?"

Kathy stood beside me now, tears from her violet eyes slashing dark streaks into the gray material of her jacket. I didn't realize I'd been there long enough for Kathy to reach me.

"You all right?"

She took a deep breath that caught crossways in her throat before it broke into pieces and went down. "Think so."

Several years earlier Kathy and I had met in class at the University of Washington, where our meticulous professor had insisted we all sit in alphabetical order. Birchfield. Black. I had slipped Bishop a five-spot to take the afternoon session. It seemed a century ago. At the time she had been a law student and I had been a Seattle cop taking extension classes. Now she was an attorney and I was a private investigator. Thomas Black.

I didn't work much, but then I didn't need to. I had a fifty percent LEOFF 1 pension, my requirements were simple, and I took pride in keeping them that way.

While a student, Kathy had rented the apartment in my basement. During that time most of our friends assumed we were lovers, or had been lovers, because she was unique and ravishing and I was tall and in shape and my face hadn't been run over by too many trucks. We were not lovers, never had been, only good friends. And something more. But never lovers. It was hard telling which one of us worked harder at keeping it that way.

Picking up my hands and pulling me upright, Kathy pressed into me, a benumbed effort to feel closer to another human, to soak some of the mortality out of the situation. After a moment she pulled my arms under her armpits and pushed them around under her jacket, her lithe back soaked with sweat. We stood that way for quite some time.

"Want to stay with her a minute?"

"What are you going to do?"

"Search the house."

"For more victims?"

"Victims or murderers."

Now was the time to pull a gun out and flex my jaw muscles, but I didn't carry a gun. I knelt and, using two fingers, removed the weapon from the woman's fist and placed it high on an antique cabinet.

"But"—Kathy gestured at Margaret Pugsley—"isn't it obvious who . . . did it?"

"She makes a move on you, holler or run for it. I won't be far."

"Shouldn't we phone the police?"

"We will."

Kathy glanced down at the marble-eyed, witless woman. "Margaret? Maggie?" But the woman had signed an open-ended scholarship with the junior space cadets.

I wandered back into the kitchen and scrutinized the

body, treading in my earlier footsteps. I teetered Fred this way and that, peeping underneath. He felt like a sleeping man but, strangely, almost hollow. A hollow man. There were impressions in the blood, footprints, Margaret Pugsley's and mine, and smaller, squarish impressions, as if a handful of papers or tiles had fallen from the dead man's hands as he was dying, these papers altering the pattern of the drips and splashes. Under his left shoulder I found the cause: a picture, a Polaroid photograph. There must have been more of them, removed by somebody. The subject was a girl of about eight or nine. After a dead body it was the last thing I would have expected to find in a home in Laurelhurst.

When I rolled his shoulder back, he was very soft and still so warm he felt hot to my touch.

"Thomas?" Kathy was getting nervous.

"Yo."

"What are you looking for?"

"A racing bicycle."

"A what?"

After wiping off my feet, I took ten minutes to tour every nook and cranny of the house. There wasn't another soul in it, or any children's rooms, or a grandma's room, or signs that anybody lived here but the two otherworldly people I'd left in the care of Kathy Birchfield: one in shock and the other on an Amtrak to the afterlife.

Nor did I see any other signs of butchery.

In the master bedroom the bed was mussed but only on one side. Someone had spent the night alone. Most likely the man downstairs in his pajamas. There were other hideaways in the mansion where one could have snoozed, but if they had been used, I wasn't clever enough to detect it.

The decorator had gone hog-wild with an unlimited checking account and a hundred back issues of *House Beautiful*. It all looked tasteful and expensive, and it impressed in the same way a stroll through a furniture salesroom impressed. But I wasn't looking at the decor.

I was looking for a racing bicycle, something similar to
my Miyata. A tricked-out two-thousand-dollar stationary bicycle in the basement was as close as it got. I
doubted it had been ridden more than twice. Upstairs I
found his computer room, full of work, papers, obscure
jottings, doodles.

His den was on the second floor. It had a man's look
to it. Ebony leather furniture. A desk that hadn't been
put into order since Hoffa burgers came out. A pipe
rack. Modern hunting weapons in a glass gun case; vin-
tage Civil War rifles on the wall. A moose head. A row
of commercial stand-up video game machines shoulder
to shoulder against one wall. Paintings, all of naked
women, including two that looked to be hundred-year-
old originals belonging in a museum. I didn't recognize
the signatures, but then, I wouldn't.

I riffled through the papers on his desk and found two
items that arrested my attention. The first was a letter
on company stationery from Daryl Rittenhouse. According to recent articles in the *Post-Intelligencer*, Rittenhouse was the guiding genius behind Micro Darlings.

It began "Dear Fred" and then proceeded to get
nasty. Rittenhouse chided him for bickering with other
members of the staff and for his shoddy work habits,
then put him on probation for sixty days, after which
time, if he didn't shape up, he would get the old heave-
ho. It was signed "Sincerely yours, Daryl Rittenhouse."

So, Fred Pugsley was in danger of losing his job. And
somebody had mailed him a dead serpent. And now he
had been turned into spaghetti. Bad Day at Black Rock.
The letterhead on the stationery said Rittenhouse was
the president and owner of Micro Darlings. That gibed
with what I remembered reading in the *P-I*

When I discovered more photos of the ilk I'd found
under the body, I fell into the leather swivel chair as if
somebody had whacked the backs of my knees with a
baseball bat. I was disgusted and angered and baffled.
After a minute I shuffled through them. No matter how

I added things up, I could make no sense of what I was holding. Polaroids. A plethora of ugly images splintered my calm. I flipped the photos over, searching for scribbling on the back. Nothing. I sat and stared and thought and then stared some more. When I sorted through the rest of the papers, I found only bills and some receipts for stocks with a local brokerage house. As far as I could tell, there wasn't another Polaroid in the house besides the three up here and the one downstairs under Fred.

Maybe it was because I figured the woman had to be the most obvious suspect. The only suspect. And that since Leech, Bemis, and Ott were her attorneys, they would undoubtedly be engaged to defend her. And since I did most of their investigations, I would be called on to help. Maybe that was why I pilfered one of the photos. I didn't want to have anything to do with it, to touch it, or to look at it again, but I slipped it into my jacket, my own dirty little secret.

When a man's days end by murder, his life becomes an open suitcase, the contents of which are fair game to be sorted and stepped on by every cop, reporter, and snoop within spitting distance. Anything a man wanted concealed was sure to be dug out and hoisted to the top of the nearest flagpole. I wondered what else Fred was hiding.

Little had changed in the room off the kitchen except that Kathy had scrounged up a paisley robe and draped it over Margaret Pugsley's shoulders. I ran out to my truck, fetched a Polaroid camera of my own, jogged back inside, and took pictures of the crime scene. Then I went over to Kathy and Margaret Pugsley and stood the bloodied woman up, threw the robe off her shoulders, and snapped three pictures of her from various angles.

"That for your private album or what?"

"We don't need them, I'll burn 'em," I said. "We need 'em, and you'll be damn glad I thought of it."

"You mean somebody might try to say she had more blood on her?"

"Something like that."

The 911 operator's voice got a little shaky when I told her there'd been a murder in Laurelhurst. She was accustomed to lost kids, runaway dogs, fender benders. The papers and TV stations were going to gobble this up. The local residents would cringe and buy Dobermans that would terrorize their neighbors' children and eat cats. Door-to-door salesmen were going to have a field day hawking private alarm systems that were bound to go off unreasonably in the middle of the night when the owners were in Bermuda.

Homicide got there in fourteen minutes. I thought the morning traffic would be worse. Ralph Crum wasn't working the case, but he showed up to snoop around. A murder in Laurelhurst. It was beginning already. We went back a long ways, Ralph and I. We'd worked together while I was still a Seattle cop, but that seemed like before zippers. Though he was married and, as far as I knew, faithful, he had an undisguised hankering for Kathy.

It wasn't until we stood Margaret Pugsley up and her face had paled so that I thought she would faint that I realized she was crippled. One of her legs was next to useless. It made sense. Those bloody footprints hadn't been anywhere near symmetrical.

Crum sucked on an unlit pipe one of his kids had given him for Christmas, directed several evidence technicians to various localities in the house, then shambled over to the sofa where Kathy was comforting Margaret Pugsley. Margaret dangled her soiled hands and forearms in front of herself as if she'd been scalded.

Holding a clear plastic evidence sack up for inspection, Crum said, "What the hell is this? Looks like something a Malay street gang would use." It was the bloodied tool I'd taken out of Margaret Pugsley's hand. I was sure it had readable prints from the woman; otherwise I might have held my peace.

"She had it when we came in," I said. Kathy kicked me in the shin. "It's a sprocket remover."

"A what?"

Kathy tried to kick me again, but I sidestepped and said, "It's got her prints all over it. Besides, look at her. They're not going to have any trouble figuring out approximately what we saw when we came in." I turned to Crum. "It's a tool for taking freewheels apart. Most of them unscrew. You wrap the chain around the sprocket, hold the freewheel in a vise or use another remover, and unscrew the sprockets. You can replace a worn sprocket without the expense of getting a whole new freewheel."

"How much does a freewheel cost?"

"A Campagnolo freewheel is a hundred fifty bucks. Twenty for a cheapie."

Crum scratched a bald spot on his head with a middle finger that had a dirty nail. Squinting, he said. "What the hell's a freewheel?"

"The gear cluster on the back of a ten-speed."

"Somebody race bicycles?"

"I dabble. Far as I could tell, Fred never touched one. Didn't see a thing in the house."

"You been through the house?" Crum asked politely, shocked at both my affront and my confession.

"Needed to check the decor. I'm buying one just like it."

Crum's face deteriorated into a slow smile. He was of Dutch extraction; you could see that the minute you laid eyes on him. His name was Ralph, but he was staging a campaign to get everybody to call him Bill. Ralph William Crum.

He was short, ruddy-faced, and his features were thick and blunt, his pale blue eyes watery. His hair was thin as corn silk, and in order to make it appear thicker, he grew it obscenely long in the back, wrapping strands artistically around his pate, hoping to conceal the shiny spots in front. More often than not, several long strands took off on their own, debunking his efforts.

Soft-spoken and slow-witted to a fault, Crum usually got things right, but it almost always took awhile. He stared at my cheek as if he'd seen mustard on it and said, "We'll get a statement from each of you." He gazed over at Margaret. "Then I imagine we'll arrest her. Don't really, uh, I don't see that I have much choice. Jeezola. Do you?"

"Jeezola?" I said.

He almost grinned. "My kid says it."

"I'm her attorney," said Kathy. "I want a doctor for this woman."

Crum looked the situation over. "Sure." He took me by the elbow and steered me into another room. Kathy gave me a piercing look. She was afraid I'd blab everything and compromise her defense. I winked.

"What's your reading of this?" Crum said. "I mean, what, his old lady just get a fart caught in the tubes and decide to lambaste the poor bastard or what?"

"I don't have an opinion," I said, worrying about the photo in my jacket pocket.

"What's Kathy got in that sack?"

"You don't even want to know."

"I'll have to take a peek."

My grin was thin as soup in a boardinghouse. "Sure."

I left an hour later, after giving a statement and after they had taken plaster impressions of my shoes and Kathy's. Mrs. Pugsley and Kathy were sitting together in the back of a police cruiser, a zombie woman and a pretty lawyer. The few neighbors who had crowded around to rubberneck couldn't take their eyes off the duo.

I stopped at the car window and watched my breath do caterpillar crawls in the hazy morning air. "Sure you don't want me along?"

"I'll call," said Kathy. "When she's feeling better we'll see what she wants to do about counsel, and I'll call. L B and O won't want to touch this, but they'll take it if she insists. Right now I've got to get her a doctor. Lieutenant Crum promised they'd take us to her personal physician downtown. You be around today?"

"I'll make sure of it "

"Thomas?"

"Hey, Pancho '

She smiled, but it was sadder than a come-nither grin on a Yesler whore. "Thomas, I've never seen anything like this before. I feel all shaky and sick inside."

"Don't worry about it, sister. Me too."

"Shaky and sick? You do?"

"You don't feel that way, there's something seriously wrong." I reached through the window and tried to muss her hair, which was piled into a loose bun and pinned with wooden sticks, but she evaded my reach.

"Thanks."

As I climbed into my pickup, a gaggle of well-dressed Jehovah's Witnesses trooped up the walk, bright and cheery. They were too late for me. For the lady attorney. For Margaret Pugsley. And certainly too late for the man on the kitchen floor.

I hadn't wanted to get saddled with another case, and Kathy knew it. What I wanted was to prune my Blue Nile, thumb through a good book, and pedal a bicycle two hundred miles a week. I call it semiretirement. My neighbor Horace calls it a bum's life.

Two hours later I was in the backyard, puttering with a Tropicana, when I got a call. Kathy Birchfield.

"Can you come over now, Thomas?"

"You defending her?"

"Looks that way."

"She ready to talk?"

"In a manner of speaking. It's all so bizarre. Don't spare the horses."

"I'll kill 'em."

3   A BREEZE KICKED UP ITS HEELS. MIDDAY traffic was beginning to snarl and toot. I drove to the Grueman Building on the north edge of University Village, a quaint shopping complex down the hill from the University of Washington. An excited announcer on the truck radio was already nattering about the Laurelhurst tragedy.

A crow perched on the portico over the front door of the Grueman Building, eyeing all the visitors and periodically crapping on the welcome mat. I made sure to time it so he didn't have anything left for me. Life. It was all in the timing.

Kathy Birchfield's door was the second one on the left in the Leech, Bemis, and Ott wing. Kathy was on the phone but hung up the minute she saw me. She had fiddled with her hair, now wore it in a tight, shiny bun. The heather gray skirt, blazer, and ivory blouse were the same. Small gold oblong earrings flashed when she moved.

Pugsley had seen her doctor but still had not been arrested. I noticed a gray-haired patrolman standing in the hallway staring at all the pretty secretaries and bobbing his head to the spicy Muzak. Or maybe he was

17

just nodding off. Somebody downtown thought Margaret was unstable, or he wouldn't have been sent.

"Think she can talk a little now," said Kathy, her tone serious, her eyes low. "It wasn't much fun. She got panicky once we got downtown in the Medical-Dental Building."

"I should have come with you."

"She began flinging copies of the *New Yorker* all over the place. I was really frightened for her until the doctor gave her an injection."

"How is she now?"

"Seems all right. You saw the cop? I don't know if she'll make sense or not. We got her best friend to come down. I figured if you were going to work on this, you wanted a head start. Might as well begin now, before they charge her."

"Crum say anything to you about it?"

"Nope. But I can tell from the way he looks at her."

"What's she told you?"

"Absolutely nothing."

"They identify the body?"

"Fred Pugsley, her husband. Thomas, are you going to take this one?"

"Your bosses want me to?"

"My bosses want you to emigrate to Tanganyika. It's your attitude. None of them appreciate the way you pick and choose your jobs."

"Can't stand an independent man, huh?"

"They call you lazy. Will you take it? This might be the biggest case I've ever handled."

"Considering her position in the community, they'll probably wait a few days until they've built an airtight case, but they'll do it. Unless something comes up, they'll charge her."

"*They'll* do it. Will *you* do it?"

I bobbed my eyebrows. "Me? I'm your slave. You know that. Let's go talk." Kathy dashed around her beech desk and walked me down the carpeted aisle to a conference room that had narrow windows inset into the wall. One of the senior partner's wives had named it the Lincoln Room and tacked a brass plate on the door signifying same. Over the years the room had collected its share of Lincoln memorabilia: pennies in plastic cases; ceramic busts of Abe—most of it junk.

I knew the cop at the door by sight and nodded at him.

Margaret Pugsley had changed her clothes, and the expression of horror that had pulled at her face all morning had been swapped for one of depletion. It was almost as if she'd been interrogated in a South American jail cell or had a pet run over by a car—or murdered somebody.

Kathy followed me into the room alongside Leech, one of the senior partners, who had hustled down the corridor to squeeze through the doorway with us. He smiled, genial and patronizing. He was short and balding and vigorous, near retirement, and would be playing tennis when he was ninety. From past experience, I knew he was there as an observer and consultant. Kathy was the new person at Leech, Bemis, and Ott, and they monitored much of what she did. So far all the criminal cases had been sent her way, and she'd blown them out of the stadium, batting almost five hundred. Another lawyer acquaintance had told me that was a phenomenal percentage, especially for a beginner, though at L B and O they tended to belittle her achievements.

Specialists in corporate law, the senior partners weren't about to snatch any seedy criminal actions away from her or wet their pants at her successes.

When I saw the tawny blond woman behind Margaret Pugsley, her body made me think immediately of the boudoir. She was clad in slacks and a cherry red sweater. Early thirties. Sleek. A diamond the size of a tooth on her left ring finger.

Her blond hair fell just below the chin. Shalimar in her bloodstream and sin in her eyes. Princess eyes, an icy pale blue. But then, maybe I was reading them wrong. Maybe I was reading things into them that weren't there. She smiled politely at Kathy, clasped her scarlet-tipped fingers together, and regarded me as if I were a slug on her dinner plate. Me, I was intoxicated by the look of her. After a bit I closed my mouth.

Her name was Veronica Rogers, and when we all were seated, Kathy said, "Margaret stayed with Mrs. Rogers the last couple of nights."

I turned to Margaret for confirmation, but she only stared, bludgeoned by the morning's events.

"Fred and Maggie were having a little spat," said Veronica, avoiding my eyes and looking at Kathy. She talked as if she'd learned how from a dictionary. Perfect diction. Perfect cadence. "Early this morning Fred phoned and told her he was sorry. Said he had some good news and for her to come right over. I still cannot believe it. It sounds so . . . like something from a cheap soap opera."

"We'll need strict confidentiality when we interview our client," Mr. Leech announced from the head of the table in a surprisingly fatherly tone.

Unctuously she strode to the door and then pivoted, knob in her tanned hand. "Certainly," said Veronica. "Margaret and I have been friends for as long as I can remember. I wouldn't want anything to jeopardize her defense. If you need me, Maggie, I'll be outside."

I thought it was apparent she had already mentally convicted Margaret. But then, so had we. Nobody had said a word, but what we all were casting about for were mitigating circumstances, excuses for an insanity or diminished capacity plea, or some other bugaboo to befuddle the DA. They hang people in this state. I knew that for a fact, had seen it happen three days earlier. Through the window of the conference room I observed Veronica Rogers saunter across the foyer, exchange a few words with Beulah, the overweight receptionist, then seat herself on a low sofa. She didn't bother to page through a magazine but stared at her knee, same as I was doing.

When I turned back to the group seated around the maple table, Kathy was looking at me, chewing her lower lip, eyes empty.

I said, "Mrs. Pugsley, I know this will be difficult for you, but please tell us everything that happened this morning. Begin when you woke up."

Surprisingly she snapped out of her trance and focused on me. "You see, I hated Fred. I'm glad he's dead."

The silence in the room grew.

"No, Christ, I, uh, didn't mean that. Pretend you didn't hear that." She glanced around the table at our faces. "At least I don't think I meant it. I'm so confused. I sound almost as if I murdered him. Damn." Her eyes were dark wet buttons. "You don't think I killed him, do you?"

We glanced guiltily at each other, and I knew the two lawyers in the room didn't want to field the question. I said, "We can't answer that, Mrs. Pugsley. Only you can."

She shook her head rapidly, "No, of course you can't."

"Did you? Did you kill your husband?"

She blinked and bowed her head so that we strained to hear her statement. "I don't remember a goddamned thing. I wanted a divorce, and I don't remember a goddamned thing."

"I'm sorry, Mrs. Pugsley, I'm having trouble hearing you."

Louder she said, "I might have. I certainly fantasized about it. Do you think I could have killed him, then forgotten?"

Kathy looked up at me, a tear flowering in one violet eye. "What was the last thing you remember before finding the body?"

"I don't remember anything. I got in the car at Veronica's in Bellevue, and then all of a sudden I was throwing a fit in the doctor's office." She tipped her face up, the brown eyes glistening. "I don't remember any of it. Do you think I killed him?"

Kathy spoke gently. "Start from the beginning, and tell us what you do remember."

For all the movement of her body Margaret Pugsley might have been a paraplegic. Her soft-looking cheeks, heavily rouged and powdered, were drooping, and her throat was aging quicker than the rest of her, though after this morning the rest might catch up in a rush. An aura of fragility enveloped her, as if she'd grown accustomed to abuse, verbal and otherwise. Take a dog you've been whipping for years and put it in a tub, give it a shampoo, sprinkle cologne all over it, and it still looks like a dog you've been whipping for years.

Kathy had spruced her up, had put her into a green suit she wore stiffly as if it were made out of tinfoil. Even her nutmeg eyes had cleared a little. Damp tendrils of hair clung to her temples where the blood had been scrubbed off.

"Fred and I aren't getting along. All of this still isn't sinking in. *Weren't* getting along! I forget. Forgive what I said. Please? I've been drugged. You know that. I'm, uh, not glad he's dead. Nobody should ever be glad somebody's dead. It was, um, a horrid thing to say. I'm just so . . . overwhelmed." Something behind her eyes went blank again. The porch light was on, but nobody was home.

Mr. Leech spoke to Kathy. "Under no circumstances is this woman to give a statement to the police. We will prepare something."

"Mrs. Pugsley?" I scooted my chair closer. "Margaret?"

"I'm sorry. I'm sleepy. Dr. Rutenhower said I'd be drowsy. I made such a fool of myself."

"Tell us what happened this morning between you and your husband."

"I got a call, early. Fred. All excited. Said things were going to change. He had something . . . wouldn't tell me what. Just he had something, and things were going to change for the better. Something about Micro Darlings. He wanted me to come right over. He wanted to . . ."

We waited, and finally Kathy asked, "What? Margaret? He wanted to what?"

Her voice was strangling. "He wanted to make love."

Tipping her head forward, she wept quietly. The three of us sat and watched, studiously avoiding one another's eyes. No group activity I know of is slower than folding your hands and sitting around a table watching a woman cry.

Mr. Leech's kindly voice pulled her out of it. "Mrs. Pugsley, as you know, we're liquidating some assets for you. In a couple of hours we should have enough to make almost any bond. I doubt if you'll have to spend a night in jail. Minute they charge you, let us know. We'll get a Gernstein hearing before a magistrate and have you out. But if we're going to defend you, our investigator needs something to work on. Please try to continue."

Sniffling, she said, "Certainly. Where was I? Make love. Right. He wanted to make love. I was shaky as a schoolgirl. Don't ask me why, after all Fred's done. A divorce was all I could think about until that phone call. I dunno, I guess I'm just a big chump. I got in the car at Veronica's, and that's the last thing I recall. It really is." The light behind her eyes dimmed. "No, uh, I remember driving across the floating bridge. And I was standing on the front porch for a minute. I don't know why. Then I went back in. Then you people were there."

"That's it?" I asked.

"I don't recall anything else until I was in the doctor's office making a spectacle of myself. I'm so embarrassed."

"Don't be," said Kathy. "You had quite a shock."

"A tremendous shock," added Leech, fingering his hoary sideburns. He looked at me and whispered, "Hypnosis?"

"It would be a lot better if she remembered on her own. We can always use it as a last resort."

"But don't you need to know things now? Right away?"

I shrugged. To tell the truth, I didn't think there would be much to this investigation. Margaret Pugsley sniffed and wiped her nose on the back of her wan hand, then glanced around to see if we'd spotted the indiscretion. If she were going to fret over indiscretions, she'd better skip the little stuff.

"Margaret," I said, glancing at some notes I had penciled on a pad, "did Fred have any enemies?"

"None that I know of."

"Everybody's got some enemies."

"I don't know of any. He squabbled with everyone; that's just the way he was. He couldn't park a car without yelling at somebody on the street. No real enemies, though."

"How were things going at work?"

"Fred's always been a star at work."

"No trouble? He wasn't in danger of losing his job? No dissension in the ranks?"

"Lose his job?" She was incredulous. "Of course not. Fred was one of the founders of Micro Darlings. They'd be lost without him."

"You didn't see a letter from Rittenhouse putting him on probation?"

"A letter? Is there one?" I wondered what else he'd kept to himself.

"Is he a co-owner?"

"Not exactly. Owns stock. Daryl is the actual owner. He's always kept fifty-one percent."

"Daryl Rittenhouse?"

"Why, yes. Do you know him?"

"What about the snake?"

"Oh, the snake. The damn snake. That's why we quarreled. It came in Saturday's mail. A dead rattlesnake. Can you believe it? I almost fainted when I opened the package. Thought it was alive at first." Remembered fear was beginning to inject life into her voice.

"Did Fred have any idea who sent it?"

"Had every idea. Eric Castle sent it. It brought up all sorts of hideous things. The incident. All the rest of that turmoil from five years ago." Suddenly Margaret Pugsley stopped speaking, twisted her head around, and said, "Veronica?"

Kathy spoke soothingly. "She's just outside. We'll get her if you need her."

"Who is Eric Castle?" I asked.

"Until five years ago he was Fred's best friend. I don't know that they've said ten words to each other since the incident. Eric, actually, uh, Eric helped found Micro Darlings. He used to have stock in it, but I don't know what happened to that. They fired him five years ago."

"What incident?"

"It's not important. Ancient history. And I don't really know that Fred had any enemies. Maybe Eric Castle, but no one else. Oh, he could be obnoxious from time to time, but enemies? I don't think so." Tears trekked down her face until her eyes were overflowing and she couldn't focus on me. "Please, what else do you want? I'm coming apart. I don't think I can stand much more."

"Under the—in your kitchen this morning I found a picture of a young girl, eight, maybe nine years old. Does that ring a bell?"

"Girl?"

"You have any kids? Maybe Fred had children from an earlier marriage?"

"Children? I wanted them, but Fred thought I was being frivolous. I'm crippled, you know. A birth defect. No matter what the doctors said, Fred wouldn't agree that I should have a child. Least that was his excuse. I offered to adopt, but that was out. Fred didn't like kids. He talks about—talked about retroactive abortion as if it were a big joke. He used to say the three worst words in the language were 'The rabbit died.' I guess, uh, I didn't tell—I didn't tell you Fred could be insensitive, did I?''

"Margaret? You have any pictures of a child in your house? Perhaps a friend's, a niece?''

"Not that I recall.''

"You folks own a Polaroid camera?''

"I don't think so. No.''

"Do you know where Eric Castle lives?''

She hunched over, picked up her purse, and rummaged through it. "Sure. Fred kept track. He moves around a lot, but Fred always kept track. The incident was an obsession with Fred. I thought . . .''

"What?''

"I thought perhaps Fred should seek professional help over it. A therapist or something.''

"How did Fred take that suggestion?''

"Are you kidding? I would never dare say a thing like that to his face. It's just what I thought.'' She brought out a small address book and read the street number to me. I scrawled it on a card with my other notes. It was on Capitol Hill near The Harvard Exit, a local cinema, about a ten-minute drive from the Grueman Building.

"Now, Mrs. Pugsley, tell me what the incident was.''

"Also,'' she said, ignoring my question, "I don't want you bothering Veronica about any of this. She's been an angel and practically my best friend in the whole world, and she's been through her own traumas. She doesn't need to be bothered. I'm standing firm on that. Veronica's overcome a lot the last few years, and I want her to stay out of this hideous business. Is that clear?''

"Perfectly.'' Leech leaned forward and looked daggers at me. He knew from past experience that prohibiting me from doing something was the surest way to goad me into it.

I winked at him because I knew he hated that and said, "The incident?''

"I can't talk about it now. I'm just not up to it."

"One last thing, Margaret, and I don't really know how to ask this without sounding rude."

"Go ahead. After this morning nothing could shock me."

"How was your sex life together, yours and Fred's?" Kathy elbowed me and gave me a hard blue look as if I were a pooch and about to do something distasteful on the carpet.

"Our sex life? You mean . . . well, I don't know. I suppose, uh, no, no supposing. I guess you could positively say it wasn't what it should have been. I won't fool you, Mr. Black. Fred cheated on me. More than once. I've known about it for years. It was just his nature. I guess I wasn't the wife I could have been. He was always looking over the fence, so to speak."

Kathy whispered to me, "There, satisfied?"

"You don't happen to . . . know anybody he slept with, do you?"

Gazing down into her lap, she shook her head, and I noticed the part in her hair was crooked. She wore two simple silver earrings, but the left one was about to drop off. Before I left, I put a comforting hand on her shoulder, which, under her jacket, felt like a piece of dead meat.

I waited in Kathy's office, where we could map out an initial strategy and arrange finances. I purposely left the door ajar, peering down the corridor as Veronica Rogers, the silver-haired cop, Mr. Leech, and a hobbling Margaret Pugsley all went into another office. Unless they soon found some additional evidence, like a blood-soaked maniac in the bushes outside the Pugsley house, the SPD would clap Margaret into cuffs and charge her.

Originally Kathy had wangled most of the day off, was plotting to introduce me to Fred Pugsley first thing in the morning, then help kick off the first event of Seattle's annual weeklong celebration of Fat Tuesday down in Pioneer Square. The waiter's race. It was a week of drinking contests, mock beauty pageants, fireworks, local musicians and comedians, a week of mind-boggling events designed to give otherwise normal people an excuse to act like lunatics—just the sort of thing Kathy lived for. She leaped at any feeble excuse to masquerade and would dress up as a clown during the celebrations. She was good: juggling; sleight of hand; pantomime; pratfalls; razzmatazz.

First Fred and then Fat Tuesday. But things had become complicated.

When she came back, her face was whited out, the razor-sharp black lines in place, everything but the bulb nose. Whiteface and Chaplin clothes from a secondhand store. Fat Tuesday, here I come. Clown attorney. She closed the door behind herself and dropped her skirt to the floor. "Kathy!"

"Don't be so squeamish. We're practically related. I mean, after all, how many times have we slept together and not made with the two-backed beast?" I plugged my ears. She jumped into her Chaplin pants and then began unbuttoning her blouse. I heeled away and watched a boy on a skateboard bouncing off parked cars in the parking lot below.

When she tapped me on the shoulder to turn me around, I said, "How do you do the whiteface so fast?"

"I told Veronica we'd hire a service to go over and clean the place up. The cops are through with it."

"They usually take longer."

"We ready?"

"What are you talking about?"

"The investigation? I have the day off, remember?"

"You're not coming. Remember the last time you came on an investigation with me. We almost got killed."

"This'll be different. What's first? Micro Darlings? Grill the neighbors? Down to the courthouse and sort through some musty old files?"

"How about a dunk in the lake, bozo? You expect

me to conduct serious interviews with you dressed like that?''

Her voice dropped out of the giggly stratosphere and plummeted toward dead clients and blood thinned with Starbucks coffee. She moved close and wiped grease-paint on my jacket. I thought she was fooling around at first until I heard her quivering voice. ''Just—just . . . Thomas, just take me around for a couple of hours, okay. I'm really shaky. I want to be with you.''

I noticed, as I always did when Kathy hugged me, that she fitted against me as if she belonged there. But then, that was part of her special appeal. She could make any man feel as if he were the one.

''Two hours, Pancho. Then you ride off into the sunset by yourself.''

''Deal. By the way, you big stinker, why did you have to ask her about her sex life? I thought you were—''

I took out the photo I'd confiscated from Fred Pugsley's den and handed it to her. I might as well have goosed her at her wedding. It was another Polaroid of the same little girl who'd been in the photo under Fred. She was posing, and it wasn't pretty. To make matters worse, she was stark naked. Kiddie porn. And it hadn't been clipped from a magazine. This was the real deal.

4 "Judas priest!" said Kathy. "Fred had this?"

"One under the body and three up in his den. I had the feeling there had been more around the body, but that they had been removed."

"Who's the little girl?"

"I don't think, at this point, that it matters to our investigation. It might later, but not right now."

Kids weren't polluted enough to pose like that on their own. Grown-ups had to cajole or threaten them. Kathy and I both knew that. Openmouthed, hands shaking, she tried to steady the Polaroid. I told her about the square patterns in the blood, about the letter from Daryl Rittenhouse threatening to fire Fred if he didn't shape up, about the lack of a racing bicycle.

"Margaret doesn't know about these awful pictures, does she?"

I shrugged. "You heard me ask about a camera. She was a little too deep in shock for me to bring this up. I'll talk to her in a day or so when she gets her wiring restrung."

"You say one of these was under the body?"

"The left shoulder."

"Then the cops have it?"

"As well as the others in the den."

"Thomas, did she do it? I mean, it looked like she did it this morning. The cops thought she did. I thought she did. Didn't you?"

"The truth?"

"Be honest."

"Course she did it. We walk into the house. The guy's brains are splattered over the fridge and the microwave. She's up to her funny bone in blood, the murder weapon in her hands. Says she can't remember. Bullshit. Somebody picked up a bunch of these photos and did something with them. Maybe flushed them down the toilet. Torched them in the fireplace. Whatever. She gave quite a performance out there. She remembers. On some level remembers it all."

"She looked bad at the doctor's."

"Murder is a stressful hobby."

"I don't know, Thomas. Despite what we saw, I don't think she's guilty."

"We'll poke around and see what we come up with. Maybe a forensic specialist can do something with the blood patterns. They may indicate he was killed by somebody taller, or shorter, or whatever. You never know what'll come out if you do enough tinkering. Where'd you pick up her friend?"

"Veronica Rogers?" She giggled. "Forget it, brother. She's married. Or didn't you see that oyster of a ring? The way you saw everything else, I'm surprised you don't need a sling for your eyeballs."

"Funny."

"Maggie gave me Veronica's number, and I called her from the Medical-Dental Building. It was nice to have her there, but she really wasn't much help. Had to dress and clean up Maggie virtually by myself. I got the distinct feeling Veronica didn't want to muss her outfit. Thinks the sun doesn't rise until she gets out of bed."

I shrugged and looked at my watch. "What time did she get up this morning?"

Kathy almost smiled and then whispered like an assassin, "She's callous. Women that beautiful are always callous."

"You dope." I pressed my index finger into the tip of the red bulb nose she had just screwed on. Kathy surreptitiously honked a horn in her coat pocket. "You're not callous." She giggled again, the sound rustling over me like a breeze across tall, dry grass.

When Kathy got into the truck the first thing she did was reach under the seat and hang my umbrella in the gun rack in the back window. "I wish you wouldn't do that."

" 'Fraid all the girlies'll think your gun's only good for rainy days?"

Montlake Boulevard took us south past Husky Stadium, through the midmorning traffic across the Montlake Bridge and up Twenty-fourth. I took Interlaken up the hill through the potholes and switchbacks in the woods. Interlaken was surrounded by greenbelt, mostly damp and soggy in February. We didn't see another vehicle until we came out on Galer at the top of the hill. According to Mrs. Pugsley, Eric Castle lived on Boylston Avenue. The odds were against his being home at this time of day.

I ate up most of the trip thinking about all the dirty little secrets people spent their lives hiding. Years earlier, when I was a cop, a man came up to my car and confessed to shooting six of his neighbor's dogs over a period of years. He said the guilt and anxiety had finally gotten too much for him to handle and he had to make a clean breast of things. Then he fled before I could cuff him. We had a Frenchman come into the precinct once and admit poisoning his wife thirty years earlier. He couldn't stand it anymore. Dirty little secrets. Me, I was already worried I'd get knocked unconscious in a car wreck and somebody'd find that photo. It was one of the reasons I'd shown it to Kathy. A witness to attest that this dirty little secret was really someone else's.

As I jockeyed up and down Boylston, looking for a

spot large enough to squeeze the Ford into, Kathy said, "You really think I should be callous?"

"You mean, do I really think you're beautiful? You turn enough heads."

"Including yours?"

"Want me to say it?"

"Once in a while might be nice."

"You're beautiful."

"Har, har."

"Now listen to you. I say it and you laugh."

The wet streets were oily and narrow, as traffic rushed along in torrents of steel, glass, and rubber. After I'd wrangled the truck into a slot three blocks away, we got out and walked to Eric Castle's place. Kathy's costume attracted some notice. Two lanky male students cantering along in jogging sweats, breath coming out in beams, made silly faces at her. She honked the brass car horn she kept in her pocket.

It was a communal house, a large, weather-beaten three-story affair with a holly hedge surrounding it, a spiked iron fence inside the hedge; grandeur overgrown. One of those places that rented out rooms and kitchen privileges. My guess was ten or twelve renters lived here. Every university district had them, and Capitol Hill had its share.

Garbed in a peacoat, a chubby, sad-looking girl with a shiny root for a nose came out the front door. She told us Eric Castle had gone to the store minutes earlier, would no doubt be back directly. She did not invite us inside but locked the door behind herself.

"What do you want with that pervert?" she asked as she trudged off.

I bobbled my eyebrows at the clown, but the clown studied the house and ignored me. We waited, basked in a lazy flow of woodsmoke from a nearby residence, and listened in the windless afternoon as someone nearby tapped out classical music on a spinet.

They returned a few minutes later, our man and a young boy, strolling along the damp sidewalks at the back of the house, talking and laughing, each toting a bundle of groceries. At least I guessed he was our man. They disappeared into the yard through a squeaky back gate. I hustled around the house through the slimy, un-mown February grass and caught the back door before it clicked shut on its pneumatic pump, then waited for Kathy.

Oversize skull, slanted eyes, the boy with Eric Castle was no ordinary kid, had a clumsy look about him, though unlike other children I'd seen in that strait, he was dressed well and lovingly, by somebody who cared. Down's syndrome. They used to call them Mongolian idiots because they had slight Asian casts to their fea-tures. A lot of parents paid little attention to how they dressed special children. I was glad to see that was not the case here. He was nine, maybe ten.

When Kathy caught up, we went in.

It was the basement. A room at the end of the cramped hallway was open, a yawning padlock on a paint-chipped latch. Cheapest room in the house I'd wa-ger. Scotch-taped to the door was a scrap of paper that said, "Eric Castle—computer consultant."

Damp, shabbier than a longshoreman's underwear, it smelled like an old doghouse. The cold concrete floor was painted navy gray. He was no housekeeper. Two racing bicycles: a Colnago and a Davidson; expensive toys, considering his environs. A computer with eight-inch disk drives. A dresser and, stuffed into a low-ceilinged nook nobody but a midget or a kid would be able to stand upright in, a rumpled bed. I couldn't fig-ure how they had jammed the bed in.

The man was gone.

Sitting on the edge of the bed, the kid took us in with swollen, wary eyes. Kathy was what got to him. A real clown up close and personal right there in his own room. Jeezola.

By the time Eric returned from stashing the groceries upstairs, she had the child mesmerized, chuckling, grinning, clapping his hands to her mute antics. She juggled beanbags and kept losing one under her squashed top hat. When she tried to pull it out, she got a stuffed turquoise rabbit instead. The second time her hand came out with a spray of paper flowers. It was a stunt I hadn't seen before. I used to know all her routines.

"Can I help you?" Eric Castle stood in the corridor behind us, his voice frosty with alarm. I stepped aside so he could see Kathy and realize we were harmless.

"Eric Castle?"

When he nodded, I told him who I was and what I wanted. We shook hands. Kathy shook his hand, too, and said hello. The kid on the bed squinted, head twisting this way and that, going crazy trying to figure out how this mime had learned to talk. Brushing past me into the cramped room, Eric Castle went over to the discombobulated boy and festooned an arm around his shoulders. Eric grinned wider than I would have.

"This is my son, Schuyler," he said. The stubborn pride in his voice was enough to bring tears to your eyes.

"You know a guy named Fred Pugsley?"

"Sure." He was too cheery to have heard the news.

"Somebody bashed his brains out this morning."

"What?" Rattled, Eric Castle slumped on the bed beside his grinning son. "You kidding me?"

I shook my head.

"He's dead?"

"As a froggie on the freeway." Kathy shot me a look that was equal parts reprimand and resentment. She rarely tolerated my gallows humor, and she was still deeply affected by what we'd seen this morning.

Eric was a good-looking man, about thirty, to judge by the age of his boy, and had one of those youthful, impish faces women talking among themselves would call cute. He was small and light, five-six, five-eight, almost spindly, but moved with the ease and confidence of a conditioned athlete. Both of the bikes in the corner had seen a lot of roadwork. In fact, I thought I recog-

nized him from Lake Washington Boulevard, one of the
more popular riding routes in the city.

"We want to talk to you about it, Eric."

"Me? Sure. I guess." His eyes narrowed. "Jeez.
Fred? They catch the guy did it?"

"What makes you think it was a guy?"

"Catch anybody?"

"The police have a suspect, but nobody's been arrested. You care to answer a few questions?"

"Yeah. But why me?" I could only think of my fruit-
less search through the Pugsley household for a racing
bicycle. There were two in this room.

"We have reason to believe you threatened Fred recently."

"Threatened? What are you talking about?"

"Dead rattlesnakes."

"Look, if the cops want to talk to me, send them."
His eyes were dark and tight, looked like punctures in
a cardboard face.

"You have something to hide?"

He shrugged and ran a hand through his cropped dark
hair. Somebody had cut it raggedly into a Caesar style.
My guess was he'd done it himself to save money. His
trousers needed patches.

"Sure I know about that snake. Somebody put it in
my bed. Five days ago. I usually go upstairs in the
evening and watch TV in the common room, and when
I do, I leave this room open. Least I used to. The outer
doors are always locked."

"Who did it?"

"I thought Fred, obviously. Still don't know how he
got in."

"We got in," I said.

"Yeah. I guess you did."

"Schuyler live here with you?"

"Stays with my folks out in north Seattle." Noting
that the boy's ears had pricked up at the mention of his
name, Eric grabbed Schuyler's shoulders and rough-
housed him goodnaturedly. It had the air of ritual. The

boy preened under the attention. Schuyler didn'· seem
to be following much of the conversation.

"What made you think it was Fred?"

"Just did. Fred always had a thing for snakes."

"The snake alive when you found it?"

"Hell, yes. He put it there, slipped it under my pillow. It would have got me good if it hadn't decided to
slither around under the sheets. I came down after
watching TV and was drinking a beer and banging away
on my computer when I noticed something out the side
of my eye. I write free-lance programs. Got a couple
in the hopper now that might get me out of here." His
dark eyes almost got dreamy. "Maybe get me some
other things, too. Gawd, it blew me away. A rattler
under my sheets."

He was living like fungus on the bottom of last year's
pumpkin, yet he had almost three thousand dollars'
worth of bicycles tilted up against the wall, and I don't
know how many dollars tied up in that computer. I was
struck by the intelligence radiating from his face, a face
that seemed to take in everything. Yet there was something else, too, a malevolence I couldn't quite put my
finger on. I wasn't sure I trusted him. Schuyler helped,
but he wasn't quite enough.

"Scared the shit out of me. I killed it with a Zefal
floor pump."

Rattlesnakes are not indigenous to western Washington, but somebody might have gone east of the Cas-
cades to get one. The only problem with that theory
was that in February snakes hibernated.

"You get a note with it?"

"You mean a little message tied around its neck with
a pink ribbon? No. Didn't have a bell on it either."

"Why did Fred hate you?"

"Been fired from three jobs in six months. Somebody's been harassing my employers until it's more
trouble to have me around than it is to let me go."

"Fred?"

"Has to be."

Out of the blue Schuyler boasted, "My dad makes hamburgers."

Eric Castle had to think about it. "That's right," he said, ruffling Schuyler's hair. "They call me king of the coronary bypass special."

"King of the corny bypass special," parroted Schuyler ineptly.

I thought I saw the remnants of sorrow in Eric's eyes, either for the child or for the fact that he was frying beef patties. Eric looked and sounded much too intelligent to be a fry cook.

"Can't prove anything. Always does it anonymously on the phone."

"What is said?"

"Bad things."

"Tell me about it."

"None of my employers has ever come right out and repeated it." I knew he was lying. He'd had the remarks repeated to him—more than once. I could see it in the way his cheeks colored.

"Could it have been somebody other than Fred?"

"Maybe." He shrugged, unable or unwilling to travel any farther down that path. I made a mental note to look up his former employers and get the scoop. I asked him to give me some names and addresses, and he did, confident I wouldn't follow up.

"Look," he said, glancing at his watch, "I gotta get going. Gotta have Schuyler back to my folks in half an hour. Then I gotta ride. Haven't been out in a few days. I'm hurtin'. Maybe late this afternoon we can get together? Or tomorrow morning?"

"How far you going?"

"On the bike? Thirty probably."

"I'll ride with you. We can talk. Drop down the hill and meet me on the Montlake Bridge. How's that?"

"You race?" he asked.

"I'll keep up."

He gave me a dubious look but agreed to meet me on the bridge at one-thirty.

The corker came on the way out when I requested the names of some friends or acquaintances.

"Don't have any friends," he said, cheerfully grinning up at me. I couldn't tell how much of it was jubilance and how much was an iconoclastic and deprecating humor.

"Surely . . ."

"Haven't had a date in five years."

"Acquaintances?"

He only looked grim.

"One last question," I said, glancing around the hovel. "What could anybody gain from harassing you? Fred? Anybody?"

His tone was flat, deadpan, and remarkably doleful. "Revenge," he said. "Plain and simple. Revenge."

5 ON THE WAY OUT KATHY GAVE SCHUYLER
a spray of paper flowers she pretended to
pull out of her ear. When he clasped them to his bosom,
his smile was wide enough to slide a 747 into. Kathy
asked me to drop her off on Broadway, claimed she had
to find a costume shop. As she gamboled off into the
freakish hordes on Broadway, she didn't attract nearly
as much attention in her whiteface as she would have
downtown or even in the U District. On the corner a
handsome man with a tenor voice was singing loudly
about his own suicide attempts.

I thought about Eric. Revenge. Revenge for what?
What could he possibly have done to get Fred or anyone
else so riled?

All three of Eric Castle's most recent employers were
within eight blocks of Broadway and John. Two restau-
rants and a movie theater. The theater wasn't open yet.
At the first restaurant, Mario's, the owner was off for
the day with what they told me was a touch of Smir-
noff's flu.

After hiking down Broadway six blocks to a hole-in-
the-wall restaurant called Terrell's Terrace, I got lucky.

At first I thought he was a volcano on a cart, but a
second glance told me it was only a fat man smoking a

cigar and rolling toward me in a wheelchair. He was barrel-chested, in black slacks and an open-necked white shirt. Named Finnegan, he was somewhere between forty-five and a hundred. His pale face had the same texture as a new cake of soap, and his hair looked like a brush. I showed him my PI license and some other ID and gave him a number in the SPD he could call if he wanted to hear somebody vouch for me.

With a casual wave of his stubby hand Finnegan told me it wasn't necessary. Smoke billowed around us and engulfed my face. He screwed his black eyes deeper into his skull, squinted up at me, and said, "Eric Castle? Sure, I remember him. Good kid."

We were blocking restaurant traffic in the corridor between the kitchen and the belly of the restaurant, so he invited me down a dark hallway and into a cell-like room, where he backed his wheelchair into a cluttered corner. I stood. By the time he got the cigar stoked up and the wheelchair into the small office we might as well have been inside a wood stove. "Eric? Yeah, I remember Eric. What you wanna know?"

"He was here about . . . ?"

"Left last summer. I'd say he worked for me two, three months. Just decided to up and take off."

"Why did he leave Mr. Finnegan? You didn't get any phone calls about him?"

"Let's see. Yeah, matter of fact, I did. Some trash about something Eric had done. Soon as I found out what it was, I hung up on the fucker."

"They call again?"

"Few times. Like I said, soon as I realized what it was all about, I hung up on the fucker."

"You recognize the voice?"

"Nope."

"How far apart were they? Man or woman?"

"About a week. A man. That's all I recall."

"Can you relate any of what they said? It might be important."

"Hell, I coulda, maybe, last summer. Not now. The gist was Eric was a bum. Like I said, hung up on 'em."

"Eric told me you fired him over those phone calls."

Finnegan compressed his thick features as if a flashbulb had gone off in his face. "Me? Hell, I never fired the kid. I told him he had a friend that was no friend makin' these here phone calls. Next day he quit."

"Why would he say you fired him?"

"Better ask him. I never did. Fact, I told him his private life was none of my affair, long as he did his job around here and kept his nose clean. He was a good worker. Conscientious. Smart as a whip. Was considering promoting him to morning manager. Hell, now that I think of it, I told him same time I told him about the phone calls. That I wanted to make him the morning manager, soon as he got a little more experience under his belt. Must have scared him. Getting a raise and all."

"Success does that sometimes."

"Funny about them calls. I really didn't give them much credence, but Eric kept pestering me about what the guy said and looking at me all hangdoglike. Told him what I told you. Didn't stay on the line long enough to hear the spiel. Want to know the truth, I think he probably did do something a little kinked. He sure as hell looked guilty. Kept staring right through my eyes and into my brain, if you know what I mean. Spooky. I still would have made him a manager. Don't get many workers like him."

"If you didn't fire him, how did he come to quit?"

"Day after I told him about the calls he didn't show up. Phoned his place to make certain he was all right, and he said he was going to school in another state. Won some sort of scholarship. I know he was lying, 'cause I seen him on the street a few weeks back."

"You think he was lying, huh?"

"I know he was. Got to talking to some of the help. They said he lied all over the place. Told some girl here he used to be best friends with Jack Nicholson. Can you believe it? Here a whopper, there a whopper, everywhere a whopper. Old MacDonald.''

Before I left Terrell's, I used the manager's phone and called one of my oldest friends from the SPD, Smithers, a chubby, good-natured man I'd mustered in with. He was still a patrolman and did favors from time to time. His tastes ran to the exotic and the overweight, and as long as I kept introducing him to women who bought their clothes from Omar the tentmaker, he would do almost anything for me. I was saving the bounteous receptionist at Leech, Bemis, and Ott for a special surprise. I asked him to run Eric Castle's name through the computer and call me at home. On the way down Broadway I scanned the busy sidewalks for Kathy, but she was gone.

At home I checked my answer machine, then erased the dirty joke some teenaged prankster had put on it. I was in the spare bedroom, pumping up my bike tires, when Smithers called back. "What'd you find?"

"Clean as a priest's dick. You sound anxious. This important? Don't have a thing on him.''

I had hoped I could find something right away, something that might be a start in clearing Margaret Pugsley. After all, Eric had a racing bicycle, he knew Fred, and he didn't get along with him. He also appeared to have something in his past worth concealing. And there was more. I kept thinking about what the girl in front of the house had called Eric. Pervert.

"Not even a couple of FIRs?''

"Nothing. I'll check NCIC when I go to work tonight. Call ya back.''

"Thanks, Smitty.''

"What's this about?''

"Probably nothing.''

"I heard you found that stiff this morning in Laurelhurst.''

"Kathy and I. Don't tease her about it. She's going to have nightmares for a long time as it is.''

"How about yourself?''

"Me? I always have nightmares. This won't make any difference. I'll put another Mickey night-light in the bedroom."

"Sounded bad. Chessman was out there snooping around. You on a hot case?"

"It started off slow, but it's beginning to show some intriguing twists."

"Like what?"

"Tell you about it later."

I suited up in cleated shoes, wool tights, gloves, then pedaled across to Seventeenth, freewheeled down through the University of Washington campus and came out at the Montlake cut. I was three minutes early for our appointment, and I ended up waiting almost half an hour. When Eric finally showed up, I was shivering, angry, and tired of watching the sparse winter boat traffic below the bridge, of feeling the slight rocking of the bridge as cars raced across the steel grating. His former employer had said he was dependable. I wondered if he was just trying to avoid me. I had only peeked through a window into his life, but so far it was all chaos.

We agreed on a route, and I warmed up while he drafted me in the Arboretum. "I was pretty good once," he said, yelling over my shoulder. "Almost got second in the Nationals."

I kept up with most of the cycling publications, and I'd never heard of Eric Castle. Second in the Nationals? And he knew Jack Nicholson? And he was a computer consultant? He must have pegged me for a dope.

When we dropped down beside the windswept water on Lake Washington Boulevard, we rode side by side until a car approached, and then we singled out long enough to let it breeze past. Despite his lies, Eric was conversant with cycling etiquette, had the look and feel of somebody who'd been riding a few years, rode a nice line and signaled potholes, broken glass, and dog doo when he was in front.

I wasn't surprised that Eric seemed to be laboring to keep up. He had heavy clincher wheels and I was riding racing sewups, so it was going to be a little tougher for him all along, especially on the hills. When we got to the slope on the way back, I would gun it and burn him. Things like that kept a ride interesting.

"I understand you worked for Micro Darlings?"

"Helped found it. Me, Fred, Daryl Rittenhouse, Ashley Phillips, and Gunnar. Those were the days. But I'll get back in the chips. I'm almost there. My writing is going real well. Hell, ask any of them. I was the one wrote all those early programs. I practically made Micro myself. Kidpro? That was all my doing. Combining video games with educational programs in a meaningful way. We were first with that, and it was mostly my doing. Later on Micro Darlings sued me to stop me from doing anything else with it. With my own programs! That's like telling Linda Ronstadt she can't sing in the key of B."

"They win?"

"Hell, I didn't fight it. I figured they can have it if they need it so damn bad. I'll move on and come up with something even better."

"How's that working out?"

"Almost there. Think I've got a buyer for a totally new concept in education."

"Was the lawsuit the reason you left Micro? Artistic integrity and all that?"

"Ask them." We were pedaling in 42 × 17s, moving at a good clip.

"You telling me you don't know why you left Micro?"

"I'm not telling you anything. Ask them."

"I will. You said something on the hill about revenge. What was that about?"

"You're not going to find that out from me, man."

"Why not?"

"You're just not."

"How long you been divorced?"

"Binnie left me about the time I quit Micro. Five years ago. When the shit hits the fan . . ."

"Let's assume for a moment that Fred didn't send you this snake and didn't make the phone calls. Who else would want revenge badly enough to put a poisonous snake in your bed? Or phone your employers to get you fired? Your ex-wife?"

"Hell, just Fred. We used to be best friends. When we parted, it wasn't exactly on amicable terms."

"How so?"

"Fred had a temper. He was mad at me."

"For five years?"

"He was never what you'd call mature."

"Why was he angry?"

"You figure it out."

"I can if I have to, but it would be a whole lot easier for both of us if you decided to tell me."

"I've never done anything the easy way, Black. Why start now?"

"And this is all tied in with why you left Micro Darlings?" He shrugged. "If somebody was going to do something, why didn't they do it five years ago?"

"Listen, Black, I'm not going to talk about Micro anymore. You keep asking, and I'll peel off and ride alone. You ask them about it if you want to know so bad. Look, I'll level with you. I lost the right to visit my kids. Schuyler I can see, but I've got two younger kids living with their mother in Bellevue. It's killing me." He turned to look at me, and I thought for just an instant that I could commiserate with him. His hair was windblown, his eyes were watery, and his face had lost its pallor.

"A guy can live with losing a woman. That happens. But kids . . . They're growing, man. They're doing things they'll never do again. I never got to see my boy learn to ride a bike. I don't have much money, so affording a lawyer to get my kids back isn't easy. Plus I'm paying child support. The cops get on me for something, it's going to break me financially. I just got this new job, and I can't afford to lose it."

"Why can't you see your other two kids?"

"Long story. 'Sides, I doubt if any of this has anything at all to do with Fred's death."

"You say somebody made calls to your employers
and they fired you?"

"Fred. I don't have any proof, but it was him."

"What'd you do? Get him drunk and pull all his
teeth?" He stared at the macadam in front of our spinning wheels, and I could see that he wasn't going to
reply. "I spoke to one of your employers. Finnegan.
He said you quit. Said you were a liar."

"Yeah, so maybe I did walk out on him. But he would
have axed me anyway. Somebody tries to knock your
head off with a sledgehammer and you fall down trying
to escape, they'd be nuts to say you were going to skin
your shins anyway. I figured, What the hell. Lookit,
Black. People have been bugging me for a long time.
I've had people shoot at me from cars. Had all the
windows in my Toyota knocked out three different
times. A guy tried to run me off the road right here in
a blue van just last week. If I hadn't seen him in time,
I think he would have killed me. Get these hate letters
in the mail."

I wasn't certain how much of this I could believe.
After all, there wasn't a cyclist in town who hadn't had
run-ins with cars. He almost got second in the National-
als, his best friend used to be Jack Nicholson, he'd made
Micro Darlings single-handedly, and somebody was
trying to kill him. Sure.

"Save any of 'em? The hate letters?"

"Hell, no. Save that stuff, and it's like sticking pins
in your own voodoo doll. I burn it."

"So where's the evidence?"

"Got none."

"What about witnesses? Anybody else see any of
this? You ever call the police?"

"I didn't take names. I don't need any. I know what
he was doing to me. And I got no use for cops. I don't
have to prove it to you. You want to know why, you
figure it out."

"When we went to your house, a young woman there
called you a pervert."

"Theresa? Looks like somebody stapled her lower lip
to her chin?" She had been slightly cross-eyed as well,
and he turned to me and mimicked that. I laughed in
spite of myself. "Theresa used to have the room across
from mine in the basement. She would come over in
her nightgown and try to get something going. Smelled
like toe jam."

"And you didn't want any part of it?"

"I'm—" Eric hawked and spit into a tree as we
passed. A poodle came bounding out of the underbrush
and nipped at his pedals until he popped it with his
pump. Yelping, the dog did a somersault and scampered back where it had come from. The bite wasn't
what hurt. It was when the mutt touched your front
wheel and the wheel stopped and you went over the
handlebars and your teeth hit the pavement at twenty
miles an hour. That part hurt. After he had fitted the
hand pump into his frame and pedaled a few hard
strokes to catch me, he said, "I'm not really interested
in women until I get my children back."

"Sounds like you want your wife back as well."

"Her, too. Yeah," he said, his voice trailing off into
the wind. "That would be great. But she's remarried.
She's gone."

"So Theresa called you a pervert because you turned
her down?"

"Basically. Made some kind of fool of herself trying
to get me to . . . you know."

"Yeah," I said. "I got women chasing me all over
the place, too."

"Okay, don't believe me. Bastard."

"Kind of a feisty guy, aren't you?"

Eric Castle pulled even with me, looked over, and
laughed. I couldn't help myself. The way he did it—it
was contagious. I laughed, too. He was devious as a
gypsy with a handful of raffle tickets, but all of a sudden
he seemed like a younger brother to me.

"Tell me about these other attempts on your life."

"You know that footbridge in the Arboretum? Somebody dropped a car battery off it a month ago."

"You see 'em?"

"It was dark. The danged battery brushed my shoulder and scared me so bad I crashed. Bent a nice Super champion rim. By the time I got up whoever did it was gone."

"Could have been juveniles."

"Hell," he said, "it wasn't juvies."

"Okay, it wasn't juvies. What about the van? See who was in it?"

"Somebody in a ski mask."

"Let's move on to something else. Why can't you visit your kids?"

"That's . . . a long story. And none of your business. It's between Binnie and myself. She's a good woman, but she's a little confused. Leave her out of this. She doesn't have anything at all to do with any of this. She's a decent woman trying to make a new life for herself. For her everything's coming up roses, and I don't want you spoiling it."

"You know Margaret Pugsley?"

"Sure. Of course."

"Looks like they're going to pin it on her."

"Fred, you mean? She killed Fred?"

"That's what they say."

"Hell, Maggie wouldn't swat a fly. Why she ever stayed with Fred and took all that abuse, I'll never know." Eric said more, but I couldn't hear him. Nor could I catch him. We were heading back and were on our way up Madrona. Instead of staying on Lake Washington Boulevard, he'd taken the steeper hill, and I'd been glad, until he stood up, dancing on the pedalo, throwing his bike frame from side to side. Tires whispering loudly, I kept up with him for almost half a block; but my thighs were beginning to burn, and he was accelerating, moving away rapidly.

At first I could see the tears in his wool tights and

then just his tights, then his silhouette through the sweat
in my eyes, and after a while he was a mere blur in the
distance. He made it look so damn easy. The customers
on a Metro bus gaped at him. He was moving. So was
I, on my lighter, faster equipment, but by the time the
crazy fool in the truck almost sideswiped me Eric was
just a speck.

Actually it was a van. I was tired and my legs were
aching and my lungs were pumping overtime and I was
trying to figure where Eric had gotten all that power
when it occurred to me. A blue van.

Eric said he'd almost been clobbered last week by a
blue van.

By the time my brain, retarded by overwork and fa-
tigue, figured it out, the van was too far away for me
to get the license. I wasn't quite to the crest of the hill
when I heard the clamor. It was coming from the spot
where Eric should have been.

A whining engine. And then something else. Back-
fires. No.

Gunshots.

Three shots.
I know. I counted.

It was an ambush. Lord help Eric.

I pedaled harder, dropped the chain down onto the fifteen cog, and threw my whole body into it, sizzing my rear tire on some wet leaves. The shots sounded like a small-caliber revolver fired from a vehicle.

Screeching rubber. Tires howling. An engine roaring off into the distance. Could have been a TV show on any network except PBS.

When I crested the hill, Eric had vanished.

I scanned the vicinity for the van, but it looked like a Tinkertoy in the distance, sooty deposits of exhaust wafting behind it. I dropped into my saddle and freewheeled, zigzagging, looking for some trace of Eric.

Fresh black tire tracks had bisected the curb at an angle, then become muddy smudges in a grass strip. I wondered if he'd been kidnapped or flattened. Wouldn't that take the cake? First on the scene to two murders in one day. That would be my record almost.

He was supine in the wet grass beyond the sidewalk.

The body was motionless, sprawled on its back, a sheen of perspiration on the face, cropped dark hair matted. Twenty-five feet away his bicycle was upside down in a shrub. Eric had leaped the curb to escape the van—no easy feat on a thin-wheeled racing bicycle—and the van had lurched over the curb behind him. It looked as if the van tires had spun in the grass, divots and slick burnt-chocolate spots marring the lawn. I looked for tire tracks across his body. They had tried to make him a Frisbee, had taken at least two swipes at him.

His chest was heaving. Good. He was alive. I couldn't see any blood. Nor could I tell if he was winded because of our quick ascent of the hill or because of his brush with an early grave.

When I knelt beside his head, we both were sweating, the droplets sluicing off my nose and chin into the grass. For some reason I felt guilty, as if I'd stood by and watched my little brother get his arm twisted. "You okay?"

He was already trying to struggle to his feet, mouth pretzeled in pain. "Still think I'm lying?"

"Heard shots. You see who it was?"

Castle was small enough that I could have picked him up bodily, the way one would pick up a child. I tried to help him to his feet, but he fended my hands away, coughed and choked on the nippy February afternoon. "Lemme alone."

"Sure, pal."

Except for a bent brake lever, his Colnago was undamaged. I checked the wheels, picked up the frame, and spun them. In his haste to scramble away from the deranged van driver, he must have heaved the twenty-one-pound bicycle into the shrubs. "Your rear wheel lost its true. Broke a spoke," I said.

Eric was on his feet now, hunched low, hands braced on his knees. "No, I didn't see the bastard. And he shot at me. Some sort of pistol out the window when he saw he wasn't going to run me down. The bastard had a ski mask on. Windows all smoked and grimy. Never got the license either. Too busy saving my butt."

"How many people?"

"Just the one."

"How big?"

"Medium to small, I guess. Hard to tell. Could have been a kid, even a woman."

"I didn't get a good make on it either," I said. "Late sixties or early seventies. Sky blue. A Chevy. Maybe a Dodge. Must be a million of them in the state." I would have said more, but I spotted the lopsided star engraved on Eric's aluminum seat post. Another one was painted on the down tube of his frame. Neither star was precisely identical to the one on the sprocket tool that had killed Fred Pugsley, but they were close enough for government work. When I turned around to confront him with my knowledge, he was vomiting. Some of it was breakfast; most of it was blood.

After jerking his water bottle out of his frame, I rushed over. "All right," he said, swigging from the bottle, eyes teary, nose dripping. "Happens all the time. I'm all right."

"We gotta get you to a hospital, buddy." My shoes were beginning to absorb wetness from the grass, and my feet were feeling icy. "You're bringing up blood. Did he hit you?"

"Leave me alone, goddammit. Told you this happens all the time." The vomitus in the grass contained coffee-ground material. Old blood. It had been in his gut long before the van came on the scene. Jaunty as he pretended to be, inside he was dying. Probably had been sick for some time. The poor nincompoop had an ulcer. After tapping his cleats clean and fitting his pump, he climbed onto his bike, all the while pretending nothing of consequence had occurred.

Before he launched out, he stood high on his pedals, searched up and down the street three or four times warily, and eased his wheels over the curb, then sat on his Brooks saddle and kicked his cleated feet into the toe clips.

As long as we had been moving, the wind cooling us, we had kept an equilibrium. But now, because of our sudden halt, the trapped heat in our bodies had found nowhere to go, and sweat was worming off our faces.

"You don't want to call the cops?"

"What for? A blue van? No license. No model. They're not going to do anything."

"Might do you some good to go on record," I said. "In case you see him again."

"Bull."

"Where were you at seven-thirty this morning, Eric?"

"Sleeping. I guess I slept till nine, nine-thirty. What? That when Fred died? You just spring these things on me, don't you?"

"The cops'd be worse. You have a sprocket tool?"

"Look, I've taken this much guff because Freddie used to be a friend and I figured I owed him. Especially if you're working with his lawyers. After all, I did mail that snake. But lay off, okay?"

"Fred was killed with a sprocket tool, Eric." The boys downtown would be peeved at me for letting this out.

It stopped him. The rhythm of his pedaling broke. It took awhile for him to visualize it. "You mean he got whipped to death?"

"Had a star engraved on it. I noticed you've got a couple of stars on your equipment."

"Stick it on everything. My trademark."

"Got a sprocket tool?"

"In my room." His voice tightened a notch and turned rancid. "Want to come back with me and check it for blood?"

"Maybe somebody took it," I said, though I had no reason to believe that. Something in my solar plexus told me he was in it up to his skinny neck. "Maybe when they put the rattler in your bed. When was the last time you saw the tool?"

"Couple months back. We'll go look," he said. And we did, businesslike, the both of us.

After we'd clip-clopped down his narrow concrete hallway in our stiff, plastic-soled riding shoes, he dragged a toolbox out from under his rumpled bed and showed me a sprocket tool, sure enough, engraved with a lopsided star. From the bottom of the box he dragged out a second tool, marked indentically, the handles on both tools made of pressed aluminum. The haft of the one I'd picked out of Margaret Pugsley's hands that morning was a cruder version of the same tool, constructed with a heavier, steel handle that was round and felt like a piece of pipe. The older ones made deadly weapons.

As was the case with most efficient bike mechanics, he kept two of them. That way he didn't have to use a vise and possibly damage sprocket teeth. "You ever lose one of these?" I asked.

For an instant I thought he was going to slash me. Then he sat back and stared a hole into the wall. "Ever had another one of these, Eric?"

"This is it," he said, but I noticed his hand was trembling as he held the tools out. "Just these two. Bet my life on that."

"You might be doing just that. Know anybody else marks equipment with a star?"

He shook his head. He was sitting on his bed, sweating. "I want only one thing in my life. Can't you understand that? I want my kids back. Tad and Lucretia."

"And your wife?"

Peeling his cycling jacket off and draping it over a chair inside out to let it dry, he narrowed his midnight eyes on me. "Yeah, I miss her. It's that obvious?"

"Maybe not to everyone."

"Still think I was lying?" He scrubbed his face in a towel. "About the van and the battery and all?"

"Still think it was Fred? That'd be a pretty neat trick, sneaking off the medical examiner's table and climbing into that van."

He grinned. Under other circumstances, we might have become friends.

Gambling on his goodwill, I pulled out a Polaroid photograph. "Ever see this before?"

"Out! Get the hell out of here! And don't come back." He was outraged, no doubt about that, but he wasn't shocked. He'd seen the photo before, or one similar. He punctuated my exit. "Asshole!"

"Love you, too," I said. It took seven blocks to dry off enough so that I wasn't freezing. Spinning low gears, I scanned the streets for blue vans. At home in my kitchen I stripped off my outer layers and, after gulping down a glassful of cold water, dialed Ralph Crum in homicide.

"Ralph, my boy," I said.

"What? Think of something you forgot to fess up to this morning?"

"Not really. What have you found out from the evidence boys?"

"You know I can't tell you any of that." I explained enough about Eric Castle that he'd have to investigate him. "Jeezola, that was ugly this morning. I've seen a lot, but those kind never get easy. Makes your eyes dim just thinking about it." He suddenly got solicitous. "How's Kathy taking it?"

"Hasn't said much, but not well, methinks."

"Of course, you know we have to check this Eric Castle out, but I don't think much'll come of it. We pretty much have our man."

"Woman, you mean."

"Whatever. Caught red-handed, so to speak."

"Castle deserves a look-see."

"Sure. We'll interview him. You know that. You ask him what he was doing this morning about seven-thirty? Could have an alibi."

"I asked. Charge her yet?"

"Tomorrow. Next day maybe."

"What are you waiting for? Building the suspense so she'll crack?"

Crum only sloughed that off with a mean-spirited laugh. At least Margaret Pugsley would have thought it mean-spirited. Me, I laughed with him and then regretted it. He was a plodding and reasonably scrupulous worker, and I hoped a chat with Eric Castle might slow him down some. He wasn't doing the busy work for the case, but he was overseeing it. Any team working murders in Laurelhurst would send daily reports to the chief. They needed all the overseeing they could stand.

Later I phoned Kathy Birchfield, thinking I'd take her to dinner at one of the bawdy and raucous Fat Tuesday establishments. Fat Tuesday was Seattle's own scaled-down Mardi Gras. The first year it was held I was still a cop and it'd been hell: riots and bottle throwing and lawsuits. Since then it had settled down. "Sorry. Going out clowning with friends at the Fat celebration," she said. "What'd you find out so far, Thomas?" Without going into detail, I filled her in. When I had finished, she said, "You think Eric had anything to do with it?"

"If he didn't, I don't know where Margaret picked up that sprocket remover. I'll bet money she's never been on a racing bike in her life."

"You call her yet?"

"A few minutes ago. No answer."

In the shower, standing under the hot needle spray suddenly realized Kathy had given me the brushoff. He voice had been squirrely, and I knew her well enough to realize it was because she'd fibbed. She wasn't going out clowning; she was avoiding me.

Once as a child I had been forced to bury five kittens my dog had killed. I had been very young, and it had been raining and dark, and the task had been worse than distasteful, a performance it had taken me years to forget. I fancied that I could smell death all around me that night and that, while I was digging, the smell was climbing into my blue flannel shirt. Until I outgrew that shirt, I could think of nothing except dead kittens when I saw it. In some small way maybe that was how Kathy was feeling about me. She had discovered Fred Pugsley's savagely mauled body in my company. I was her blue flannel shirt.

Next morning I waited for a decent hour and drove to Laurelhurst from my place off Roosevelt. It was a short drive, my second trip in two days. A squat, businesslike female nurse with savage green eyes and plump cheeks answered the Pugsley door.

"Mrs. Pugsley's asleep. Probably will be until late this afternoon. Doctor came over early this morning and gave her an injection. It's been quite a shock for her. I guess she was okay, not sleeping but okay, until she opened the microwave in the middle of the night and found it full of blood."

"How long have you been here?"

"Few hours. Doctor called at four-thirty."

"Anybody else here?" She shook her head. She was as compact as a hundred-pound sack of flour. "You here for the duration?"

"Just until she wakes up and gets oriented. Least that's how it stands for now."

I thanked her, and she stood in the doorway and watched me leave. I spent twenty minutes grilling the neighbors, all of whom were over sixty and wanted to hash the case over, hypothesizing, conjecturing, and ruminating endlessly. I bit my tongue and held my peace. Nothing as thrilling or as gory as this had ever infected their sleepy street before. The woman Kathy and I had spotted yesterday over the kitchen sink was the best witness I could find. She had been at the sink all morning, peeling apples. She claimed nothing had driven past except Mrs. Pugsley's BMW and my truck.

"In this neighborhood I hear a car a block away," she said boastfully. "Maggie was the only one who came until you showed up." If she realized what sort of straitjacket she was putting on Maggie's future, she gave no indication of it.

"Pedestrians? See anybody walking?"

"I look up from the sink every few minutes. Habit.

ı would have seen someone. I certainly would have seen someone walking in.''

I drove up the hill and away from Laurelhurst, past Children's Orthopedic and into the U District mid-morning crush. Without thinking about it, I drove across the Evergreen Point Floating Bridge. Jumping off 520 at 104th Northeast, I proceeded to NE Eighth Street, hung a right, and promptly got lost. Bellevue had always been unfathomable and Byzantine to me. After I had pulled to the side of the road and studied a map, I decided she lived near Goat Point, in a clustered development overlooking Lake Washington, the north end of Mercer Island, and, to the west, Seattle's jagged skyline.

It was a big house on a big lot on a street full of big houses on big lots. Beside the house sat a garage that was as large as my entire spread, as well as a concrete driveway that ran around back, probably to a carport for those rainy days when the lady didn't want to get her mink damp.

Ritzy homes. Large yards. Ranch-style houses. Volvos and Saabs and Lincolns in the garages. Everything was so homogeneous I expected they branded the pets to tell them apart. I pulled up in front of the Rogers house.

Using the glass in the storm door for a mirror, I ran my fingers through my hair and thumbed the chimes. I looked pretty damned good in fuzzy glass doors. An onyx plate beside the door said, ''Gunnar and Veronica Rogers.'' I'm not good at scents, but even out in the nippy breeze the house smelled of a hybrid between an antique drawer and an Avon lady who'd been hit by a bus.

Veronica Rogers looked somehow more glamorous this morning, as if her face had just been peeled off the cover of a fashion magazine. She made me feel right at home.

''Oh, you.''

I grinned.

"Your name again? I can't quite place it."

"Thomas Black." Jeezola, I remembered hers. I remembered everything about her.

While she chewed that over, she held the door and reluctantly let me in. A gust of February shouldered its way into the house behind me, and she shivered. "I'm sorry. I wasn't expecting you. The lawyers said you wouldn't want to question me."

"Afraid I do."

"I'll do what I can to help Maggie." The way she said it flip-flopped the words into an accusation, against Margaret and somehow, incredibly, against me. "Mind if I run a little errand first?"

"Not at all. Can I use your phone while I'm waiting?" I noticed a mod plastic pineapple telephone in the entranceway. It seemed odd, in poor taste compared to the rest of the furnishings. She shrugged at it and walked away. I watched.

It had been nagging at me for a while, but I hadn't called my office in the Piscule Building. I might have a whole ton of leads on my answer machine. The sweet, elderly blue-haired lady who shared the office with me had once accidentally erased one of my tapes. The first message was another random dirty joke from the foul-mouthed teenager who'd been laying dirty jokes on my tapes for almost a year. When I caught him, Seattle's supply of Ivory would be low for a month.

Another call was from some bozo trying to sell me shares in a miniature golf course. A relative wanted to borrow money again. Mr. Soft Touch, that's what they called me. And then Desiree came on the line. Typically Desiree used two or three spots to record her messages. She was a big bad biker mama. "I'm going to make you feel like a man," she warbled. "I'll suck your face until your brain turns to a raisin and your teeth sweat. Ever had something you wanted somebody to try, I'm your girl. Thomas . . ." The tape ran out. Never fear. She'd be on the next. And the next.

Through with her errands, Veronica Rogers came back into the hall and watched my face turn pink.

Mrs. Rogers had short blond hair and a tan that, considering the Northwest's winters, had probably been nursed under a sunlamp. She was one of those women who made you wonder how far the tan extended. You felt impolite wondering, but you wondered all the same. She wore a loose print blouse under a waist-length jacket and expensively faded charcoal jeans that were tight enough to make you remember them but not so tight as to beg fashion. Her high-heeled shoes were a bright cherry red, her sockless feet evenly brown.

"Desiree Nash, Thomas. I don't want anything, just your pleasure. Guarantee you'll never forget it. Anything you want. Name it. Anything. Any time." I hung up and almost broke the pineapple.

"Sorry," I said, wondering if she'd heard any of it. Desiree's sheepherder voice should have been audible in Yakima.

Veronica Rogers led me through a walkway lined with tall tropical plants and ferns and into a formal dining room, through that and into a smaller sitting room. Shorter than I'd thought at first, she didn't wiggle a bit. She rode those cherry red heels like a sergeant at arms. Chrome-plated figures on several trophies in the dining room hinted that she played tennis to keep firm. I recognized paintings on the wall from a local artist. Investments. Fifteen hundred dollars a crack.

She gestured for me to sit on an aqua sofa that was so pristine and satiny I felt as if I were deflowering a virgin. She sat across from me on a straight-backed chair. I said, "Veronica . . ."

Crossing her legs primly, she folded her hands on top of one squashed but firm thigh, waiting until I was through watching. She had a very keen sense of her own attractiveness. Her voice wafted through the room, outlining her station in life. "Do me a big favor? Call me Mrs. Rogers."

She would have done less damage if she'd smacked me in the skull with a steel-toed boot. She was better than I had run up against in a long time.

7

"TELL ME ABOUT MAGGIE AND FRED. SHE'D been here two days?"

"The kids call it Maggie's room, downstairs." Kids? I hadn't seen a kid track anywhere on the premises.

"What prompted this last visit?"

"Same thing prompted all of them. Fred screamed at her. Or Fred slapped her. Or Fred dumped a bowl of soup over her head at The Butcher. Whatever. This time I thought sure she was going to fly to Reno. It just seemed like the last straw."

"Was she angry or just hurt?"

"Both."

"How about that morning?"

"I didn't see her. But she'd had it with him for quite some time."

"You think she did it, don't you?"

"Me?" Her words were flat and precise, a perfunctory genuflection to a long-standing friend. "No, of course not. Margaret isn't capable of something like that."

"Mrs. Rogers," I said, "does somebody in this household own a bicycle?"

"We all do."

"A racing bicycle. With tools and the whole gig."

"Nothing like that. No."

"How well did you know Fred?"

"Known him for years. My husband used to work for Micro Darlings, was in at the inception. We went to their parties, and they came to ours. Fred was godfather to one of my children."

"And Maggie's your best friend?"

"One of many good friends."

"Fred have any enemies?"

"He could be abrasive. I wouldn't know of any enemies though." It was incredible how clearly she could intimate that Margaret was the killer, using nothing but body language and tone of voice. She'd make a perfectly lousy witness for the defense.

Something gray-blue flashed past the half-closed draperies, and I heard a loud motor outside, tooting through a broken muffler. Veronica Rogers wasn't surprised, didn't even incline her regal head toward the window.

Footsteps in back of the house. Somebody was coming our way, several somebodies. Then, clean-shaven and deferential, a skinny young man of about seventeen stubbed through the dining room, trailed by two children, a towheaded boy and a little girl of about seven with the darkest red hair I'd seen in a long while. Until I saw the boy, I'd assumed Veronica Rogers bleached her hair, but the boy's was the same white-wine shade.

"My stepson, Dennis, and my two children." Both the younger kids were dressed out like royalty on parade, and neither one had played in those clothes. Or ever would. Wooden soldiers, they stood, apprehensive and alert, awaiting their mother's white glove inspection.

Veronica Rogers's mouth turned up at the corners, but I couldn't tell if it was a counterfeit smile or something uglier. Neither could the tense kids. I wanted to say, "Ease up, lady," but it was none of my affair. She explained, "The furnace went out at school." She scrutinized them. "Do you have your homework?"

The younger boy said, "Yes, Mother."

"There's a stain on your dress, young lady." The girl peered down guiltily.

"Michelle did it."

"Lucy." Veronica Rogers's tone was controlled, but the message stung. Lucy turned around obediently and marched away behind the two boys. She didn't need spurs for these kids. Like a Comanche warrior on horseback, she had them trained to knee commands.

After they left, I said, "Wonder if I could take a peek at the room Margaret stayed in."

"Is that necessary?"

"If you don't mind."

Silently she led me out of the room and down a narrow, carpeted stairway to the lower level, the basement, reserved for children and guests. I caught a glimpse of pixie-eyed Lucy as she vanished around a corner.

As we passed a window, I saw Dennis outside in the backyard, clomping around in rubber boots and hauling a sudsy bucket and hose to his van. An older van, it was blue. And shabby. Sky blue. I stopped in my tracks. From this angle I couldn't see enough to tell if it was the one that had attacked Eric.

"Come this way," Veronica Rogers said, pointing at the door with the chilled politeness of an airline hostess suffering a migraine.

Now that I thought about it, I couldn't be sure yesterday's vehicle had been that shade of blue at all. Maybe it was, but I couldn't swear it in court. It didn't make any sense. No sense whatsoever. Dennis, her stepson? Why would that skinny kid ambush Eric Castle? But maybe it hadn't been Dennis. It could have been anybody. Her husband, Gunnar. Veronica herself. Or any of a million other van owners. I was weaving fantasies.

Or—more fantasies—I wondered if they let friends borrow their vehicles. But then, Margaret's afternoon could easily have been accounted for. Undoubtedly she had spent time with the attorneys and police. Besides, her distress had not, I thought, been faked. She would have been in no condition to drive, much less attempt murder. I would find out. And then again, maybe I was waltzing off on a tangent. Perhaps this was just a bizarre coincidence.

All eyes, I followed her into the bedroom, wallowing in her closeness. A small bedroom, it was used partially for storage, a single bed, a dresser, a trunk on the floor with books ricked up on it, and a bathroom at the back. Several cardboard boxes marked "Xmas ornaments" and "Xmas lights" stood in a corner. To judge by the number of boxes, in December they ignited the joint so half the state could see it.

"Nice," I said, glancing out at the blue van again, a Chevy. Veronica circled around and blocked my view.

"If there's nothing else . . ." A phone rang in another section of the house. Instantly she was off in a frantic rush. "Darn. Let me get that. I'll just be a minute."

She might as well have left a dope fiend in a roomful of morphine. Working feverishly, I systematically rifled every drawer, closet, and cupboard in the room. I tossed the mattress and found a dog-eared pornographic magazine the stepson must have hidden. I threw it into a bottom drawer under some old drapes. That would panic him.

The payoff was in a shabby Overland trunk, black and battered, the lock broken. I knelt and hurriedly clamped a row of paperback mysteries between my hands and lifted them off, bookends and all. The movement disturbed a thin layer of dust. I could hear Veronica Rogers talking on the phone in another room. "I. Magnin . . . Oh, yes, Brit. . . . It was on sale. . . . Maggie? No, I haven't spoken to her since last night."

The trunk was bulging, trophies and medals—and letters. Love letters. The trophies were packed carefully, the letters sandwiched down along one side next to some old computer texts. I quickly pawed through the trophies until I found the tools underneath. No sprocket remover, but there were crank removers, a spoke wrench, and some Sugino chain rings. One trophy was inscribed "2nd place—Rose Festival—Eric Castle."

Something funny was going on.

I rifled through the letters, all addressed to Veronica Salter, McCarty Hall, at the University of Washington. I read one. It began "Dearest Binnie, Last night after the game was the rarest and most beautiful thing that ever happened to me."

It took me a few seconds for the implications of what I'd discovered to stop rebounding in my skull.

"What are you doing?"

I looked up. She stood in the doorway, giving me an acerbic and somewhat amusing look, short and cute as a button, her locks flopping across one eye. "Lucretia?"

"Mommy calls me Lucy. How did you know my name was Lucretia?"

"I met your father yesterday."

"My father? Gunnar?"

"Your real father. Eric."

"Eric?"

"You remember him? We rode bicycles together yesterday. He used to be a racer, didn't he?"

Before she could stop herself, she blurted, "We went to bicycle races every Wednesday night. It was fun. Do you really know my father? I don't remember very much, but Tad tells me about it. I don't see Daddy anymore."

"That's too bad." I was thinking the next time she saw him might be on the news when he got arrested.

"What the hell do you think you're doing?"

It was Veronica hulking in the doorway above her daughter, examining me and the trunk and the love letters in my hands. The green eyes became vortices. I was a dolt. "I'm sure we've finished our interview, Mr. Black. Lucy, you go to your room and don't come out."

Lucy backed up out of her mother's vision but not

out of the fray. She had a stake in this, and she sensed it.

"Nice kids, Binnie. I'd hate to see them cheated out of a father who loved them."

Her words came out like machined and polished bolts on a conveyor belt. "They have a father who loves them, and I stopped cheating them the day I left that other person. I made a mistake letting you in. It's a mistake I won't repeat. You have sixty seconds to vacate the premises."

"You were married to Eric Castle, weren't you?"

"What gives you the right to paw through my personal possessions?" Her outrage got the best of her composure, and she almost broke into tears. Her bulwarks weren't as thick as I had thought or as she pretended. She was right. I had overstepped the bounds of propriety, something I often did on cases.

"I'm sorry."

"I doubt you've ever been sorry in your life. You creep. Know who you remind me of? My ex-husband, Eric."

"I overstepped myself, Mrs. Rogers. I really want to apologize. Sometimes I turn into an imbecile."

"Margaret will be upset to hear about this." It was a quiet threat, almost an afterthought, from a person who knew how to get things done, had seen strings pulled. The implication was that I'd soon be out of work.

"I've been fired before, Veronica."

"I asked you not to call me that."

"Mrs. Rogers, yesterday somebody came painfully close to killing Eric."

She had been studying a lamp in the corner, but she looked up now, her green eyes becoming moist. I couldn't tell if it was remnants of rage or what I'd said about Eric. Lucretia was still watching from the other room. I winked at the kid, and she, surprisingly, winked back. For seven, she had spunk. I winked again, but she was gone.

"Eric's been telling stories like that for years. He's the biggest liar you'll ever meet."

"I was there. I saw it." Stretching the truth a bit wouldn't hurt. The truth was elastic. But even as I spoke, I wondered if Eric might have hired someone to trump up the skirmish. It had been awfully convenient for him to race up the hill like that, putting me out of sight just at the moment of the ambush. I'd seen divorced husbands do screwier things. "Somebody tried to run over him in a blue van. I thought it was a Dodge, but I could be wrong about that. Could have been a Chevy. When that didn't work, they fired a couple of pistol shots at him."

It took awhile for the implications of my tale to sink in. Then it took all her willpower to keep from looking out the window at her stepson's van. "Just leave, Mr. Black."

She walked across the room and led me in the general direction of the front door.

"Eric didn't want me to come here." She stopped and looked at me, really looked at me for the first time since I'd entered her house. For some goofy reason, my indiscretion and my ties to her husband had actually, I thought, brought us closer. My voice sounded foggy. "He loves you very much. He warned me several times not to come here. Didn't want you bothered. He loves the children, too. Seeing them again is all he thinks about. And you."

"Eric has always loved children." Her words were as smooth as the skin of a peach, but underneath they had a slashing bite. She continued toward the front door, up the stairs, and into the front room.

I noticed there was a wiggle this time. It was the kind of hootchy-kootchy stuff that made knocking sounds in the hollow of your chest. "I'll appreciate it if you don't bother me again. In fact, I'll phone the police if you do."

"Veronica. You don't—" But she shut the door on me; didn't slam it, just closed it. She was a class act

all the way, and I had blown it. Sometimes this job was
the last thing I wanted to do. I spotted a mop of red
hair in a downstairs window. I waved, but Lucy was
gone.

The contrast between the way Veronica lived and the
way Eric Castle subsisted in his damp basement with
the navy gray paint on the floor was almost laughable.
It was difficult to imagine the goddess inside this house
sleeping with the bedraggled, down-on-his-luck computer programmer I'd gone riding with yesterday. Yet
she'd had three children by him. I couldn't help thinking
that instead of living with his grandparents, Schuyler
might enjoy this Bellevue life-style. Private schools.
Soccer twice a week in the fall. Tennis lessons.

My expectation was that Veronica would peek out the
window to see whether I'd left the neighborhood, but
when she didn't, I hopped out of the truck and hiked
up the steep drive. I didn't want to, but I was too close
to pass it up. In another neighborhood I might get shot
for this kind of stunt; but I wasn't in another neighborhood, and I'd already made a fool of myself. There was
no way I could feel any more foolish than I'd felt when
Veronica caught me digging in that trunk.

A burgundy two-tone Lincoln Continental sporting a
sunroof sat behind the windows in the closed garage.
Sudsy water trickled down the driveway. I skipped over
the stream. Dennis was nowhere to be seen. When I
got to the van, I wrote down the license number, which
was mostly obscured with sludge. The right rear fender
was blashed in. So was the left rear. It was a beater
van, a teenager's first car, and the stereo speakers
blasted away, tarnishing my thoughts. There was really
only one way to tell if this was the vehicle used in the
attack yesterday.

I knelt. If somebody had been spinning the tires in
the grass yesterday, chances were I'd find evidence underneath. Mud in the wheel wells, grass divots trapped
under the frame. I peered under the Chevy. What I saw
was a pair of huge brown eyes.

Dennis Rogers.

He was on a creeper, scrubbing underneath the vehicle. Who the heck washed the underside of a beater van?

"Morning," I said, my grin lopsided.

He was shaky but resolute, courageous for a kid who was probably still suffering the indignities of high school.

"Mother was just out. She said you weren't to prowl around. *Mother! Mother!*"

"Okay, okay," I said, holding my hands up. "I'm leaving. I'm leaving. Nice van. Yours?"

He didn't know how to answer my question, so he nodded. He had crawled out now and was facing me, brandishing a long-handled scrubbrush.

"You driving around in it yesterday afternoon?"

"Don't answer that, Denny." A spray of water splashed the back of my jacket and whipped up my neck into my hair like ice. Behind me Veronica Rogers wielded the garden hose. I ran and ducked, but she got my trousers, too.

It wasn't bad. If I kept the heater at full blast, I might dry out in half an hour. When I climbed into the Ford, Veronica Castle Rogers and Dennis were at the top of the driveway, watching.

Micro Darlings wasn't far. I couldn't
see anywhere else to go. I'd already spoken
to the neighbors at the murder scene and to the mailer
of snakes. Margaret wouldn't be available for a while,
and even so, I had my doubts about her ability to improve on her story. So I headed toward Micro.

I could see the modern steel and dark glass building
from the freeway, but I couldn't figure out how actually
to ferret my way into the parking lot until I'd cruised
up and down Bellevue's streets for fifteen minutes and
talked to a bunch of smirking gas jockeys wearing baseball caps backward. When I was done futzing around,
I pulled into a huge parking area beneath a chrome and
black enamel sign on top of the building. It said MICRO
DARLINGS in neon. I'd be ahead of the game if these
people didn't hose me down.

Still damp when I slid out of the pickup, I found
myself scanning the enormous population of vehicles in
the lot for blue vans. Surprisingly, out of several hundred choices, I located only two. One was so new as to
exclude it, and the other had primer on the back half. I
sauntered over and checked it anyway. The primer was
old. The Rogerses' van was still the best bet.

By dint of my brown eyes and my tenuous connection

to Maggie Pugsley, I quickly talked my way into the inner sanctum. It was the fifth and top story, with a view that encapsulated some of Lake Washington and a snatch of Seattle's skyline. The receptionist who escorted me up in the elevator wore backless heels and panty hose that rustled like a kite in a breeze. The contagion of excitement surrounding the recent death had to be the reason for the personal touch.

Straining not to look at the wet spots on my clothing, she cooed when she spoke. "Just a minute and I'll see if Mr. Rittenhouse has a minute to talk to you about Fred Pugsley."

"Sure thing."

She left me standing next to a desk in a fancy foyer on the fifth floor. Several offices jutted off this space. A woman sitting at the nearby desk tapped her teeth with the soft end of a pencil and glanced around to see if we were being observed. She whispered. "Fred Pugsley?"

I nodded, and she motioned for me to lean closer.

She had mousy brown hair, heavy glasses, and a beak of a nose. I guessed she gargled with Scope at every break, kept a copy of *Miss Manners' Guide to Excruciatingly Correct Behavior* in a drawer, and maybe taught a youth group for the YWCA. I guessed wrong. She turned out to be a bit of a ghoul. A natural giggle was firmly lodged in her voice, a giggle that the thought of a murdered co-worker couldn't eradicate.

"I'm Fred's secretary. Isn't it awful?"

"How long you been here?"

"At this desk?"

"The company."

"Six years."

"Did you know Eric Castle?"

"Eric? I was his secretary, too. Fred sort of inherited me after . . . Eric broke off with the company."

"So you knew them both?"

She nodded, her tone conspiratorial. "I still can't believe this is happening around here. Fred Pugsley getting murdered like that. I hear his wife did it.''

"Where'd you hear that?''

"Everybody's talking about it. The whole building. I think Brittany Phillips was telling about it before work when she brought her husband in. His car's on the fritz.'' Brittany Phillips? Veronica Castle Rogers had spoken on the phone to somebody named Brit. If they were the same person, the same Brit, I wondered how much of her information came directly from Veronica Rogers.

"Tell me about Fred.''

"Fred was a great boss. He really was. We're going to miss him. Such a tragic thing. But he—he had some problems.''

"Name a couple.''

"This is confidential?''

"Absolutely.''

"He used to proposition me about once a week. And he was serious. Played around with anything in a skirt. The secretaries used to say, 'Heaven help a Scotsman if he comes in here.' I shouldn't be talking like this about him, but it's true.''

"Have any enemies?''

"He ticked everyone off at one time or another. He was in trouble, you know. They were going to fire him.''

"What about Fred and Eric?''

"Well, gee, Fred and Eric used to be about the best friends of anyone around. They got most of the credit for the Kidpro programs in the early years. That's why they called it Micro Darlings. Most of the early stuff was programs or games for kids. Fred designed OrbitGlaze. Or Eric did. I forget which. Did you know that? They really made this company, mostly Fred—he's some sort of genius, you know—and Eric was his ace number one helper. And Ashley's written some stuff.''

The receptionist who'd guided me upstairs emerged from Rittenhouse's office and said, "He'll see you in a moment. If you'll have a seat?'' She gestured at a set of modern pastel furniture backed up against one wall.

"Thanks." After she had rustled off and the elevator swallowed her, I turned back to the secretary at the desk. A nameplate in front of an unopened paperback romance novel said "Sheila Balzac."

"Sheila?"

She nodded, eyes wide, peripheral vision fine-tuned.

"How do the people around here feel about Eric?"

"Eric?" I nodded. "Feel? If he sashayed through that door right now, I don't think more than fifteen people in the building would recognize him. We've expanded so much since he left. And it was mostly because of the work he started with Fred. Too bad he wasn't able to hang around and collect some of the rewards."

"What happened?"

"You'd better talk to Daryl about that problem. I don't think poor Fred ever got over the whole thing, you know. They were, uh, best friends, Fred and Eric. Fred felt so betrayed when it happened. Hit Eric. Poor Fred. I still can't believe it. It was supposed to be awful, the way he died. Five years ago I didn't see it, but I heard he hit Eric. He hit him so hard he knocked some of his teeth out. Then he tossed all Eric's junk off the roof.

"Actually," Sheila Balzac said, "I shouldn't probably tell you this, but I think Fred had an obsession about the problem five years ago. Really did. You a newspaper reporter or what?"

"Private detective."

"That's what we had here the day it happened. A private detective. That's two I've met in my life. I'll bet most people never meet any."

"Bet they don't."

He had a large chest, and he barreled out of the office, pumping my hand with a conviction and grip from another era. I couldn't match either. He had made his mark in the world, and I was a simple, unknown private investigator. Hell, the guy didn't even wear any sappy jewelry or a watch he could have hocked for a Winnebago.

"Daryl Rittenhouse," he said, nudging the heavy, black-rimmed glasses up a notch on his nose with his free hand. He wore a starchy white shirt emblazoned with plaid squares, sleeves rolled up, knit tie swinging loose. I recognized him from a hundred TV interviews and magazine pieces. He was the hottest entrepreneur of computer goods on the planet, the hyping huckster of computer software. "You wanted to talk about Fred Pugsley?"

"Thomas Black," I said. "I'm a private detective."

"That's two I've met in my life," he said, and Sheila Balzac's grin cracked the morning wide. We exchanged looks, and her smile followed me into the office behind Rittenhouse.

Rittenhouse closed the door gently and gestured at a piece of modern furniture formed out of curved chrome pipes. He was younger than I expected. His hair was styled but untended and windblown. It was the color of a copper penny that'd been in the dirt and rain for a few years, except that it was shiny. He was a few inches shorter than my six-one, a couple of pounds heavier than my one-eighty. A few more heavy barbells, a bit more fat. The shirt and slacks were immaculate, but his shoes were worn to nubbins and rounded at the sides of the heels. The slacks were a pinch too long like those of a schoolboy whose mother bought everything for him to grow into.

An expensive home gym was set up in the corner. I noticed his bread-loaf chest was out of proportion to the rest of him. He'd been doing too many bench presses. Reminded me of a young man I knew who tanned only the front half of his body.

"Here about Fred, huh? Terrible thing. Don't know what this damn world is coming to. You expect to hear about something like that in Chile or the Mideast, not Laurelhurst. God, it was such a shock," he said when I was settled and he had scooted his rear end onto his glass-topped desk, dangling his legs. He was a man who believed in eye contact, gray and dim, but eye contact all the same. There was an intensity about the man that gave a glimpse into the reasons for his success. "You really working for Margaret Pugsley's attorneys?"

I nodded. "I understand you knew Fred quite well?"

"Horrible thing. We had a company meeting and said a prayer for him. But what can you say? None of us are religious except Ashley. And he was too shook up to speak. Shocked us all out of our socks. Founded the company with me. Fred, the genius. Eric. Ashley Phillips, our idea man. And Gunnar, who got on the bandwagon after it was rolling along pretty good."

"Gunnar Rogers?"

"Yeah, uh, you know him?"

"Know his wife. Veronica and I have played water sports together."

"Really? Hell of a nice guy. He's joined another outfit here in town, but we keep in touch. Fact, they do our press. Go hunting with him couple of times a year. He's the only one worked in this company really had what you'd—just between you and me—call a nut sack. I get the distinct feeling that this modern civilization of ours has softened us up to the point at which if we actually had to scramble for a living, uh, you know, like people did, say, two hundred years ago in Tennessee or some other part of what was then the Far West, a substantial portion of the population would simply curl up and die."

"Good point." I noted several compound bows in a rack on one wall. Another wall over a series of computers, all of which were turned on and running, was studded with photographs of Rittenhouse in the woods, squatting on an elk cadaver, a moose, a bear, holding up a monstrous fish. The smiles in the pictures were jungle-proud. Also, photos of Rittenhouse beside three or four different aircraft.

Seeing where my eyes rested, Rittenhouse said, "Fly

a bit since the company really got on its feet. Became almost a necessity. Went scud running just this weekend. Used to take Fred up.''

"What about Fred?''

"The police were here, you know.''

"Figured they would be. They talk much?''

"Not as long and as arduous as one might suppose, actually, given the extreme circumstances of their visit.'' He rocked back on his coccyx and clasped his knuckles on one knee, balancing like a sailboat in a tricky tacking maneuver. "At one time Fred and Eric and I—that's Eric Castle, you don't know him—were nearly inseparable. We rode the STP about six years ago, and Eric must have pulled half the ride. You know what the STP is?''

"Seattle to Portland. I rode it one year.''

"Break ten hours?''

"Nope.''

"Eric Castle broke ten hours by himself on training clinchers. No shit. We're talking major animal here . . . where was I?''

"Fred go with you? He didn't look in condition for anything strenuous.''

"Ashley went on that. Uh, Fred's main physical activity seemed to be having sex with other people's wives and girlfriends. I know he's dead, but that was just a fact of his life. Anyway, yeah, uh. When we started, we were all dirt-poor, tinkered on computers over at the U. Fred was in engineering, I was in business, and Eric was a math major. Full scholarship. You can say what you want about him, but at what he does I've never seen better. In fact, if it weren't for a few things that happened, I'd like Eric back. If it were just me, he would be back. He gets some royalties on the first Kidpro games, but that all goes to his ex-wife for child support. Hell, last time I talked to Eric he was picking up garbage in a park. Sad story.''

"I keep hearing about something in Eric's past. What was it, and did it have anything to do with Fred?''

"Hadda do with all of us." Rittenhouse got a far-away look in his gray eyes. He didn't seem to mind trashing a dead man's reputation, and I couldn't help thinking about the vitriolic letter he'd written Fred. But then, there was a candid, man-to-man air about him, too, an air that made me think he was telling the truth and nothing but.

"We were like the Three Musketeers. Used to spend eighteen hours a day in Fred's rooming house near the U. Dirt poor. In some ways I was happier back then. We hacked; we programmed; we did it all. Don't think there was a major computer bank anywhere on the West Coast we hadn't broken into. Eventually, I suppose, we would have landed in the calaboose. Fact, several of our colleagues from those years are in prison at this very minute. One in Colorado. Ever hear of Theodore Watts?"

"Nope."

"Actually quite infamous in computer circles. I may hire him when he gets paroled." He shoved his glasses higher on his nose. "Another genius. Eric was the one who came up with the first game. He was programming in Pascal at first. Just the niftiest little program you ever saw. The Asteroid Tunnels we called it. They still play it at most universities.

"We screwed up, though, and it became public domain. All of us were green as God's little apples, didn't know a thing about copyrights or what have you. Didn't care at first. Anyway, I got to a prof I knew and had him outline what we had to do, and we brainstormed for forty-eight hours, coffee and Coca-Cola and a joint or two, until we got something we thought we could copyright. It was the first Kidpro program. Wrote it for an Apple and then just went from there. We knew we had something when, six weeks after we got a rather remedial version out on the market, Software Simpatico of Dallas offered two hundred grand for it.

"Eventually I got out of writing and left that to Fred and Eric. They were kind of like McCartney and Len-

non. Never was a pair like them. Alone Fred cooked
up some nice stuff, but there was something about the
chemistry between those two.''

"And then something came along?''

Daryl Rittenhouse snapped back into this world from
some hazy time warp. "A child was molested in our
office. Sometimes the office staff would bring their children in if they couldn't get baby-sitters. We had a girl
working here name of Deirdre Zabronski. Her sister,
Brittany, still works in cost analysis. Fact, she's expecting a baby of her own.

"Deirdre brought her two-year-old daughter in one
day, and somehow in the hustle and bustle she lost track
of her for a couple of hours. When she got back to the
little one, it was glaringly apparent that all was not as
it should have been. The child simply was not reacting
the way one would have expected under those circumstances.''

Rittenhouse butted his heavy glasses higher onto the
bridge of his nose with one knuckle and looked away.
Even at this late date the tale bothered him. Bothered
him a lot. I'd been suspecting something like this all
along, and it bothered me, too.

"When all was said and done and the child and the
parents had all three undergone several rather hectic
days trying to ascertain precisely what was wrong, they
finally took her to a series of doctors. . . . '' Rittenhouse's voice plummeted down a shaft of memories until it was almost inaudible. "And they found that she
had been physically assaulted. Sexually assaulted. Sick
world, isn't it?''

"And?''

"Understandably distraught, we went over the whole
scenario, all of us together, Brittany, Sheila outside,
Ashley, Deirdre, Eric, Fred, Gunnar, and all the rest
who were working for us at the time. Nobody seemed
to know what had happened. The police were next to
useless. The gist of it was—and this was the general
consensus for quite some time—that whatever had been

done to the child had been done by a stranger, one of our customers or any of a dozen people who were in and out of the building on that particular day. At one time we tabulated everyone who'd been through here, and it was nothing short of ridiculous.''

"How could a kid disappear for two hours? Where was the mother? Drunk?''

"I'm glad she didn't hear you say that. You have to understand in those days we worked in a different building in cramped little offices and we had all sorts of cubbyholes. Deirdre claims she never left Jessie—that was her name—for more than ten minutes at a pop. But it happened. Don't think we didn't feel lower than whale shit. All of us.''

"What became of the little girl?''

"Physically, at least, she was okay. Psychologically, nobody knows. Her mother says she's different. Her father thinks she's forgotten all about it. But you know, a thing like that has to leave some psychological scarring. A real shame.''

"How does this affect Eric?''

" 'Bout two months later, after everybody here swore they didn't know shit from Shinola and the police came up blank, one of the secretaries came to work one morning, opened the place up, and found a Polaroid down behind her desk by the front door. She knew it hadn't been there the day before, and she figured, and this is probably a reasonable reconstruction of the events, that it fell out of somebody's briefcase as he was leaving the night before and fluttered back behind her desk. Maybe even out of his pocket.''

"You didn't have any janitorial service then?''

"We did. Twice a week. They hadn't come in the night before, though. Nobody had been in the building overnight.''

"Go on.''

"The secretary about literally had a seizure when she saw the picture. Of Deirdre's child, Jessie. She brought it to me, and we decided to wait until everybody came in, one by one, and confront them all with it. You know, I looked at that thing, and I just wanted to get a gun and kill somebody. I just . . . for a few moments went crazy. I still get mad thinking about the whole thing.''

"No fingerprints or anything?''

"Didn't think of that until it was too late. And that's something I've never stopped regretting, not that there's any doubt about who the real pervert was, but finger-prints or something might have gotten him convicted.''

"Nobody was convicted?''

"One by one we assembled them until we had every worker in this cramped little conference room. I'll tell you something. You want a hard job, you stand up in front of a bunch of people you know and like and have worked with for almost a year and tell them you think one of them is a child molester. Ain't easy. Emotions were running pretty high.''

"Somehow I have the feeling this all leads up to Eric Castle.''

"Lie detector tests. That's what we decided on. The police came and left. What could they do? We could have been here for weeks, trying to figure out whose picture it was. Know who came up with it?''

"Let me guess. Fred Pugsley?''

"Eric. You know what a psychopath is? That's Eric Castle. Lies about everything. He lies so hard and so often that he believes his lies himself. He actually be-lieved that he could fool a polygraph. He volunteered to be one of the first.''

"And he didn't do so well?''

"The investigator came into the room holding the graph paper readout and said, ''This is the one. He did it.''

"What was Eric's reaction?''

"Denied it up one side and down the other. And he might have been okay if he'd left it at that. Hell, I be-lieved him. The lady did the testing told us before she began that those machines weren't infallible. Fred believed him. Those of us who knew him believed him. But then he went and put his foot in it. Psychopaths are like that.''

9

"HOW DO YOU MEAN HE PUT HIS FOOT IN it?"

Daryl Rittenhouse whisked his heavy glasses off and buffed them on a handkerchief. "Eric swore he had never molested a kid in his life. Had most of us convinced. Made us turn his office upside down. Wouldn't give us any peace until we turned over every scrap of paper, emptied every drawer looking for more pictures.

"We tossed it. Nothing incriminating. Now listen to how nuts this guy was. He asked Deirdre if she thought he'd touched Jessie. Deirdre let a few seconds pass and then spit in his face. I don't think she did it intentionally. It was impulsive, the cumulation of a lot of pent-up hostility with nowhere to vent it. It turned the trick. Eric said he wanted us all out to his house. If we thought he was molesting kids and taking pictures of it, he wanted us to go through his house with a fine-tooth comb and see for ourselves. I don't know. Maybe he was bluffing, figured we'd never take him up on it."

"What would that prove? Searching his house. Couldn't he have dumped anything the night before or early that morning?"

"That was the beauty of it. Nobody knew we'd found the photograph until it was too late to do anything. No-

84

body. Our secretary found it. She was crying at her desk when I came in. We were the only two people in the building. So we just sat there in shock, and when everybody arrived, one by one we herded them into the cramped little conference room. Never gave a hint what it was all about. Didn't start the meeting until everyone was inside. Remember, the child thing was two months old by now.''

"Everybody show up for work that day?''

"All but Lisa, from Tacoma. She's gone to New York to get into publishing. Couldn't have been involved.''

"You searched his house?''

"After he'd unlocked it. It was a junky little place on the lake—none of us had much money then—and he had it rigged with electronic invasion detectors, he called them No way anybody could have gotten in without him there to punch the right combination. Had a little electronic box right on the front door. Burglar-proof, he called it. He and his wife were the only ones knew the combination.''

"So you went in?''

"Yeah, uh, we went in. About six of us. What a strange bird. In some ways I can't believe he's still alive.''

"I'm assuming you found more pictures in his house.''

"Found some commercial porno downstairs, but that didn't amount to much. Had the bad stuff cubbyholed in the attic. Bunch of pictures of Jessie. Some other kids.''

"What'd he say?''

"Nothing. Not a damned thing. One minute he's claiming he's innocent, as if he really believes it, and the next minute he shuts up like a dead man.''

"I heard Fred had some words for him.''

"Fred didn't get there till after we'd found the stuff. He flew off the handle. Knocked almost all Eric's front teeth out. One blow.''

"Maybe that's why Eric didn't say much.''

Rittenhouse laughed. "He had plenty of time to talk before that, the way he was flimflamming us all at the office."

"So what came of the police investigation?"

Leaning back and thumbing his intercom, Rittenhouse said, "Sheila, do me a favor, honey? Get Ashley up here, would you? I think he'd want to talk to this investigator."

"Sure," she said.

"Came of it? The criminal case fell apart. I don't know how hard the Bellevue police tried, but they came up with zilch. By the time they got around to performing their own legal search of Eric's place, they found nothing. And none of us had thought to keep any of the pictures. Nobody really had any hard evidence. For a while there Deirdre and her husband were suing Eric. But that fell apart. Deirdre had some sort of breakdown because of the whole thing, and they moved to Maine. Live on one of those islands off the coast. Flew out there last summer. They're both working at a resort. Getting by. Deirdre's sister still works here—on maternity leave. Brittany. She's married to the man you're about to meet. Ashley Phillips."

As if he'd just received his cue, a tall, thin, impeccably attired man in a dark, pin-striped suit strode into the room. From what Rittenhouse had told me, I assumed Eric and Fred and Ashley were all about the same age. But Ashley looked twenty, a good ten years younger than the others. Good living. When he hit fifty, he'd look thirty. A well-thought-out diet and virtuous thoughts. I'd have to remember that, monkey with my diet a little.

"Ashley Phillips," he announced in mellow tones. When I stood to shake hands with him, I realized he was a good four or five inches taller than my six-one. But I doubted he weighed an ounce more than I did. "I understand you're a private detective? Hope you're the one working for Maggie. I've been worried about her. I might be able to help."

"How'd you know she had a detective working for her?"

He smiled and sat behind Rittenhouse's desk. There was an easy camaraderie between the two. Just looking at him, I could see Phillips was the kind of man who had a lot of friends. At his funeral it would be standing room only. "Wife told me. She's friends with Maggie. Think Maggie's up to receiving visitors yet?"

"Have no idea," I said.

"We'd like to be with her. Let her know we're behind her one hundred percent."

"I almost can't blame her," said Rittenhouse. "I mean, I've known women who would have butchered him a long time ago."

Ashley was deeply offended by that. Dark hair without a cut mark on it, a smile that was all toothpaste-ad teeth.

"Christ," continued Rittenhouse, "she shoulda de-balled him while she was at it."

"She didn't do it, Daryl, and don't say she did. I mean that." There was a threat in his voice. "You keep trying to imply that somehow she might be guilty. That's a very poor attitude to take."

"I'm not implying shit," shouted Rittenhouse. "I'm saying it. Right out. She killed Fred, and I don't blame her a bit. Way I heard it, they found her in the house, covered with blood, holding the murder weapon. Get realistic. Of course she did it."

Turning his large dark cow eyes on me, Ashley Phillips said, "I refuse to believe something like that about Maggie. Brit and I are on her side until she tells us otherwise."

He was the type of friend you wanted in a jam like that. Sometimes I almost wished I had friends like that. One, maybe two, in case the first one was out of town a lot, that's all you would need.

Ashley Phillips angled the executive chair backward and propped his feet on the top of Rittenhouse's desk. "Down deep," he said, "Fred was an all right person.

In fact, he really had a lot of love in his heart." Rittenhouse snorted. "He really did. He just was afraid to
show it. So he was always putting on this gruff exterior.
Sometimes people were frightened by it. It got him a
reputation."

"Who? Who was frightened?"

"Business acquaintances. Various people. Nobody I
could name."

"You gotta understand," said Rittenhouse, adjusting
his thick spectacles and casting a look over his shoulder
at Ashley, goading. "You gotta understand. It could
have been any husband or boyfriend on the East Side,
and maybe half of Seattle, too. Fred was a cocksman.
Cuckolded every man jack he could. His theory was,
all women were aching for it. What he had to do was
proposition every woman he ran across, and sooner or
later one or two would relent. After push-ups, cuckold-
ing was his favorite sport."

"How did Fred's theory work in practice?" I asked.
"Fred wasn't any Robert Redford, judging by the pictures in their house."

"You send out a thousand valentines, you're bound
to get a few in return. Send out a thousand more, a few
more returns. He was a busy man. His program writing. Philandering. I heard he even propositioned your
wife, Ashley."

Phillips didn't bat an eyelash. "That's not true. Simply not true."

"I heard he told her he thought pregnant women
made the best lovers."

"Get outa here," Phillips said. His calm was contagious. I could think of situations over the past few
years where having him around might have saved me a
fat lip.

"Fred doing anything different these past few
weeks?" I asked.

Ashley said, "No."

Rittenhouse chewed it over before he corrected him.
"The scuttlebutt has it he was on a minor rampage.

Ever since Eric was found out five years ago, the incident's bugged Fred. I guess Fred and Eric were closer than any of the rest of us. I guess he kept thinking there must be some more proof of guilt. Something more than what we found in his house.''

"Either of you know anything about Fred threatening Eric? Or vice versa?''

They shook their heads.

Looking as if the whole subject were more distasteful than he could bear, Phillips said, "It was really a shock. Almost collapsed the company. The thing of it was, Eric never, ever showed that sort of inclination to any of us. What it made you wonder, I guess, was what the rest of us were hiding.'' The room got quiet, and we all knew we were thinking about dirty little secrets, ours and others we'd heard about.

"Sure,'' said Rittenhouse, not wanting to pursue that. "But you have to remember. That's the nature of a psychopath. They can convince almost anybody of almost anything. Eric's one of the best.''

Ashley Phillips lowered his voice. "He needed help. It's too bad society doesn't have more assistance available for people like him.''

"Too bad they don't ram a tent stake between their earholes,'' Rittenhouse said bitterly. "Think about it, Ashley. If he was molesting kids five years ago, he's molesting kids today. They should have got him, not Fred. Somebody should have put out his candle long ago.''

"Sounds like something you've put some thought into,'' I prompted, but Rittenhouse just looked at me.

Ashley Phillips shook his head. "It was tragic.''

"Either of you have the names of any women Fred carried on with?''

They exchanged glances. Ashley only shook his head no. Rittenhouse said, "Barking up the wrong tree. You wanta start making a list, I'll let you borrow one of our computers. Fred chased anything that moved, and if it had a hole and he caught it, he planked it.''

"Daryl, he's dead, for godsakes. Have some respect."

"It's the truth. Can't see sugarcoating a man's rep just because he's dead."

"Nobody wants to see Maggie off the hook more than I do," said Ashley, adjusting his tie and tugging at the pointed hankie in his breast pocket. "I don't think I slept more than twenty minutes last night worrying about Maggie. Imagine what she's been through. Steps through her door to make up with her husband and . . . Then she finds herself suddenly accused. Poor thing. It's not like life has ever been easy for her. But chasing down Fred's women just would not be productive. Besides, myself, I tried to keep out of it. I liked Maggie, and I didn't want to know if she asked me something. I just really have a hard time lying to people."

"Me, too," said Rittenhouse, sarcasm bleeding through his tones.

When I left the office, Ashley Phillips left with me, moving like an athlete. They all were athletes, all the Micro founders. Daryl the hunter. Eric the biker. Fred the bed bouncer.

"You a runner?" I asked when we were alone outside Rittenhouse's office.

"Shows, huh? Managed to squeeze into the top one hundred at last year's Torchlight." He was all aw shucks and apple pie. The Torchlight was a 10k footrace held every August on the Seafair Parade route before the parade.

"Good for you," I said, confident that cyclists were in better shape than runners. I was vain, too.

"Listen," he said, stroking his dark hair with an open palm, his long fingers and manicured nails only just skirting pretty. "About what Daryl said in there. Don't pay any attention to him, huh? Doesn't mean half of what he says. He wouldn't hurt a fly."

"Or a moose or a bear?"

It took Phillips four beats to decide I was ribbing him. He laughed, easy and mellow.

"What he told you about somebody's doing away with Eric Castle. You want the truth, he loved Eric. We were just all so embittered to find out. It shocked us then, and it shocks us now to think about it. But we loved Eric. We still do. If he came in here now, Daryl would welcome him with open arms. So don't pay any attention to his tough-guy posturing. That's just the way he feels he has to be in front of people. Especially other men. You being a detective and all. My wife says he needs a machoectomy."

"Thanks for the tip."

"And if there's anything . . ." Ashley Phillips tugged his dark silk handkerchief out and mopped his glistening eyes with it. I noticed tiny concave jellyfish floating on his eyeballs, contact lenses. "What a horrible thing to have happen to one of your best friends. And Maggie." He put a gentle hand on my shoulder. "If there's anything, anything at all I can do to help you extricate Maggie from this jam, just tell me what it is, 'kay? I mean that. I'll do anything. Money. Time. We were thinking of organizing a support fund. If you want me to come with you and try to find out some of the women Fred was, you know, intimate with, I'll do it."

"I'll keep you in mind."

On the way out Sheila Balzac ambushed me at the elevators. I had been planning to use the stairs, but she was going down and wanted to talk. She smelled like wildflowers and mouthwash. She fingered the door open button for a moment and peeped around my shoulder at Phillips's receding figure, at his long-legged strides.

Phillips did seem to be special. I could see how with his élan, Rittenhouse'n drive, and a McCartney-Lennon writing team of Eric and Fred, even if they were both off kilter, Micro had gotten off to such a brilliant beginning. The elevator took us down, leaving our stomachs a floor and a half behind. When we got to the cafeteria, I leaned against the door close button. "What was Fred doing this last week?"

"What do you mean?"

"What was he working on?"

"Some project. Our new ChildPlay programs for schools. Nothing real difficult."

"You said he propositioned you?"

The blood rushed to her face. "Fred propositioned everybody. I probably never should have mentioned that."

"And you slept with him?"

"I won't say."

She already had. "What about Brittany Phillips?"

"You know about that?"

"I'd heard something."

"Isn't that bizarre? Coming on to a pregnant woman? Brit's got the kind of class to handle something like that, though. I don't really know that it happened, but a little birdie was flitting around a couple of weeks ago, saying it had."

"Ashley know about it?"

"Sure."

"You were here five years ago, right?"

"Gosh, yes. You mean the incident?"

"Who was the most upset?"

"Most upset? I've never thought about it that way. I always thought I was, but I guess that wasn't really true. Daryl wanted to kill him. He threatened it several times. And of course, Fred slugged him. But I think Ashley was the most upset."

"What makes you say so?"

"It really hurt Ashley, poisoned his faith in human nature. I guess he felt betrayed. We all did, but he felt it the most, I'd say. And of course, Eric's wife. Saw those pictures, and she was gone. Divorced him overnight."

"And Fred Pugsley pursued this?"

"Always running down rumors of where there might be some final, conclusive evidence about Eric. He pestered the investigation company that ran the lie detector tests until they wouldn't speak to him anymore.''

"Ever come up with anything?"

"Not that I know of. There did seem to be an extra flurry of activity last week, though. He was digging into it again. Know what he used to do? Search offices around here. I warned him. . . . Were you there?"

"Pardon?"

"At the murder scene. One of the girls said she read in the *P-I* that a lawyer and a detective found the body. Was that you?"

"We found him."

"What was it like?"

"Do me a favor, would you?" I let the elevator doors slide open. "Tell me where Brittany Phillips lives."

She did so, stepped out, then twiddled a necklace and a ceramic pendant that looked suspiciously like an emergency suppository. Whispering, she said, "What was it really like? At my aunt's funeral, it was just like she was asleep . . ." I shrugged and left.

10

ASHLEY AND BRITTANY PHILLIPS
resided in a luxury condominium on
Lakeside. A pie-eyed fly fisherman could have opened
their living room window and laid a Royal Coachman
on the water. Storms from the east might pump waves
into the room, except that in Seattle storms rarely blew
from the east. Ironically, Eric Castle and I had pedaled
past it yesterday afternoon.

I found their name on a mailbox and buzzed. She
was pregnant all right, and as soon as I saw her, I
prayed she wouldn't deliver while I was there.

In her own way she was as meticulous as her husband. They fitted together, salt and pepper. Brittany
Phillips had big, brown, moony eyes and a short but
precise mop of hair, the color of which matched her
eyes. Her smooth, flawless complexion matched her
husband's. Almost as tall as I was, she was thin to a
fault. Their children would look like walking chop-
sticks.

"Come in. You're working for Maggie, I hear."

"Word spreads fast."

Her smile buttery and sweet, she offered me a seat
in the living room, then eased herself onto a straight-

backed chair. "I can't get out of the sofa," she said, patting her enormous belly, "once I get in it."

It was a two-story unit, the main floor on ground level. I smiled. She smiled. Through the living room window the lake looked as if it were under a giant magnifying glass, taupe waves, gray, green, then a blanket of teal-colored waves slapping into the dock outside the window and splashing white. Foam slobbered across the short dock. It was more wickedly hypnotic than any fireplace.

"When are you due?"

"Any day now "

"Your first?"

She nodded, basking in an inner glow pregnant women seemed to have a copyright on. "Ashley and I have been trying for so long, and now it's almost here. It's so exciting."

"I'm glad for you," I said. "I spoke to your husband a short while ago."

"I know. He called." I couldn't help noticing when I came in that one of her ears was redder than the other, as if she had hung up the phone to answer the door. The pundits and gossips were burning up the lines at Micro Darlings these days. And why not? It wasn't often that one of the top officers in a local corporation was murdered in his kitchen. According to the news report I'd heard in the truck on the way over, the police still hadn't officially laid the blame on anyone. Speculation would be rife until they did.

I said, "I understand you and Ashley were close to the Pugsleys?"

"Very. Ashley's been so upset over this. He hasn't eaten a thing. He was nervous enough about the baby, but now he's a wreck. I'm not much better, but at least I know I have to stay calm for the baby's sake. If it's a boy, we'll call him Freddie. That was Ashley's idea. Maybe it will even make Maggie feel better."

Not if she's in prison, I thought. "You tried to see Maggie?"

"Not yet. But we're going over after work today."

"I'm interested in Fred's . . . womanizing."

"Yes." She straightened her jumper, a corduroy affair in dark green. "Well, Fred was certainly that. A womanizer. We keep hearing that Maggie did it. Could it be true?"

"Nobody knows," I said, soft-pedaling the facts. "How did she feel when Fred stepped out on her?"

"I think from the time they were dating at the U, when he got a chance, he took it. Maggie always knew that. That's what surprises me. Why would she get outraged and kill him now? She has her own job in the travel agency downtown. Just got a promotion a few months ago. She could have left Fred and found somebody else."

"Is that what you told her?"

"Ashley and I both tried to stay neutral. After all, it was sort of tricky. He worked with Fred."

I mulled it over, staring out at some intrepid sailors a quarter mile away on the lake, the multicolored sails billowing in the wind, antlike figures scrabbling at the lines. "Know anything about Fred's investigations into Eric Castle?"

"You mean how he thought there was more to that horrible thing with Eric a few years back? Never called him Eric after that, by the way. Always 'that stinkin' little pervert.' It really bothered Eric's ex-wife. And Fred knew that. He used it to taunt her. Do you know Veronica?"

"We've met."

"When she was still married to Eric, Fred launched a campaign to get her into bed. I think maybe I'm the only one she told. She got so flustered she even mentioned once hiring someone to break his legs. Kidding, of course."

"Of course."

"Yet he was best friends with her husband?"

"Ironic, wasn't it? I've been thinking about why somebody would want to kill Fred, and the only thing

ı can come up with is a disgruntled boyfriend or husband. Or Maggie.''

''The way I understand things, your sister's daughter
was assaulted?'' She nodded and tucked her thin upper
lip under her teeth, reluctant to expound. ''And then
they tried to sue and, when that didn't pan out, moved
out of state?''

''Now they just want to forget.''

''What happened with the lawsuit? Why did they give
up?''

''My sister . . . It's rather complicated and personal.
Didn't have anything at all to do with whether they could
have nailed him because they could have. Deirdre had
a, uh, what they call a nervous breakdown. She lost her
mind for a while there. The pressure.''

''And what about Eric and Veronica?''

''That's another ball of wax. Veronica decided after
she'd married Gunnar that she didn't want Eric visiting
the kids anymore, so they got their lawyers to pull some
strings, and now the whole thing's in the courts. Eric's
suing them. Can you believe that?''

''For the right to see his children?''

''Precisely.''

''Tell me about Gunnar. How soon after the divorce
did Veronica meet him?''

''Gunnar worked for Micro. We all did. Me, Ashley,
Fred, Daryl, Eric, and Gunnar. Veronica would have,
too, I suppose, but she was taking care of the babies
and still finishing up in school. She and Gunnar knew
each other for years before they got married. Gunnar
was a little older than the rest of us. He was the public
relations expert Daryl brought in. He's got his own
company now down in the Joshua Green Building. 'Course, their biggest client is Micro.''

''Did Veronica marry him soon after her divorce?''

''Not soon. She's really an awfully nice person. From
what I gather, Gunnar was the one who went off the
deep end about Eric's seeing the kids. He didn't think
it was right. Ranted and raved about it for weeks, but

then, when he put his foot down, it was really down.
In fact, Eric went over there one day and tried to see
them. Veronica said he was crying like a baby. Gunnar
picked him up and threw him down the hill in front of
their house. That was it! Veronica turned the garden
hose on him. In that neighborhood it was really kind of
embarrassing.''

"A thing like that could really damage a guy's pride.''

"It was the last time Eric ever tried to see the kids.
After that he hired a lawyer and started some sort of
action. From what Veronica tells me, so far he hasn't
been very successful, and no wonder, considering. . . .
Do you know, after Veronica divorced him, he sent her
love letters? Never got over her. Veronica says a lot of
his behavior is compulsory. He just gets these obses-
sions. Actually that's why he was such a good program
writer, too. It's funny how a trait can make some people
successful and turn other people into criminals, isn't
it?''

It was something I'd thought about a lot, but now
wasn't the time to delve into it. On the way out the
door, as she teetered her bulk on her stilt legs, I noticed
a photograph of herself and Ashley, taken years ago.
Both were younger, their complexions even milkier.
Brittany's hair hung almost to her waist. Other than that,
they looked like a pair of sleek whippets, standing arm
in arm beside a sailing boat called *The Glass Slipper*.
A stunning couple.

"You sail?''

"It was only a friend's,'' she said.

"One last thing.'' She looked at me expectantly, her
brown eyes almost level with mine. "How does Gunnar
feel about Eric?''

"Outrage. Exasperation. The same way we all feel.
It was all such a waste. He shouldn't be out there on
the streets. I know one thing.''

"What's that?''

"If Veronica and Gunnar are forced to let Eric see

their kids, it's going to kill them. You can't believe how livid they were when they found out Eric had filed suit."

I believed it. The one actor in this play everybody wanted to see on another planet was Eric Castle. Snakes. Blue vans. Telephone calls to his employers. Car batteries dropped on him from overpasses. With this crowd after him it was a wonder he didn't drop dead just from all their malicious thoughts. I was beginning to wish he'd go away myself. Go away or perhaps drop into a deep hole and disappear. Nobody was going to miss him, nobody except Schuyler and the taxman.

On a hunch I stopped at a pay phone outside a grocery store two blocks away and dialed my answer machine at home. Kathy answered. "Thomas, sweetheart."

"What the hell are you doing in my house?"

"I knew you'd check in. How's it going?"

"Don't they miss you at work when you skip out? You're going to get fired if you keep playing hooky."

"Don't be silly. I talked to Maggie Pugsley. She's ready to talk."

"She remember anything?"

"Didn't say. Come and pick me up."

"Not on your life."

"Please? You can fill me in. We'll kick it around, see what you've got so far. Maybe we can have lunch down at Fat Tuesday afterward. The Miss No Fat prelims are being held today."

"Maybe." Now that I thought about it, I often came up with brainstorms booting things around with Kathy. Anyway, the Miss No Fat contest probably wouldn't damage my retinas. I'd never been to one, but I'd heard tales. And if Margaret Pugsley were anywhere as shattered as she had been yesterday, it might be good to have a sympathetic female along, somebody to help assuage her fears, loosen her up, comfort her.

When I got to my house off Roosevelt, I parked in front. My plan had been to toot until Kathy came run-

ning out, but there were complications. Her sports car
sat in the humped driveway. So did a Harley-Davidson,
a gang bike, chopped and stripped. On top of the sissy
bar sat a monkey's skull.

"Oh, brother," I said. Kathy was never going to let
me live this down.

THE MOTORCYCLE IN THE DRIVEWAY
belonged to the wife of a brute I'd
arrested years before when I was still a cop. She had
been leaving nasty messages on my answer machine all
week.

Hangings weren't my favorite pastime, but John
Coulter Nash, a triple murderer, had done everything
but beg me to attend his. He wrote letters. Had his
lawyers write. Implored the warden to write. Sent a
telegram and finally, when I didn't respond, phoned
me, a pleading note in his rich, deadly baritone.

"Black?"

"Who's this?"

"Jack Nash. Don't hang up. Look, they're going to
give me the big drop. I want you there." I kicked that
around while the long-distance lines hummed. John
Coulter Nash had meant next to nothing in my life.
"Look, Black, my wife is going to be there. I don't
want a bunch of jerk-off reporters taking notes and
laughing and ruining it for her."

"I'm sure it'll be a very solemn occasion."

"Just the same. I want someone there . . . someone
I respect to keep the goobers in line."

What could I say? How many of these bizarre invi-

tations does a man get in a lifetime? Great small talk
for that flat spot at parties when nobody knows any
more jokes. "Pass the chips. By the way, I ever tell you
about the time I watched the governor hang a man?"

Years earlier I'd collared John Coulter Nash running
a stop sign, fed his name through the computer, and
learned of an outstanding warrant for rape. He waited
with me for the radio report and then tried to dent my
skull with a length of pipe. As we tangoed, I used a
step on him that wasn't in the police skills manual. It
put him down for the count and instilled a grudging
respect for me.

Through several meetings in criminal court we
formed a half-assed bond, the way some screws do with
their cons. After two years in the Monroe Penitentiary
he was freed, whereupon he promptly retraced his path
and murdered three of the witnesses who had testified
against him during his first trial, raping two of them
before hacking them up with a kitchen knife. The best
I could tell, he was a homicidal maniac.

It was the first official killing in the state in years,
and the *P-I* and *Times* and the television stations edi-
torialized it to death, bloated with good cheer, all.

I'd seen my share of hangings, mostly impromptu
affairs, suicides until now, so this wasn't much. Lord
only knows why Nash wanted me there. It gave me a
great sorrow. There was a time when I'd have been
happy to drape the noose around his neck with my own
hands. Not now. Maybe I was getting soft.

Eight reporters, several prison officials, Nash's lawyer, Desiree, his wife, and myself had constituted the
sparse crowd. There was no animosity in the building,
only cold detachment and some fetid curiosity. It didn't
do much for me, nor for Desiree, Nash's wife, who
looked as if she might drown a kitten every morning
before breakfast just to get her day headed in the right
direction. Nash's lawyer turned the color of chlorophyll.
Desiree watched with sleepy blue eyes and popped a
wad of gum under her molars. Desiree was what you

might call a motorcycle mama, a handsome woman riding under the Jolly Roger colors.

After her husband's execution I met her at the motel where we were both staying. She was in Walla Walla alone and needed someone to commiserate with. I was alone, too, had some free time, and figured, what the hey. We all have to make sacrifices.

Desiree broke down and wept. Our conversations droned on long into the night, and she told me her life story. Since junior high school, when a teacher had "sort of" seduced her, she'd slept with half the U.S. Navy and every ambulatory biker on the West Coast, as well as a few in wheelchairs. She'd done some armed robberies, cocaine, smack, some fencing of stolen goods, and then she told me a few things she was ashamed of.

When she boasted that she wanted to screw my brains out, I retreated to my motel room, bolted the door, and forced a chair under the knob. She apparently thought sex was like chewing gum: rip open the package and pass it around. That had been last weekend. I had almost forgotten about her until I got the messages on my answer machine that morning.

I strode up the steps to my house and unlocked the front door. It was Desiree's motorcycle in the driveway. I recognized the monkey skull mounted on the sissy bar.

"Hello."

"In here." It was Kathy's voice in the kitchen. Slowly I proceeded through the dining room.

Desiree stood hipshot beside the open refrigerator door. Kathy remained out of sight, sitting at the table, I presumed. "You ain't been answering my calls, bub."

"Desiree, I told you. I'm not interested."

"Like hell you ain't. You're a man, ain't you?"

Built along the lines of a goblet, pipestem legs and an overly developed upper torso, Desiree looked at me, as had her late husband, out of eyes that were a deceptively gentle blue. Her face was comely in a rugged,

boyish way; four earrings in one ear and a heavy coin
on a hook dangling from the other. Her black hair fell
in wet-looking ringlets and though she had smelled like
a biker in Walla Walla, she smelled like Arpège now.
About fifteen ounces of it. Probably had shoplifted a
bottle at Pay'n Save on the way over and baptized herself.

She had boasted of posing for biker mags. She wore
thick boots with ankle buckles, dirty jeans, a black
leather jacket, and under the jacket a skimpy white lace
chemise that was barely held together by slack laces. A
tattoo of a heart was splotched against the inside of one
of her astronomical globes. Probably been there since
her teens. The tattoo, I mean.

"Well," Desiree said.

"Well."

"I've never had a cop before."

"I'm not a cop anymore."

"What are you?"

"Private detective."

"Never had one of those either."

Desiree reached into the refrigerator, removed a con-
tainer of milk, unfolded the waxed cardboard top, and
gulped deeply. Kathy Birchfield stepped into the doorway and smirked wickedly, eyes brazed onto the motorcycle queen. "Thomas. I guess lunch is off then. I
mean—"

"It's not off, and you know it. Damn it, Desiree,
scat. I've got things to do. I'm working a murder investigation."

"Honey, try me. Your tongue'll be cramped up for a
week."

Kathy began laughing.

"You the wife or what?" asked Desiree flatly. After
giving me a devilish scowl, Kathy exploded into more
buttonbusting laughter, a contingency Desiree Nash
hadn't planned on. Desiree's face began to look like
something on a hungry rat. She stepped forward and

grasped Kathy by the collar. "Listen, Miss little I. Magnin slut, I got—"

"Whoa there." I pried Desiree's broken-nailed fingers off Kathy's collar and inserted my body between the women. It was a sorry move because it gave Desiree an excuse to crowd me.

The roar of half a dozen Harleys broke up our ménage à trois. Six or eight of them chewed up the still afternoon in the narrow drive between my property and Horace's, the proximity of the houses creating a makeshift echo chamber. Gouts of blue smoke swirled past the kitchen window in the overcast afternoon. Horace, my grumpy retired neighbor, was going to love this. He wouldn't have a bowel movement for a week.

Desiree broke off the melee and strutted to the back porch. She shouted names as the last of the ignitions were switched off. Steel Cranium. Bug Eyes. Butt Crack. Zeke. Paddy. She had zipped her jacket and put more deceit into her swagger.

"Come to fetch you home," said a tall, rangy specimen wearing Jolly Roger colors on the back of a cutdown jeans jacket. Arms bared to the air, he must have been freezing. A tattoo of a swastika was emblazoned onto the back of his right hand.

All sweetness and honey, Desiree said, "Paddy, you asshole, I come home when I get there. I'm still in mourning for my ex. Can't you see that?"

"Don't look like no mourning to me, chick," said Paddy as his cohorts burst into gritty laughter.

Paddy clomped up onto the porch and gripped Desiree firmly around one wrist, wrenching it to and fro. They struggled wordlessly.

"How'd you know where to find her?" I said, stepping outside.

Looking me up and down, Paddy flung Desiree down the porch steps. She landed hard but was unhurt, as if she'd performed the stunt before. "You must be the pig."

"Let's get it right. Ex-pig."

"Bacon is bacon." He was standing far too close, and though it wasn't yet noon, his breath was fetid with beer. He was taller than I am but not much heavier. Desiree had already gotten to her feet, straightened herself up, and fitted herself onto the tiny seat of her hog.

His nose four inches from mine, Paddy glared the way a professional boxer glared before a bout. I came nearer than I had in a long while to dropping somebody with a sucker punch. That was my specialty, the patented Thomas Black sucker punch.

I should have let fly.

Instead, I watched Kathy tiptoe into the kitchen, carrying my .45 auto. She knew how to use it, but from where she was standing she couldn't see the rest of the bikers, and they couldn't see her. Those astonishing violet eyes looked as if they were made out of molten glass. I shook my head at her, and she lowered the pistol, trembling. Though nothing was visible, I was certain there were at least five guns in my driveway to answer anything she did. We didn't need to make a racket. Horace was going to be upset enough when he saw what I was saving for this year's Fourth.

Paddy got a good grip on me, and I thought I heard an echo in my heart. It was the porch railing coming out by its roots. It cracked, broke, and I landed on my buttocks in the cold earth on top of my Diamond Jubilee. I shook my head to clear the cobwebs. Damn. I had been meaning to reinforce that rail. I staggered to my feet, and the thorns in the Blue Nile nibbled my calf through my brown cords.

They were waiting for me to escalate the fracas. I knocked the crud off my cords and smiled, painful as that was. "You gentlemen got what you came for. Why not motor on out?"

Even as I watched a couple of them snigger, I felt a strange sort of oppressive melancholy for them, misfits and runts all. John Coulter Nash's jerky exit had tainted my life.

A minute later they were gone in a welter of smoke

and machismo. As they sallied forth into the street, heading the wrong direction on Roosevelt, a one-way street, horns beeped and tires shrieked. Desiree gave me one last lascivious stare over her shoulder.

I didn't like taking guff or getting tossed off my own porch; but it had been a long week, and it was only half over. I had seen a man hanged. I had consoled a fresh widow. Two fresh widows. I had driven hundreds of miles from eastern Washington. I didn't feel like knocking skulls with a moron. I had already let enough morons lump my skull.

"Are you all right, Thomas? Look at your roses."

"They'll be okay," I said, kneeling beside the Blue Nile. I noticed all of Horace's curtains were being hurriedly drawn. "I gotta prune these suckers."

"You sounded bad, Thomas. You losing your touch? I thought you were going to take care of him. I had the gun. Why didn't you do something?"

"The gun isn't loaded, sister."

"I loaded it. Why didn't you do something?"

"It's been too cold to prune."

"With those hoods, you dope. You could have thrown him on the roof if you wanted."

"I don't need to get broken teeth to prove I'm tough."

"You've already proved you're tough?"

"I've already had broken teeth."

We drove in my truck. To aggravate me, Kathy inserted the umbrella in the gun rack but was strangely quiet about Desiree. Ordinarily she would have gone on for days. I wondered what was holding her back. I gave her a quick and succinct rundown on what I'd found out so far about Micro Darlings, the incident of five years ago, and the former employer who'd called Eric Castle a liar. I left only a few things out. As we coasted down the long hill on Forty-fifth from the university, Kathy said, "Who was that woman?"

"Were you listening to any of this?"

"Every word. Who was that woman, and where did

she have that plastic surgery done? Puerto Rico? They must have put a small island under each pocket.''

"Remember the guy the governor strung up last weekend? His wife. And no plastic surgery. They're real.''

"How do you know?''

"You sound jealous.''

"Of that?''

Laurelhurst was as quiet as ever. Maggie Pugsley answered the door herself, and we entered without talk. The nurse was gone.

Maggie had dark sacs under her eyes and wore a robe similar to the one Kathy had scrounged up for her yesterday. Hobbling in front of us, she led us through the walkway, and we all got comfortable in the living room. I sat on the sofa beside her, and Kathy took a chair across from us.

"What's going on?'' she asked.

"Maggie,'' I said, "I'd like permission to go through your house. To search it.''

"Search?'' She didn't seem disoriented, but her speech was slow, slurred. "Maybe later. I'm not up to thinking about it now.''

"Then answer this, now that you're feeling better: Did you kill your husband?''

Stirring, Kathy said, "Subtle as ever.''

"Did I kill my husband? I can't say.''

"Why not?''

"I just can't. I have to think about it. I don't think so.''

"That's better than yesterday. You can't tell us whether you killed your husband, but you think you didn't?''

"Something like that.''

Kathy cleared her throat. "We're going to be honest with you, Maggie. They haven't charged you with murder yet, but that's a miracle. Any minute now you can expect to be dragged downtown and booked.''

"You'll take care of me, won't you?''

"We can't do much if we don't have the facts. We need your cooperation, Maggie. I'm sure if Thomas wants to search your house, there's a good reason."

"The police have already been through everything, even my underwear. When I got home, everything was mussed. Our financial records, everything. I felt so . . . violated. I can't believe this is my life." Despite her weary and beaten voice, Maggie wasn't anywhere near tears. Perhaps she was cried out. "Will they really charge me?"

"Count on it," I said. "Unless you can talk somebody else into confessing. My feeling is they're building a case on you they don't think can be broken."

Straightening her skirt, Kathy said, "They've asked you to undergo a lie detector test, Maggie."

"Have they?"

"Detective Baldacci suggested it."

I reached over and touched Maggie's knee. "It would be silly to do one for the Seattle police without trying you out on someone more sympathetic first. If you want to go ahead with it, I know a woman in Pioneer Square who runs a nice test. If the one for us doesn't work out, we'll skip the cops."

All of a sudden Maggie realized she was with people. She patted her hair, touched her face, and pulled the robe tight at the neck. "I must look a fright."

"You look just fine." Kathy reassured her.

"Fred researched them."

"Researched what, Maggie?"

"Lie detectors. Polygraphs. They use them mostly for employee problems, theft, that sort of thing. Fred said experts rated their accuracy anywhere from ninety-five percent at best down to seventy percent. He thought they could be very misleading."

I looked at Kathy. "What you say is true. However, if you show up well on the polygraph, it could get the police off your back. They think you're innocent, they're liable to concentrate their energies elsewhere. Right now it's all directed at you."

"Fred researched them. They're not always accurate."

"Why would Fred bother to learn about polygraphs? Did this have something to do with the test they all took five years ago? Did Fred think there might be something screwy about it?"

"They didn't all take it. Eric was one of the first. They didn't see any point in putting anyone else through it after his results. Fred didn't take it. Daryl didn't. Hardly anybody did."

"Perhaps Fred didn't think Eric Castle was guilty?" She shrugged. "Is that why he spent so much time investigating? He was trying to clear Eric?"

"Fred would never have admitted that," said Maggie, a tear sitting like a jewel in the corner of one eye. "Not even to me. Fred had to be tough, and he had to be right. His public position was that he was trying to hang the dirty little pervert. I've often suspected Fred had never come to terms with Eric's wickedness, that he was unconsciously trying to find evidence of his innocence. Something crazy like that. Yes, I think Fred was trying to clear Eric. Hopeless as that was. Eric was the best friend he'd ever had. They were so different but so close. Eric was one of the few people around who didn't judge Fred all the time." She examined our faces to see if we were understanding any of it. "Fred liked to shock you with how uncouth he was, and if that worked, well, then he went right on shocking you. If he couldn't work his wiles, why, he gave up and was himself. That's how he was with Eric. Himself."

"And with you," said Kathy.

"Yes. With me. Most of the time."

"You didn't kill your husband, did you?" Kathy asked in a soft monotone.

"Me? Why on earth would I kill Fred? Just because he belittled me in public? Because I woke up one morning and found him going at it on our couch with a girl he'd picked up the night before in a Belltown tavern? Me, kill Fred? I only thought about it once, and I got

so scared I threw every knife in the house out. That was
how I thought of it. A knife in the back. It was the only
way I ever thought of it. The tool he got killed with
. . . I don't even know what that was. But he wasn't as
bad . . . Fred liked to pretend he'd had a lot of women.
He exaggerated, and he was convincing. In our entire
marriage he only stepped out on me four or five times.
I realize for some women that would have been four or
five times too many. But . . . I don't know. He loved
me. I know, he told me after each one, asked me to
forgive him.''

Kathy said, ''Would you agree to a polygraph? If
only a trial test with a sympathetic examiner?'' All of
us sat quietly and listened to the ticking of a regulator
clock in the other room. Maggie pondered the suggestion. She didn't blink. She didn't move. The look on
her face was similar to the look I'd seen when I found
her yesterday, covered in blood and half naked, her
hubby in the adjoining room, slaughtered and cooling.
What sort of rage had it taken to maul him like that? A
fifth or sixth marital indiscretion?

When it became clear Maggie wasn't ready to give
us an answer, I said, ''Maggie, if Eric wasn't the one
at the company, chances are whoever really did it is
still there. Not very many people have been fatuous
enough to get off the Micro Darlings boat.''

Kathy said, ''Why are you harping on this?''

''Fred was harping on it, and Fred got killed. I have
to think whatever was concerning him during his last
weeks might have had something to do with his death.
In theory, if I could retrace Fred's steps perfectly, I
could find out who killed him.''

And then I began thinking about how much evidence
they had on Eric, how well cemented in he was. They
found pictures in his house, and his house was supposedly burglarproof. Only he and his wife knew the combination. But then, the whole company was full of
computer geniuses. Could one of them have broken the

code? He failed a lie detector test. He lied. In fact, he was a chronic liar.

Slipping out of her daze, Maggie said, "I tried to humor Fred, but we all knew Eric was guilty as sin. Poor dear, his life must be such a mess."

"Yours isn't much better. I've got a few more things to run down. But when I come back, I want to go through Fred's things. In the meantime, don't fool around with any of it, no matter how insignificant you might think it is. Okay?"

"Sure."

"One last item."

"Yes."

"Margaret, where were you yesterday afternoon after I left you at Leech, Bemis, and Ott?"

"Yesterday? Veronica took me to her place for the afternoon. I was there until, oh, fiveish."

"Was the van in the driveway."

"Dennis's van? I didn't notice."

Outside, in the cab of my truck, Kathy scooted over beside me until our thighs touched. "Thomas, I've never felt so acutely aware that somebody's life was in my hands. Our hands."

"Makes you want to be good at what you do, doesn't it?"

"I could never get used to this feeling."

"We might nudge things along a little, but by and large, people determine their own fates."

"What she said about Fred's thinking Eric was innocent. Could that be possible?"

"I doubt it. I think that was a wife hoping her husband wasn't as full of hate as he appeared to be."

"From what you've said, Fred made a habit of getting people upset. Don't you think he might have provoked somebody we haven't turned up yet?"

"Things are going in so many directions I'm going to chase them down one at a time. Right now it's this incident five years ago. Fred seemed keen on it, even if he was barking up the wrong tree."

"Yes, and if Eric thought Fred was out to prove him guilty, maybe Eric sneaked over here and killed Fred." Kathy shuddered as she thought about Fred's murder again. I hadn't told Kathy about the tools and memorabilia I'd found at Veronica's. Odd. Eric's ex-wife detested him, yet she kept his old bicycle racing trophies. Nor had I told Kathy about the dousing Veronica Rogers had given me. She didn't need more ammunition. The scrap with Desiree and her friends would last for months.

We had lunch at Swannie's, and the Miss No Fat prelims had just finished when we got there. We walked in the door as three women hustled past in various stages of undress, all three oiled down as if for a muscle pose off. "Shoot," I said.

"We'll be here for the finals," Kathy promised, winking lewdly.

It was a long lunch, and we talked about a lot of things, none of them related to the case. When I dropped her off in front of my house, I said, "Don't they miss you at work sometimes?"

"I'm not gone that much. They know I'm working on the case. And I saw a murder yesterday. They understand."

Though I didn't say it, I wasn't so sure the stodgy, workaholic partners at Leech, Bemis, and Ott did understand. She had been right about still being affected by the murder. She wasn't nearly as lighthearted as usual. At lunch she mentioned Desiree only three times.

I drove downtown and found a meter near the Joshua Green Building, plugged two quarters in, and went inside to find Gunnar Rogers.

**12** "WHAT SORT OF JERK-OFF ARE
you?" Gunnar Rogers glowered
from behind his desk.

"Nice to meet you."

"My wife phoned, told me all about your visit."

"Those phone lines are hot."

"Jerk-off."

"Me?"

"See anybody else in this room?"

His workplace was stylishly small, and the only thing
in it that wasn't flawless was the detective in front of
his glass-topped desk. The suite comprised three offices, a couple of conference rooms, and a waiting area,
where a receptionist who resembled one of my grade
school teachers stood watch, her lacquered hair stiff as
a wicker basket. A bag at her feet entombed a book
titled *No More Hot Flashes*.

We were on the sixth floor of the Joshua Green Building, which overlooked two other high-rises, Elliott Bay
beyond them. In one of the skyscrapers opposite us a
man sat at a desk, staring at us. An Indonesian tanker
in need of paint bobbed in the quiet bay. A white and
green ferry steamed toward Bremerton. Somebody had
once said that the sound was a joke from God and the

ferries were the punch line. In this office visitors were the joke. I was the punch line.

"I wish she hadn't called you."

"Jerk-offs like you are why people put locks on their doors and insurance on their cars."

"You're going to keep piling this up, maybe I should get my galoshes?"

Gunnar Rogers could have been a male model for Neiman-Marcus men's fashions twenty years earlier. Hell, he could have been a model yesterday. In his mid-forties he was easily fifteen years older than Veronica.

Ice-blue eyes, sculpted blond hair tinged silver, just the proper amount of sideburns, Gunnar was chesty and solid, without being fat. Handball and saunas. I'd bet my truck on it.

"Afraid I offended your wife."

"If I'd been there," whispered Gunnar, inhaling his anger, "there would have been hell to pay."

"Your wife does all right by herself."

"There must be regulatory agencies for people like you. We intend to get in touch with them."

"Mr. Rogers, I'm working for the attorney who represents Margaret Pugsley. She hasn't been charged yet, but she's heavily implicated in her husband's death. We found her there at the house, near the body. We're trying to uncover some facts that might help her defense."

"I suppose that means talking to you?"

"Letters would be a little slow."

"Sit down." He gesticulated at a walnut-handled chair. I sat. "We're not used to private detectives and their back-alley ways. Do me a favor. Don't spit on the rug. You want to play straight with us, we'll play straight with you. Ten to one, you asked Veronica to look in that trunk, she'd have opened it for you."

His conjecture was tommyrot, and we both knew it. She would have told me to take a flying fuck at a rolling doughnut. "I'll keep that in mind."

"Now, what is it you want to know?"

"You were working at Micro at the time of the thing with Eric Castle?"

"I was there. Why on earth would you want to know about that?" He raked his blunt-tipped fingers through his hair. The action neither ruffled nor tidied the moussed locks. They were impervious to damage.

"Fred seemed overly concerned about Eric Castle during his last days."

"The only thing Fred was concerned about was Fred. Besides, that incident was his hobby, had been ever since it happened. Talked about it. Joked about it. It wasn't important to him, just incidental. There were two things important to Fred: money and any two-legged mammal in a skirt."

"Just the same, he seemed to be poking around recently. He speak to you about it?"

"Why would he?"

"What about Eric? Have you been in touch with him lately?"

"That bastard? The only time we hear from him is through his lawyers."

"I take it you're not fond of him?"

"Eric?" Gunnar nodded at a deer head mounted on the wall behind me. "I'd just as soon put him up there on the wall."

I grinned tightly, the way you would at the funeral of an important person you didn't know. "Have you threatened him?"

"That pipsqueak knows what I'll do if I catch him skulking around. I threw him out of our yard once already. I should have broken him in half when I had the chance. Maybe you don't understand about Eric," said Gunnar, lowering his voice the way some people did when speaking of deviants. "He's a child molester. It's only by a freak happenstance that he isn't in prison. They know how to treat child molesters in prison."

"I know about Eric."

"Dirty little freak wants us to send the kids over. Can you believe that? We're keeping records for when it gets into court."

The hatred in his voice made me think of an incident years ago when I was in the SPD. Somebody shotgunned a gentleman in an apartment near Greenlake. Five twelve-gauge blasts point-blank into his torso. Nobody wanted to talk. Not the neighbors. Not the relatives. Not the employer. It turned out the victim was a convicted child molester. They never solved it, not that the boys in homicide got all sweaty trying.

"Hell," said Gunnar, fixing his blue-gray on me. "You know what I think? I mean, if you're really pursuing Fred and investigating this the way it should be done? I think Fred got the goods on Eric. That's what he wanted, you know, to get the goods on Eric. I think he got the goods on him, Eric learned of it somehow and went over there and murdered him. That's what I think."

"Interesting," I said. I had been entertaining similar theories myself.

"Listen, Black." Gunnar's voice grew gruff as he leaned across his desk on thick elbows, shirtsleeves rolled into starched envelopes on his heavy forearms. "I'm in publicity and promotion, so I have to be able to read people fast. It can make the difference between earning three grand a year or three hundred grand. Eric was maladjusted. Only thing he could do was program. And I'll tell you this: Maybe the others don't know it yet, but Eric, much as I despise him, was what made Micro. He was the only real hotshot programming genius there. Hell, they're still running on fumes from his brain stews. He gave ideas away like they were candy. Still can't figure out why he did that. Something deep inside was twisted. Despite his genius, his whole life was a lie. Ever know a pathological liar?"

"A few."

"Know who you should talk to? Eric's parents in Greenwood. They'll tell you about him. Then you'll know what I mean."

I asked for their names and addresses, but all he could remember was the old man's Christian name. After making a mental note to look it up in the phone book, I said, "Schuyler lives with them?"

Gunnar Rogers grimaced. "Schuyler? Yeah, he lives there."

"Why?"

"He just does."

"Veronica's firstborn?"

"Umm."

As we contemplated Schuyler and Veronica, the room began to take on an uncomfortable silence, a silence I wasn't about to shatter. It was apparent that Veronica had emotionally jettisoned Schuyler. Finally Gunnar said, "I'll never forget the day Brit found that photo. What a hell of a thing. If she hadn't found it, Deirdre would probably still be here instead of on the East Coast, Eric would still be working at Micro, Veronica would be married to Eric, and I might still be with my first wife, Cindy. Who knows? Fred might be alive even."

"I thought a secretary found that photo."

"She did."

"You said Brit found it."

"Brittany Phillips was a secretary in those days."

"One last item. Fred approached your wife. Did you know that?"

"What do you mean, approached?"

"He tried to get her into bed."

The laughter rattled my teeth. When he tipped his head back, I could see the silver-gold mixture on the backs of his capped incisors. "Fred and Veronica? You think I took that seriously? Veronica? Fred?" He chortled again, but it was beginning to sound forced and phony. Under the skin of his mirth I sensed a deep insecurity concerning his wife.

On my way out Rogers didn't bother to shake my hand, merely stood behind his desk as if to make certain I didn't try to pilfer anything. "People don't trifle with Gunnar Rogers. Keep away from my home and my family. Visit Veronica again, I'll break you in half."

"Wouldn't dream of seeing her."

In the outer room the lady under the lacquered hair glanced up from her typewriter. "What can I do for you?"

"Gun and I were just talking and I forget . . ." I snapped my fingers. "I'd go back in and ask, but I don't want to bother him. He had a meeting with somebody yesterday afternoon between, what, one-thirty and three, did he? Mentioned something about that. Was that yesterday?"

She scooted her executive's chair across the rolling board and broke open a black appointment book. "Don't see anything. Believe Mr. Rogers took the afternoon off on personal business."

"Oh, yeah. The friend of his who got killed. I forgot about that. Must have been with the family, huh?"

Typing now, the IBM element whirring, she spoke over her shoulder. "I don't think so. I believe he said something about getting his son's van fixed. Had a broken muffler."

That disclosure took me all the way down the elevator, outside, and to my truck. Good old Gunnar had been out all yesterday afternoon? I wondered if he had been driving his son's beat-up old blue Chevy van on Lake Washington Boulevard. I wondered if he owned a pistol.

Bad day at Black Rock. Gunnar had threatened me. Desiree had ruined my reputation with a lady I admired. Paddy had thrown me off my own back porch. Horace, my neighbor, was going to be crotchety and irascible for weeks. And a beautiful Bellevue woman with green eyes had turned a garden hose on me. Hell, it wasn't the worst thing that had happened on a case. Last summer I had dropped through a lawn into a rotten septic tank and almost died. Even the cat had shunned me.

Twenty-five minutes later I was speaking to Eric Castle's parents, a drab duo in their early seventies. They answered my questions as if I were a grand jury. From the looks of her she had been a housewife since the Civil War. Eric's father had worked for Burlington Northern. Sitting side by side on a worn-out davenport that they must have been sitting side by side on for fifty years, they both wore interchangeable bifocals, and neither one smiled, looked as if they had never been taught how.

Resembling an emigrant from another planet, Schuyler waved to me from a tree outside the window. I had to work at it to keep from laughing at his antics. A flattened spray of paper flowers jutted from his rear pants pocket. He was still dressed well, and I realized as I surveyed his grandparents, they weren't responsible for his OshKosh jeans or Nike shoes.

"Veronica buys Schuyler's clothes?" I asked.

"Veronica?" said the old man.

"Means Binnie," said his wife in a near shout.

"Binnie? Nah. Never bothers to come. Don't have no use for Schuyler. Eric buys 'em. Buys all Schuyler's clothes. Won't get a rag for hisself. Lord knows, Eric ain't got a dime to spare. And the boy don't know the difference."

"Now, Grampa," said his wife.

"I suppose you know why Eric was forced to leave Micro Darlings?"

The old man peered at me through his bifocals as the old lady's veined, leathery hand patted his knee, calming. "We know."

How do you ask a pair of golden-agers if they raised a degenerate? "You have any thoughts on the subject?" I asked, rather lamely.

"You mean, did Eric do them things? Have to ask him. We ain't spoken of it."

"Never?"

"Not a once. And we ain't goin' to. Ma couldn't stand it." But Ma looked plenty tough to me. It was Pa who had thin skin.

"How often does Eric see Schuyler?"

"Near every day," said the old man.

I nodded. "How about friends? I can't seem to get a line on any of Eric's friends. I need to talk to some of them."

"You seen Aaron?"

"Who?"

"Aaron Barbour. Practically brothers. Folks used to live right next door here." He gestured out the window but didn't see Schuyler, who hadn't stopped clowning. He was putting twigs behind his ears, scratching at his armpit and making animal sounds. "Eric and Aaron known each other 'bout thirty years. Fact, Eric took Binnie away from Aaron in high school."

"Poo, he didn't," chided the old woman. "She just decided she wanted to go out with Eric, was all. A woman's got a mind of her own, Pa."

"One man's got a woman, his best friend comes along and gets that woman, he's takin' her away," said the old man solemnly. "Ain't no other way to look at it. Caused some real hard feelings at the time, you recall."

"Poo."

They gave me an address for Aaron Barbour. "He'll be home," said the old man. And then he said something Horace was always saying about me. "He don't work much."

"Mr. and Mrs. Castle, was Eric ever molested as a child?" I had read somewhere that many abusers had been abused themselves as children.

Neither one of them spoke. The old man swallowed and managed to look blind. We sat like that for some time while, outside the window, Schuyler swung from a branch and scratched under his arm. I winked, scratched under my arm, and let myself out, armed with a name and an address that would take me across the sound.

I stopped at a booth near the Ridgemont Theatre and made some phone calls. First, I woke up Smithers, who was home with a cold. "Hey, old man," I said.

"This case you're working on is big stuff, Thomas. You see that story on last night's news?"

"Must've missed it. Look, Smitty, I know you're not feeling well, but could you do me a couple of favors? I've got a great dame for you. She's going with somebody, but I think they're about to break up."

"She better be slicker than Babs. Talk about a nut case. You know, she would rather make out in the back seat of my car than in the bedroom. Got damn cold out there last winter."

"This lady is pretty, Smitty."

"Big?"

"I got on a teeter-totter with her, I'd land in Kansas City. All woman."

"What do you want?"

"Byron and Myrtle Castle. Got that?" I gave him their Greenwood address. "I want to know if either one of them has a record in Seattle for anything."

"What else?"

"Gunnar Rogers. Veronica Rogers."

"Okay."

"Daryl Rittenhouse." I spelled it.

"The dude that runs Micro Darlings over on the East Side?"

"That's the one. And how about a kid named Dennis Rogers?"

"Those his folks?"

"Yep."

"That it?"

"For now."

Kathy was in the office when I called. "You're at work. It's a miracle."

"Been here most of the day. What's up?"

"Somebody sued Eric Castle a few years back." I gave her some approximate dates. "They never went through with it, but if you could look up the pleadings, it would be a great help. Need to find out just what sort of evidence they had."

"I'll go over to the courthouse right now." I gave her the names of everyone involved and thanked her.

"Thomas? I need to talk to you. About Fred Pugsley."

"You got something on the case?"

"I can't get it out of my mind. You know. The other morning. It's beginning to bother me."

"We'll talk."

"Tonight?"

"I'll be in Kingston the rest of the afternoon, so I might be back late."

"I have a key."

"You do?" But she had hung up on me. I couldn't even begin to count the times Kathy had pretended to turn my house key back to me. Apparently she'd had a gross of them stamped out and had been turning in duplicates over the past year.

I followed North Eighty-fifth east to the freeway and hightailed it to Edmonds to grab the ferry. Seattle was more or less in a ditch. To the east was the Cascade mountain range, where in the winter the passes got snowed in. Some, like Cayuse, were closed for months. To the west was nothing but water, and beyond that islands and the Olympic Peninsula, the Olympic Mountains. Ferries chugged to Vashon Island and small towns like Bremerton, Winslow, Kingston. When they weren't interfering with my schedule, I liked the ferries.

Mine was the last vehicle flagged on board. It was Thursday and not all that crowded. I sat inside the windows above the prow and watched the sparse boat traffic on the choppy sound. Like Kathy, I seemed to be having a difficult time ridding myself of the canvas that had been Fred Pugsley's demise.

13

THE FERRY DUMPED US UNCEREMO-
niously in Kingston, and as was the
custom, we all got exasperated and raced through town,
beeping our horns and gunning our engines. I was all
for maintaining the local customs. I didn't see anybody
hit a goose or a dog, though the last time I'd taken this
ferry, an old woman from Canada had smacked a duck
with her Gremlin and screamed like a banshee when
she saw the mess of feathers in her radiator. Aaron Barbour lived on the highway heading toward Hansville and
Point No Point.

The man who greeted me as I bounced over the mud
and ruts in the three-hundred-foot-long driveway might
have been an overgrown troll. Heavyset, his torso was
far too long for his legs, and his belly rode over his
manure-stained jeans like a huge melon. He was a head
shorter than I was. Hair sprouted from every conceiv-
able spot on his skull. Only a fleshy band around his
eyes and two peekaboo ears showed through the shock
of hair and Yosemite Sam beard. His reddish mustache
was long enough to tuck into his mouth and chew, as
he did from time to time, snaring it with his lower lip.
In his hands he held a pitchfork as if it were a javelin.

It was a small farm, picturesque and green, probably

125

not even a full-time operation. I parked in an open gravel area between the house and a ramshackle barn that should have been condemned.

Nothing about the acreage or the man spelled prosperity. Three Dodge pickups in various states of disrepair were lined up in the weeds beside the house. A stooped woman on the porch fussed with a plant. By her coloring, age, and the nylon doughnuts around her ankles, I took her to be his spouse. He was too old to be the man I was seeking. She was too old to be the wife of the man I was seeking.

I killed the engine and leaned out the driver's window in time to hear the man say, "You wanta sell that truck? How many miles ya got on it?"

"Hundred and twenty. Aaron Barbour live here?"

"On the second engine, or third? Give you six hundred cash. Who wants to know?"

"First engine. No sale. Thomas Black. I need to see Aaron." After I stepped out of the cab, I held out a hand to shake with the man. He stretched his hirsute lips tightly across his teeth and immediately got into a gripping contest with me. We went at it hot and heavy while he introduced himself.

"Name is Greg Ghee," he said, pumping furiously, eyes tiny, hard dots. "Aaron rents a shack out back. Believe he's around."

Eventually I won the contest, but almost by default, as his knuckles were cracking loudly. I could tell he wanted an immediate rematch. Me. I thought people who went in for that sort of nonsense were silly. My guess was he kept a rubber ball and sat for hours in front of the Magnavox every night, squeezing. Silly. Besides, I might lose a second skirmish.

"Mind if I talk to him?"

"You ain't here about his income tax again, are you?"

"I'm not with the IRS."

He placed two filthy fingers in his mouth and whistled, as if beckoning a sheepdog. "Be out in a minute, if he ain't whacking off." He looked at me and burst into laughter. "Peculiar kid."

If some people had cigarette voices, and once in a while a man had a cigar voice, this oversize troll had a Prestolog voice.

Greg Ghee planted the pitchfork tines into the ground between us and leaned against the handle, placing the top of the worn and dirty wood alongside his cheek. "Been here off and on since high school." Ghee's blue crystal eyes were set into plump cheeks. If he'd had a daughter with those same blazing pinprick crystals, I'd gladly fall in love with her; no trouble. He whistled again, longer this time. Something beyond the wall of the barn snorted, and I thought I felt the ground shake, but it must have been my imagination. Ghee grinned.

"Where's his shack? Maybe I could go back and find Aaron myself?" I thought I felt the ground shudder again. Maybe a bulldozer was being operated nearby, although I didn't hear a motor.

Another bearded man with black hair hanging limply to his beltline came around the corner of the barn in a crouch and stealthily tiptoed toward Greg Ghee. He was younger than Ghee, late twenties maybe. His crooked teeth poked the afternoon in a grin that was only two points off shyness, so I didn't alert Ghee, now pontificating about a baseball coach he'd thrashed in a men's room twelve years earlier. When the younger man got three paces away, he stood up straight, inserted both hands into his coveralls pockets, and spoke in a normal voice.

"Hey, old man." Ghee jumped. "You whistled?"

When he saw who it was, Ghee spit a slimy-looking stream of tobacco juice between the newcomer's feet and said, "Don't sneak up on people like that, Aaron. Give 'em a heart attack."

"Aaron Barbour?" I said. He nodded, all teeth and squinty eyes, at least what I could see of him through the whiskers and hair. For a moment I thought I'd stumbled into a commune or a wild experiment in zooplasty, but upon reflection, I decided it was only chance. One of these longhairs was hip, straight out of the late sixties and early seventies. The other, Ghee, was a terminal redneck.

"Here he is," announced Ghee gruffly. "The Hansville poster for birth control."

"Hey, old man," Aaron Barbour said, sliding into a rough-and-tumble mock sparring match. The old man was keen on games. "You better be careful. I got some stories I can tell on you." They danced and slapped at each other's beards for a few moments, and then it was over.

"Aw, you were still suckin' hind titty ten years after I got my first good stuff."

"Yeah, and I'll be sucking titty ten years after you get your last good stuff, too," Barbour laughed. It was all manly and tougher than broken glass in your toothpaste. Any minute I expected one of them to challenge the other to a gut-punching contest.

"Well," said Ghee, jerking his pitchfork out of the ground and waddling toward the barn, "I'll let you two get on with business."

I handed Aaron Barbour an embossed business card, which, to my dismay, he kept—I was running low—and said, "You related?"

"Me and Greg? Naw." Barbour's gray-blue eyes looked as if they belonged on a huge bottom fish. He was medium height and stocky. "Greg's just my landlord. I been here off and on ten years. Live out back." His smiles were forced but relentless. After each exchange he bared his ripsaw teeth.

"Understand you used to be friends with Eric Castle."

"Still am. Eric and I've been best friends since junior high school. Grade school really. Lived right next to each other." Teeth. "You here about the murder?"

"How'd you know that?"

Ghee hadn't moved out of earshot yet, and he yelled at me. "You investigating that pederast?"

"I'm investigating the murder in Laurelhurst. Fred Pugsley."

"Catch that little babyfucker, what you gonna do to him?"

"Haven't decided," I said.

"Bring his nuts to me," said Greg Ghee. He sounded serious. "We'll eat 'em. Rocky Mountain oysters." Smacking his chicken lips, he left.

Aaron beamed and said, "He don't like Eric."

"Only a saint would. How'd you know I was here about the murder?"

"I used to work at Micro. In shipping. Eric got me the job. I was really going places. One of the only companies I've worked where my hair didn't become an issue. Most bosses see this long hair and don't want me around. Too independent for them. Don't want me dealing with the public much."

"I still don't understand how you knew I was here about the murder."

"Simple. I knew Fred. Daryl Rittenhouse. The whole gang there at Micro Darlings. Used to eat lunch with Daryl." Crusty spit clung to his incisors, and a patina of what I took to be oats ringed the mouth hole in his beard. "You show me a card tells me you're a private detective. I put two and two together. Gotta be here about the murder."

We had been standing in a light mist, but now the wind was beginning to get rambunctious, and the mist was picking up weight, pasting limp strands of Barbour's hair to his pale, pimpled forehead. "Why don't you come around back? We can talk in my place. It ain't great, but it's got a roof."

Again the ground rumbled, as if heavy earth-moving machinery were tearing up the landscape nearby.

He led me through a gate, around the run-down barn, along the length of it. The ground was uneven, the mud packed into a solid path. Beyond the barn was a barbed-wire fence that enclosed a muddied yard. Fifty meters beyond the fence stood a tiny shack under a stand of leafless birch trees; the shack tilted slightly to one side. Had it been a man, I would have said he was snockered. Beside the shack's wooden porch sat an MG sports car that was almost as old as my truck.

We walked along the fence, and the ground rumbled under our feet. It brought back a dream I'd had the night after Fred Pugsley's death, a dream that Mount Rainier had erupted, spewing lava and panic all across the Northwest.

Then I heard the snorts.

I turned my head and gasped. Aaron Barbour hugged himself, both hands tucked up inside his overalls, and laughed until he was spitting out his nose.

"Looks like a Sherman tank, don't it?"

On the back side of the barn, locked in a small electrified enclosure, stood the largest animal I'd seen since my last visit to the elephant house at the Woodland Park Zoo. Creamy white, he was as tall as I was. We were only twenty-five feet away, and although we had two fences between us, I didn't like the way he was eyeballing me. He struck the ground with a front hoof. Again the ground rumbled. "We call him Aunt Mabel," said Aaron Barbour. "Looks big, don't he?"

"Never seen a bull that large."

"Ain't too many around. Twenty-nine hundred pounds. He's a Charbray."

"He looks almost like a Brahman."

"Brahmans don't get that big. Actually he's a cross between a Brahman and something else I can't remember. All meat. Greg's brother raised him to stud, but they had some trouble with him over in Redmond, so he's been here a couple of months."

"Trouble?"

"Ripped up the neighbors' cows. Killed a bunch of 'em. Some pigs, too. And a horse maybe. Fact, I think the cops are looking for this old guy."

The bull hadn't taken his eyes off us, was rattling a corner post with one pointed tip of his long, wickedly curved horns. The post was as thick as a telephone pole and quivered like a straw. I felt as if somebody were pointing a rocket launcher at my sternum. "He ever get loose?"

"Fact, he did last week. Greg's got this cattle prod gizmo on a pole he gets him back into the pen with. Uses it from his truck. I use my pellet gun on him. You oughta see that sucker hop. Don't worry. The fence is electrified. He could bust it down, but he don't. 'Sides, he'd have to go through two wire fences to get us."

"He's big enough to plow through Green Bay's locker room."

Aaron Barbour laughed and popped a breath mint into his mouth, then offered me one. I took it and crunched it and swallowed in one gulp.

"You can lead 'im around by that ring in his nose," said Aaron. "Nose is very tender."

"Anybody ever been stupid enough to try?"

"When old Aunt Mabel got loose last week, Greg's wife went out the attic and stood on the roof until Greg rounded him up. I'd been home, I would have climbed a tree and said my prayers. That sucker could run plumb through my house, he took a notion to."

The inside of the shack looked as if it'd been involved in an ongoing party for the last three or four years. It consisted of two low-ceilinged rooms, a bedroom and a main room. The main room had a torn-up couch, a hot plate, a sink, and floor-to-ceiling bookshelves on two walls. All paperbacks. Some sci-fi, but most of it was shoot-'em-ups. An adult western lay splashed face-down on an overstuffed armchair, along with a pair of heavy-framed black reading glasses. On the cover a blond woman showed a lot of cleavage to a cowpoke who held a smoking six-shooter. The blonde was too beautiful to be real, looked remarkably similar to Veronica Rogers.

After Aaron flicked some clothes off a chair, we sat down, and he offered me herb tea. He had the look of an ex-hip groover, one of those dudes who was still sweating drugs out of his system from parties fifteen years ago. When I took a raincheck on the sassafras tea, he sipped from a mug, burned his lips, and bared his crooked teeth. Every age has people who get stuck in it, frozen in time while the rest of us troop onward. He would still be listening to "Eleanor Rigby" and burning incense when he checked into a nursing home.

"Did you know Fred Pugsley well?"

"Like I said." He sipped and grinned. "I knew 'em all."

"When was the last time you were around any of them?"

"Eric I saw about a month ago. He's trying to sue his old lady—his ex old lady—so he can see the kids. It's pretty sad."

"Depends on whose point of view you're looking at it from."

"You gotta know Eric. We been friends since I helped him get away from Butch Blumcart in sixth grade. Butch was going to pound him. Sixth grade. That was the last time I got a haircut."

"What do you know about company politics? Was there much infighting at Micro?"

"Hell, yes. That's one of the reasons I got outa there. That and what happened to Eric. Not that he didn't deserve it, but I couldn't be listening to what Eric was telling me in one ear and what they were saying at Micro with the other. See, Eric came and stayed with me after it happened. Never saw a guy so crushed. I guess it was about like a guy's first few weeks in the joint. He hardly ate. *Never* slept. I used to hear him in here sobbing at night. So I gave my notice at Micro. Probably not a good move. Last spring I talked to the guy got my job. Making almost thirty-three grand a year. Can you imagine?"

"Tell me about Eric and Fred."

"Fred used Eric. I tried to tell him that a couple of times, but Eric's always been too kindhearted."

"That's not how I heard it. Used him how?"

"Fred appropriated Eric's work. They'd sit around

and talk, and Eric would think things up, and by the time he turned them loose, Fred had him convinced that he had thought them up.''

"What's the real reason you thought I was here about the murder?''

"You don't believe I just figured it out?''

"Not hardly.''

"Eric called. Told me about you.''

"And warned you not to tell me certain things?''

"Something like that.''

"What were you supposed to keep me from finding out?''

"Binnie. He didn't want me saying anything about her.''

"They started out young?''

"High school. Got married in college. She got pregnant, and he married her. That's when they had Schuyler.''

"I've met him.''

"People think he's weird, but I think he's a pretty neat little kid,'' said Aaron Barbour, kicking off his boots and stacking up his stocking feet near an electric heater. It was clear Aaron felt a moral obligation to line up on the side of anyone who was out of the mainstream. "You gotta understand about Eric. That family meant everything to him. She could divorce him legally but not spiritually. Spiritually Eric is still one with Binnie. Always will be.''

I frowned. "He was upset after he left Micro?''

"Upset isn't the word for it. He was suicidal. As far as he was concerned, the world had stopped. For a while there I thought he would never pull out of it. He just stayed out here and stared at the sky all day and watched TV all night. It was weird.''

"How'd he snap out of it?''

"He was here 'bout three months when Greg found out what he was hiding from. Greg ran him out of here with a deer rifle. Even took a couple of shots at him, from what Ida says. Then I lost track of him. I think he

hitchhiked around the country for a while. Nobody ever
formally charged him with anything. When he got back,
he seemed better. He started programming again and
trying to get his kids back. Course, by that time Binnie
had married Gunnar Rogers. That didn't help matters
as far as Eric's mental health was concerned. He wanted
Binnie bad. Everybody wants Binnie.'' He grinned.

''Even you?''

''You met her?'' I nodded. ''Neither Eric or I was
much in high school, but palling with Binnie put us on
top of the heap. Everybody wanted to be around us.
Yeah, I don't know why she went out with me in the
first place. I was the first guy she ever dated, and I
guess she just didn't know any better.'' He chuckled.

''Anybody bother Eric when he was staying here with
you?''

''Daryl Rittenhouse. He came over once, and they
got into some sort of shouting match. Didn't hear any
of it. Ashley Phillips showed up once, too.''

''He argue with Eric?''

''Naw. He came out and brought stuff of Eric's they
tried to throw away at Micro. Personal stuff. Ashley
always had a big heart.''

''What about Fred?''

''I don't know how people can turn on each other
like that. Sure, Eric proved himself a louse, but I was
his friend. I figured I owed him something.''

''You thought he was guilty as charged then?''

''No doubt about it.''

''You talk to him about it?''

''He wouldn't talk. Knowing Eric, that's proof
enough. He was always willing to talk about anything.
Yep, knowing Eric, that was proof enough.'' Aaron
Barbour stroked his scruffy oil-black beard and patted
his lap until a fat, piebald cat lurched into it. ''Fred
was a funny friend, though, I thought. He even came
out here, oh, 'bout six weeks ago looking for something
of Eric's.''

''He say what?''

"Didn't have to. He wanted evidence to put Eric in the clink. Even went around and talked to the Partridges next door to see if maybe he'd done anything funny with their kids."

"Had Eric?"

"No."

"What did Fred say to you when he came?"

" 'There's gotta be some proof.' Said it two or three times. Fred was funny."

"Not when I saw him."

14

"I SHOULD TELL YOU SOMETHING," said Aaron Barbour, stroking the mangy cat's back with one hand, his mangy beard with the other, rattling fleas all around. I'd gotten a whiff of him outside. He probably bathed every election day—provided the Democrats won.

"Being caught didn't destroy Eric. He could have handled that. It was Binnie's reaction to it. When she didn't stick by his side, he bummed out. He really believed in 'till death do us part.' Couldn't face anything else. A couple of times, when he was moping, I got on her case, but he snapped at me, wouldn't let me bad-mouth her." Barbour whistled the old *Twilight Zone* theme song. "Wouldn't let anybody, ever, put down that woman. Never knew anybody who loved like he did. His kids, too. It was almost—"

"What?"

"Psychotic, I was going to say. But that isn't right."

"Maybe it is."

"They were different. First love for both of them. I didn't count for Binnie. We only went together a couple of weeks. Never did anything but kiss a couple of times. Eric and her, they were makin' it on her mother's basement couch on their second date. And it never changed

for them. Maybe for a year or so after Schuyler was
born and they found out he was different, but then it
went back to the way it was. Torrid, man.''

"When you worked at Micro, was there anybody else
around you thought could have been a molester?''

"You mean, there might have been two of them?''

"I mean, Eric might not have been the one. It's a
million to one, but I need to consider it.''

"You're skating on clouds, man. I've known Eric for
a long time, and he was always a couple bubbles off
center. He settled down a bit when they all started up
Micro, stopped smokin' weed and getting drunk every
weekend. But he was always different. Always had a
real strong sexual component to his makeup.'' I wondered how much of this I could trust, coming from a
man who lived like a monk, with a cat in the house and
a bull in the yard, and who likened ''a strong sexual
component'' to a deviant one.

"Know what Eric needed?'' Barbour asked, throwing a swatch of that long hair behind his shoulder, rotating his head and spine as one in a practiced
semicircle.

"What?''

"A mother ''

"Yeah?''

"Binnie wouldn't be his mother anymore after it happened. She never came right out and accused him. In
fact, from what he said, she maintained his innocence.
Probably still would if you asked her.''

"Then why did she leave him?''

"You thought Binnie was the one who left? Eric was
the one. He was living here in my pad two nights after.
Said she claimed out loud he was innocent but that he
was listening to her insides and her insides were
screaming 'guilty.' ''

"Veronica stood by him?''

"All the way, man. But down deep Eric glimpsed
signs of doubt. She denied it. They fought. But he
couldn't trust her. She swore she believed him, but that

wasn't enough. He had so much comin' down on him
in those days he just couldn't take a doubting Thomas
under his own roof.''

"But she claimed she didn't doubt him."

"Right. He just didn't believe it."

"Sounds as if he expected a lot from her."

"It destroyed him to leave her. Slayed, man. No other
way to put it. She staged quite a scene when he told her
he was leaving, but I guess eventually she adjusted.''

"She's adjusted real well."

"Course, she's treated him like dirt ever since. She
took the breakup as a confession.''

On the way out I spied a diploma on the wall. He
had a Bachelor of Science degree in mathematics from
the University of Washington. As I picked my way
through the wet weeds and hard-packed earth, moving
toward the barn and the unearthly three thousand
pounds of steaks, Aaron Barbour stood in his doorway,
the door sealed behind him to trap the heat.

"Got me thinking about the old days," he said. I
turned and watched him line his crooked teeth up for
my inspection, that shy-evil smile. "Binnie? What a
woman. I remember once we went to a rock festival at
Satsop and it was hot and everybody was smoking weed
and the ladies were all taking off their tops. We were
free spirits then. She wouldn't do anything like that
now.''

"No," I said. "She wouldn't."

"Don't think I'll ever forget it. She danced to the
music as if nothing was happening. No, I'll never forget that. I imagine I'd feel different if I saw her today.''

Don't count on it, I whispered to myself. But then, I
had always been a pushover for blondes.

I went the other way around the barn to get a closer
look at Aunt Mabel, who was busy munching dinner.
Through a chute in the barn wall Greg Ghee fed him,
pouring grain into a wooden trough. Aunt Mabel's chest
almost touched the ground, as did the long hair surrounding his genitals. When he moved, the creamy hide

rippled, the musculature evident. Breath wheezed out his nostrils like smoke; humidity rose off his hide in visible whorls. Twenty-nine hundred pounds. Jeezola. He was heavier than Kathy's car. One of those horns could easily put a dent in a brick wall. And he had a reputation for meanness. Being in the same county with him made me nervous.

"Hey, Black!" It was Greg Ghee, watching me through a pair of knotholes in the side of the barn.

"Yeah?"

"What are you really here for?"

"Checking somebody's insurance claim with Aaron."

"Know what I think of that, Black?"

"No."

He rolled his eyes, signaling me to look at Aunt Mabel, whose tail was raised in pursuit of a biological function. Nature's salute to liars. Greg Ghee laughed so hard he brayed.

I had missed a lot of boats in my life, and the four-thirty ferry was just one more. I managed to grab the five-ten, remained in the truck to read a copy of the *Weekly* highlighting the Fat Tuesday events, and, as I read, resolved to take Kathy to a couple of them when I got the chance. Instead of driving straight home, I went to Capitol Hill and parked in front of Eric Castle's place. I'd been hearing a lot about him.

In slippers, jeans, and a torn T-shirt he answered the basement door when I rapped on it. He had a beer bottle in his hand, and the blur in his dark eyes told me it wasn't the first one today. "Get outa here," he said.

"I want to ask you some questions, Eric."

"Ain't talking to you. Not a word. Get out."

"You need help, Eric."

"And who's gonna give it to me? You?"

"Did you know Fred was investigating you? Did you know he had been digging around for weeks? Did you know he had some pictures? When was the last time you spoke to him?"

EARL W. EMERSON

Eric tried to hit me in the head with the beer bottle, throwing it at me; but he missed, and it sailed into the backyard and shattered against a rockery. "Ain't talkin'," he said, slamming the door and locking it. We stared at each other through the glass for a moment before he yelled, "Don't come back."

It was almost six-thirty when I got home. Kathy had been and gone, penning a note. "Ward, gone out to pick up your costume. Back in a jiffy, June."

Costume? What the hell was she talking about? If she thought I was going to wear one of those bizarre Fat Tuesday ape suits, she was LoonyTunes.

I scanned the evening *Times*, set aside the sections that dealt with the Laurelhurst murder, and called Smithers. His cold sounded worse. "Hey, old buddy," he barked. "The parents are clean as a priest's . . ."

"You sure?"

"Sure as snot in a sneezing schnauzer. When are you going to introduce me to this Humpty-Dumpty in skirts you promised?"

"Keep your pants on."

"I haven't got around to the others on the list yet. Something came up."

"Thanks again for the information, Smitty. Get well soon. Chicken soup and all that."

"The right woman would cure me."

I played my phone machine tapes back. A portrait studio in Ballard wanted to take pictures of my puss and then sell them back to me—blackmail. My truck insurance had lapsed because of a computer foul-up. Desiree had called. Six times. She had a new proposition.

Disgusted, I snapped the machine off and undressed, then climbed under a hot shower. It had been a while since a female as demented as Desiree Nash had tried to get her hooks into me. As I stood under the spray and let my thoughts roam, I wondered exactly what she had proposed. Not that I was planning to accept. When I tore open the shower curtain to splash into the other

room and play the rest of the messages, a woman in a
black sheath dress was standing in the bathroom.

"Kathy!"

"You've lost weight, Thomas." I jerked the plastic
curtain around myself. "But it looks good. More cycling, huh? What? About ten pounds?"

"Eight pounds. Kathy, damn it! Can't a guy have any
privacy? And how did you get in here? I could have
shot you."

"What with?"

"Never mind."

"Just had to leave your costume here so you could
put it on. Swannie's is going to be shoulder to shoulder
as it is without your dillydallying." She had rented a
suit for me with tails and spats and a top hat.

"Cripes," I said, "I'm not going to wear that!"

"Don't be that way. Listen to yourself."

"I'm not wearing that costume."

"You said you were going out with me, and this is
part of the package."

"Hell, you know I even hate wearing a tie. How many
times have you seen me in a tie?"

When I came out of the bathroom, she hooted the
way women hooted at male strippers. I grinned and
bowed and tipped my hat and flipped my tails. My
mouth hurt I grinned so hard.

She had on a black lamé dress that I swear had been
applied with an airless; would require a team of skilled
surgeons to extricate her. It revealed far too much pale,
swollen cleavage. Tighter than frogskin, it extended to
the floor, flaring slightly at the knee to give her just
enough room to move. Lord only knows how she
walked in it.

Her face was a mask, her lower lip dark blue, her
upper lip a lighter hue. Both eyes were cloaked in a
deep cerulean that flared dramatically out to the sides,
topped by exotic pencil-sharp slashes of black and silver. A red star on one cheek. Lightning bolt on the
other. Dangling from her ears were ragged silver coins

that seemed to have been pressed by a freight train.
People were going to stare. Even for Fat Tuesday, people were going to stare. But then, that was the whole
idea.

My big mistake was in prancing around under Kathy's admiring gaze and then disappearing into the bedroom to fuss with my hair. I couldn't help it. I hadn't
been out with her in a while, and she looked terrific.
Her admiring eyes were the jewels of my vanity.

Then I heard a noise in the other room. Some people
might have mistaken it for laughter. It had turned to
screaming, hysterical guffawing by the time I found her
in the living room. The last of Desiree's proposals was
playing on the tape machine. Tears streaming down her
cheeks, she was on the sofa, on her back, kicking her
feet with glee, her face red with it. If she hadn't calmed
herself enough to see the look on my face, she might
have laughed herself to death. As it was, it took her a
minute to wind down.

"My old fourth-grade teacher calling about the school
reunion," I said.

After erupting into hysterical, hiccuping laughter
again, Kathy said, "Tell me the truth. What happened
in Walla Walla, you big charmer? How did you get this
lady so stuck on you?"

"Nothing happened in Walla Walla."

"You've got a way with women, big fella." She
hooted and tugged at the shoulder of her gown, which
had slipped dangerously during her seizure.

"Sure," I said. "They dress me up; they laugh at
me. They talk dirty on my answer phone and have their
boyfriends throw me off the back porch. Call me Cary."

"Sure, Larry."

"That was Cary."

"Was he one of the Three Stooges, too?"

When we got outside, I could see that it wasn't driz-
zling at all, though from inside it had looked rainy.
Seattle's prestidigitation. She drove me down to Pioneer Square in her two-seater, and we parked near the

Kingdome and hiked. Kathy was wrapped in a floor-length fur she'd found at a rummage sale for ten bucks before furs came back. The cold streets were full of glad-handing half-swacked loonies, and I was relieved to see we weren't the only fools in costume. One beefy lady even wore a flesh-colored bodysuit that I swear was transparent. Kathy jerked my elbow when I turned around to reconnoiter her receding figure and dragged me into Swannie's basement.

"I was just—"

"Yeah, I know what you were doing."

Swannie's stood almost catty-cornered from the fire station and across from Waterfall park. It was noisy and smoky, and it smelled like broiled steaks and beer and women and the perfume smell you get off old money.

Kathy knew somebody who worked there from her legal practice, and we had reserved seats downstairs. Swannie's boasted live comedy four nights a week, but it doubled up on the bill during Fat Tuesday. "What is a heterosexual on Capitol Hill? . . . A tourist." The crowd broke up. I noticed Kathy garnered her share of salacious glances. She had a working dancer's well-formed body, and we all knew she wasn't wearing a stitch under that dress. She was never hard to look at, but her costume and the cerulean blue slashes around her eyes made her absolutely startling. I was glad she hadn't worn her mime makeup. The building was full of mimes. There were no other gooney birds in tails.

"You're the prettiest woman in the building," I said.

"You lie, big Tom," Kathy said unconvincingly. "But thanks anyway."

The first comic was a button-nosed woman who told off-beat jokes about her husband and her dog and a neighbor named Fat Alice who was the local prostitute and would do it for a smile and a pack of cigarettes.

Kathy said, "You look like the Cheshire cat or something in that suit. I wish I had my camera."

"So do I," I said, giving her a Groucho leer. Kathy's eyes held me like a spit.

"I'm glad you're with me, Thomas."

"Me too."

"Thanks for wearing the . . ." She nodded at my
togs. "It's not the same when I'm the only one dressing
up."

"My pleasure," I said through gritted teeth.

We had appetizers at Doc Maynard's, then squeezed
into The Borderline, where we heard a great rock band
that played too loudly. During the slow songs she bel-
lied up to me and danced close.

When nobody was looking, Kathy pressed a soft, two-
toned blue kiss against my cheek. "What's that for?"

"Just for being here."

"My pleasure."

"Let's go somewhere and talk."

"Sure."

After getting turned down at several overcrowded eat-
eries, we finally grabbed a back table at Luigi Mc-
Nasty's on First Avenue. Over dinner we chatted, while
beyond Kathy's shoulder a Japanese couple who were
already toasted stared at our getups and pretended not
to stare at our getups.

"I lucked out on that civil suit you asked me to check.
Even phoned back East, someplace in Maine, and spoke
to the couple who filed it. They didn't want to talk, but
when I told them Fred Pugsley had been murdered, they
decided I might have some more interesting tidbits. We
swapped info."

"They have a case?"

"From the pleadings? Nothing that would have stood
up in criminal court, but then, civil actions are a different matter. They flat out accused Eric Castle of being
the one who molested their child. Gave the date and
everything. They had a couple of dozen witnesses they
were planning to have testify. It was all circumstantial,
but it would have been ugly for Eric."

"Think they would have won?"

"Couldn't say. Eric's lawyer didn't put up much of
an answer in their pleadings. From the looks of it, in

court he would have been a one-legged man in an ass-kicking contest. Would have ruined Eric's life."

"He's already done that. Why did they drop the suit?"

"Deirdre was a little vague on that, but Bill, her husband, said Deirdre had been ill since her child was attacked. I guess the pressure of the lawsuit and all was more than she could bear. They decided pursuing it wasn't going to get them any peace of mind."

"That's something nobody in this whole mess seems to have."

"Including me," said Kathy. I reached across the table and held her hands. "What have you found, Thomas?"

I told her all of it, going into detail, describing each of the people I'd met and coloring their answers with my personal observations. Kathy listened, training her violet on me and nodding at the appropriate times. After I finished, she said, "Want to make a list?"

"Suspects?"

"Sure."

"Can't hurt. Two lists," I said. "Somebody killed Fred. And somebody tried to kill Eric when I was riding with him."

"You think they were trying to kill him or just scare him?"

"Kill. I had the feeling it was someone inept, actually doing their best to kill him."

"Inept?"

"An amateur. Maybe somebody who was so emotionally wrought up in their plan they couldn't think straight."

Kathy twiddled her fountain pen nervously over a scrap of paper and said, "Fred's killer. Who's first?"

"Gotta be Maggie. Could be she found one or more of the pictures I found. Added to his philandering, it could have been the straw that broke the camel's back. Especially if she thought the photos were his, that he had taken them. Then, too, they could have been Eric's, and Fred found them, and she got confused—attributed them to Fred. In fact, what the hell are those pictures all about anyway?'' Kathy wrote the name down. ''Then Eric. Eric might have got wind of the fact that Fred had some sort of concrete proof on him. Fred found the pictures, confronted Eric, and was murdered for his trouble. The weapon also points to Eric. Maggie could have walked into it after Eric left.''

''Who else?''

''Gunnar Rogers. Fred had put the make on his wife several times. Gunnar doesn't strike me as the type to take that lying down. And he hated Eric. He had access to that tool, which could have eventually been traced to Eric. It might have been his way of getting two birds with one stone: eliminate Fred; have it pinned on Eric. He could have come over, killed Fred, and spread Polaroids around as another arrow pointing at Eric. Maybe Gunnar had some Polaroids left over from when they searched Eric's house five years ago.''

''Next.''

''Daryl Rittenhouse, although that's a long shot. Daryl strikes me as one who wouldn't mind settling a grudge with a whip. The letter proved there was bad blood between the two of them. There's not much else to go on here, but I still don't want to discount him at this point.''

''Next.''

''Any one of the boyfriends or husbands, from what I can gather. Fred had his fingers in a lot of pots.''

''Nice metaphor,'' Kathy said, displaying a jaundiced frown. ''Next.''

''I guess that's it.''

''Thomas, you're such a chauvinist.''

''Me?''

''You've admitted a woman could have killed him. Maggie's at the top of your list. Don't you think there's one more logical woman to add?''

''Who?''

''Veronica Castle Rogers.''

"I don't think so."

"Why not? Listen, you've got Gunnar on there because Fred made lewd suggestions to her. She has the same motive. You've already admitted a woman could have done it, yet the only people you seem willing to put on your list are men. Why couldn't she have been offended by Fred, maybe even hurt by him somehow, and decided to get even? Maybe Fred forced himself on her. It happens, you know. She could have gotten the weapon the same way Gunnar could have. And framing Eric would have been to her advantage, too."

"Put her on," I said. "We'll see who was home the morning of the murder and who was out gallivanting around."

"Now, the list of people who might have attacked Eric."

"Dennis Rogers," I said.

"Who's that?"

"Veronica's stepson. He owns a blue van very similar to the one that was used."

"Why would he do anything like that?"

"Why comes later. Gunnar. He hates Eric. Doesn't want Eric to see his stepkids. He could have used that same van. Rittenhouse. He as much as said somebody should wipe Eric off the face of the earth. Maggie claims she has an alibi."

"That's four people. Anybody else?"

"Can't think of anyone."

"You dope. Veronica!"

"Sure. Put that sweet thing on both lists. We'll burn her for a witch, too."

"Be fair, Thomas. She could have used her stepson's van. She has reason to want Eric out of the picture."

"Okay. And there's somebody I forgot for the first list."

"People who might have killed Fred?"

"Brittany Phillips. She's ten months pregnant, and I doubt she had the strength to do it; but I've been surprised before. And her husband, Ashley Phillips. They had a slim motive. Fred propositioned Ashley's pregnant wife. That might set some people off. An argument could easily escalate into murder. Everybody at Micro Darlings seemed to know about it, though Ashley professed ignorance. The whole trouble with this murder is when it happened. At the beginning of the commute hour. Anybody could have left a little early and gone over on the way to work and whacked him.''

"Yes,'' said Kathy somberly, "but didn't that neighbor say no cars had driven in that morning except Maggie's BMW and your truck?''

"That's what she claims. And the yard's almost inaccessible from any other direction.''

"It doesn't look good. In fact, the more we dig into this, the more it looks like Maggie murdered her husband.''

"I'll talk to her again,'' I said. "If she did it, I think I can get her to fess up.''

"Why aren't we putting Brittany and Ashley on the list for Eric's attacker?''

"Good idea. They're the aunt and uncle of the injured child. It would only be natural for them to be upset and want revenge. Neither one of them talks that way, but I've been lied to before. But why wait five years? Or maybe they haven't been waiting. Maybe they've been the ones Eric claims have been harassing him.'' Even as I said it, I remembered how close we had been to their condo on Lakeside when Eric got attacked. Was it possible one of them waited until we pedaled past, clambered into the van, pulled the ski mask over his or her head, and proceeded to make the afternoon ugly? Maybe they had spotted us going out and had waited for us to return. I stood up from the table. "Excuse me a minute.''

I located a pay phone out of sight of our table and dialed my own number. It was killing me. Kathy had been giving me teasing looks all evening, and I knew she was thinking about Desiree's phone messages. I had to find out what Desiree had said. It couldn't have been as nasty as Kathy was intimating.

But it was.

I listened to all six messages, each raunchier than the last, while my intestines knotted up. "Hey, Tommy?"

Somebody had picked up my home phone.

"Who's this?"

"Don't you recognize me, baby?"

"Desiree, you're trespassing, for godsakes. I'll call the cops."

"Do that, and we'll take our clothes off and dance on the roof. How'd you like that on the late news? Bet the neighbors would die. We might say some interesting things about you while we were up there. Did it to a peckerwood in Portland once. Ended up moving out of town. When you comin' home?"

"What do you mean 'we'll take our clothes off'? Who's we?"

"Queenie's watchin' TV, but I can't promise she'll be here all night, not 'less you show up. Told her what a smooth looker you were."

"Listen. Don't touch anything. I'll be there in half an hour."

"Tommy, there's no beer in the fridge."

"Send out."

When I got back to the table, Kathy was examining the two lists we'd compiled, had acquired lines in her brow. "Marry me," I said.

It took her awhile to get a handle on that. "Pooey phooey. So who did it?"

"Did which? The murder, or the attack on Eric?"

"Either. Both."

"Damned if I know."

"You all right, Thomas?"

"Ducky."

15

"THOMAS, I'M HAVING A HARD TIME forgetting what we walked in on the other morning." Kathy's voice slipped.

"It takes everyone awhile to forget."

Kathy ran her eyes over my face, then dropped them to my hands on the table. She grabbed my thumbs and curled her fists around them. The violet twinkled. "I like you, Thomas."

All the ladies loved me tonight. I had two beauts at home, tapping their feet, counting the minutes. This one had hold of my thumbs, squeezed them in a suggestive rhythm.

"Who do you really think tried to run down Eric Castle?"

"I'm voting for Gunnar Rogers. I think he's a . . . jerk-off. And like a lot of people, he detests Eric Castle with a passion bordering on dementia. The afternoon of the attack he was out of his office. His receptionist told me he was taking his kid's van somewhere to get it fixed."

Kathy brooded. "You gonna check to see if he ever took it anywhere?"

"That's one of about a hundred items on my list. And after I talk to Maggie again, I guess that's where I am

now. Making a list and checking it twice. Lord help me
if I have to dig into Fred's dirty little sex escapades. Or
Eric's.''

Kathy smiled demurely. It turned into something else,
something she could not conceal. "What?" I said.

"I wasn't going to say this, but Mr. Leech has been
getting some calls. I guess you ruffled some feathers."

"Me?"

Desiree and a cloven-hoofed succubus named Queenie
awaited. Veronica Rogers had disgraced me in Bellevue. Kathy had eavesdropped on the salacious invita-
tions on my answer machine, giving her enough verbal
bullets to last until we were both in rockers. Gunnar
had threatened to break me in half, and he was large
enough and fit enough to worry me. My internal ther-
mometer had gone cockamamie. My ears were turning
red.

"Leech told me a very prominent socialite on the
East Side was forced to take a garden hose to you."

"It's getting a little stuffy in here, isn't it?"

"You're kidding," Kathy said, her voice almost a
scream, as she realized from my reaction that the accusation must be grounded in something more than ru-
mor. "Somebody squirted you with a garden hose?"

"Louder," I said. "Otherwise it won't make the front
page of the *P-I*."

"Sorry. Was I yelling?"

"Let's get out of here."

Outside on the sidewalk three men in Hawaiian shirts
and sunglasses nearly crashed into us. They carried a
stuffed pig that wore a lei and sunglasses, and we could
see right away that all three of them were about as sharp
as the leading edge of a bowling ball. One of them
screamed, "You seen Charlie's? Charlie's is it, and
we'll win the run, man." A second man belched and
said, "I ain't never imbibing another beer as long as I
live." Before Kathy or I could straighten them out, the
lead speaker puked on the sidewalk. His cohorts
hunched over and looked as if they could hardly wait

to join in. The annual Fat Tuesday pub run. Down a beer at a series of pubs, have your ticket validated by each bartender, dash to the next drinking establishment. Fun in the big city. The winner was the first to return to the start line after a twelve-saloon circuit.

Across the street a woozy-looking lady in pink tights roller-skated down the sidewalk, clutching her validation ticket. She had great legs. She ricocheted off a light standard and almost got clipped by a Bronco in the street. We gave directions, but they didn't hear us.

After we had climbed into her cold car, Kathy reached over as if to grab the gearshift knob but clutched my knee instead. I let her. The investigation didn't seem to be humming along the way it should. "What would you think if I opened my own office?"

"Criminal law?"

"Something along those lines."

"Risky."

"I know that. But Leech, Bemis, and Ott is pressuring me to do only business law. And I don't like business law. I guess I'm even getting somewhat of a track record. Last week a man charged with vehicular homicide actually came in and asked for me by name. Bemis wasn't thrilled."

"You knew L B and O was a business law firm when you signed on."

"I didn't know how incredibly boring it was all going to be."

Uncharacteristically I asked Kathy to drop me off at the freeway exit at Fiftieth, fobbing off her curiosity with a story about wanting to walk the dinner off. She was disappointed, had wanted to stay up late chatting, maybe even sleep over on the couch. She gave me a smile that was three parts shy and one part sly, and I thought for a bone-chilling minute she had figured out why I didn't want her driving past my place. The lights would be blazing. In the drive would be a Harley with a monkey skull impaled on the sissy bar. If Kathy figured it all out, I'd have to move out of the country.

"By the way, Thomas."

"Yeah?"

"What am I supposed to do with that damned snake?"

"Where is it?"

"I put it in the Amana at work. I stapled the sack shut, but if somebody opens it by accident

"Leave it '

"But, Thomas '

Four different student-filled cars honked at my spats and top hat. By the time I reached my homely frame house off Roosevelt, the glacial February winds had numbed my face. Only minutes in front of midnight, several lights were on at Horace's, Horace who rarely failed to get tucked in against his fat wife by nine.

Find a drunken oboist and stick one ear into the bell of his instrument when he's on a roll, have somebody else repeatedly slap your opposite ear with a piece of sheet metal, and you have a fair approximation of the cacophony issuing from my place. Horace would not soon forget this onslaught. Petitions would be circulated. It wouldn't be the first time. He had once passed around a petition to keep me from parking my truck in front of his house.

I closed the back door against the night, bumped the refrigerator door shut with a hip, switched off the radio on the kitchen counter, turned off the glowing burner on my stove, and stepped through the dining room into the small living room. The stereo and my Sony TV were still blaring. Around the corner I heard women's voices raised against the din. Time to meet Desiree and Queenie. I hated blind dates.

When I rounded the corner, a six-pack and four empty green Heineken beer bottles greeted me. So did two women in biker regalia, each clutching a beer, guffawing at a singing dog on *Johnny Carson*. Queenie saw me first, scratched at her peroxide mop, and ran her eyes distastefully over my costume. "What do we have here? The Mad Hatter? 'Twas brillig, and the . . . ' "

I could barely make out her words against the raucous television.

As tall as an NBA guard, Queenie wore a pink sweat-suit affair with about thirty belts loosely arrayed around her incredible hips. She lounged on my floor, propped up by cushions they'd pried off my couch. She quaked when she moved. Even a blind man would have said she was busty.

"Took your time, Thomas Black," said Desiree Nash. "The party of your life waiting—and you surely took your time."

"What's that horseshit he's wearing?" said Queenie.

"Forget it," said Desiree. "We'll have that off him in two winks of a twink."

I said, "You two. Up and out. Make tracks."

"Hey, boy. This is your lucky night. Desiree has opened school. And you are going to get straight A's."

"Out!"

"What'd you say?"

"Get the hell out of here. Savvy?"

"He don't gonna want us," said the blonde, lapsing into a stupor.

"Don't listen to a thing he says," purred Desiree, doffing her jeans jacket. Underneath she wore a yellow sleeveless man's T-shirt, much too small for what it was encapsulating. Crossing her arms, she grabbed it at either hipbone and quickly wriggled out of it. She took a deep breath. She had an earring through one nipple. "He don't want us out of here? Hell, he's a man, ain't he?"

I kept alert for the ululating of motorcycles outside.

Queenie sat up, was trying to focus her mutant pin-prick pupils on me. She was doped. How she'd managed to cling to Desiree on the freezing motorcycle ride over was beyond me. Desiree chewed gum like a mule and struck a hipshot pose she thought I'd appreciate. It was damn loud in that room. The TV. The pulse

pounding in my eardrums. I could barely see, it was so
loud.

"Out!"

Desiree and Queenie both widened their eyes and
looked to my right, behind me. For an instant I took it
for a joke they'd collaborated on. Pretending a boogeyman was behind me. But they seemed surprised,
genuinely startled. The acting was too good. Queenie
clawed at a boot, as if reaching for a weapon. I pivoted
to look behind. I didn't complete the turn.

The floor tilted up and grabbed me. The walls began
melting onto my face. I had been had. The side of the
house, the whole east side of the University District
exploded, taking me down with it. No pain. Not even
numbness. I was swooning, and when I reached out, I
grabbed a handful of carpet.

Desiree reached for me, then drew a revolver from
somewhere.

The big-bosomed Queenie was scrambling and bob-
bling across the cushions. From the floor I watched, my
eyes crossing. I heard the tinkling of breaking glass
under my face. The house had become an elevator, rising faster and faster, pinning me tightly against the carpet. I struggled, but nothing happened. I couldn't even
reach my knees.

There was no pain. Nor any injury that I could detect.
Nor anything but blackness and Johnny Carson. Then
females shrieking. A gunshot. At least I took it for a
gunshot. The floor shuddered. Calmer chitchat. I felt
something warm and smooth swinging loose as it
brushed my face. Desiree was bent over me, hollering
into my ear, "Black, you bastard. You die, and I'll get
even."

Then an icy wind blew over my body. Johnny was
making them laugh. I tittered. The TV people were
hee-hawing their guts out I was inside a Venus flytrap,
and it was digesting me corpuscle by corpuscle. And I
was laughing. And it grew colder. And colder. And I
was laughing.

It sounded like a drugged songstress belting out a screechy tune. Wailing. It was an electronic siren. Some idiot had left it running. Then it cut off abruptly. Movement. Horace, my retired neighbor, yawped that he was going to sue me if I didn't croak first. Or maybe I was dreaming about Horace. What was all this talk about dying? I'd be up in a minute as soon as I got my bearings. Somebody shouted in my ear. A baritone spoke in subdued tones and said, "He doesn't look good, Chuck." Somebody else whooped. A sharp object pierced the back of my hand. What were they doing now? Nailing me to a board? More wailing. I was jostled, prodded, talked over.

Somebody dropped my limp arm onto my face. A couple more of those, and I'd have a bloody nose. Half an hour passed. At least it felt like half an hour. I listened to a woman calmly tell somebody about her live-in lover's problem with his parents. It seemed they wanted him to be a doctor, and he wanted to be a goof, a ski bum, a collector of *Mad* magazines. We all had problems. Me, my problem was that I couldn't pry my eyes open.

Slumber took me on a roller coaster of phantasma. Or was it merely my own death I was experiencing? I dreamed of big-breasted women, a blonde and a brunette, stunned looks on their grimacing, ratlike faces. I dreamed Kathy Birchfield was over me, murmuring sweet nothings. I dreamed her tears splashed onto my face, that Kathy gently brushed them off and kissed my brow. Then my lips. That she laid her mane of hair on my chest and wept. It seemed to last forever. My thoughts rambled, and I dreamed about a bull named Aunt Mabel.

Later I felt myself waking up. My body didn't want to, but my brain was pulling. It seemed to take forever to force open my eyes, eyes that felt glued shut. Then I tricked myself and dreamed I was awake. Suddenly I was.

A pleasant-looking nurse in her early twenties stood over me and held my hand. Everybody loved to hold hands with Thomas Black. "Fifty-two," she said. "I guess that's all right for a pulse."

"Pretty normal for him," said another voice, another female, who must have been hiding in the closet because I couldn't see her.

"You finally decided to wake up and join the rest of the world," said the nurse. "I'll get doctor and have him check you over. By the way, your wife is here."

"Wife?" My throat was sore and dry. "What kinda funky deal is this? Don't have a wife."

It was Kathy Birchfield, worry coloring her voice. "Oh, my God. He's got amnesia." She grabbed the hand away from the nurse and pressed it up against herself. Guessing by where she pressed it, she was testing me to see if I was alive. I was.

We were alone. Kathy hovered over me, and I couldn't tell what the look on her face meant. I don't think I had ever seen one quite like it, not on her. Her shiny dark hair was pulled back into a ponytail. I hadn't seen that for a while either. Devoid of makeup, her skin had a scrubbed American-girl look. She had a way of appearing to be a different person every day, and the scrubbed glaze threw me. She wore jeans and a T-shirt, nothing under the shirt. The fur coat she'd worn to Fat Tuesday was across the room on a chair, resembling a nest.

"The Easter bunny been here yet?" I asked.

"Thomas." She wasn't going to let go of the hand. "Thomas, I was so scared. At first they wouldn't tell me a thing, and then I convinced them I was your wife, and they said you might never wake up. You were a six on the Glasgow scale, which I guess is something they use to rate comas. It seemed to worry them. They said there was a possibility you'd never wake up. They have a man up the hall who's been in a coma for three years. Weighs ninety-five pounds."

"Worried, sister?"

I must have said the wrong thing or used the wrong tone of voice because Kathy's violet eyes pooled, filled with tears, and overflowed. Speechless, she hugged my hand against her thumping heart. I was alive—no doubt about that.

"Don't cry, Dorothy. I'll get rusty." I glanced past her at the window. I was looking south and couldn't figure it out. It was dark, but I could still see a portion of the rosy sunset to the west. "What time is it?"

Sniffling, Kathy said, "Five-thirty."

"In the morning?"

"Night, dummy."

"Which night?"

"Saturday."

"Last time I checked, it was Thursday. Saturday? Jeez, it feels like I've been dozing half an hour. When did I come here?"

"Early Friday morning. About one. Your neighbor, Horace, heard shots and phoned nine-one-one. I think he was trying to get you in a jam." I tried to sit up, but Kathy forked her fingers into my chest and shoved me back down. I wasn't comfortable with how easily she'd done it. I was wasted. "He claimed a motorcycle with two women on it took off from your place. Said one of them didn't have a lot of clothes on. Horace's eyes got a little glassy when he talked about it. What happened, Thomas?"

"Let me think about that one for a while. When did you see the old grump?"

"Early Friday morning. He called the cops, and then, when he found you, he called me."

"How the hell did he get your number?"

"I gave it to him a year ago."

"Horace? That crackpot?"

"I worry about you."

"You bimbo," I said, trying to sit up again. Kathy pushed me down a second time. "You been lifting weights the past couple of days? So how long have I been here?"

"All day Friday. All day Saturday."

"How long have you been here?" My guess was she hadn't left. She had a look to her as if she'd been sleeping in a box of coat hangers.

Blubbering in earnest now, she dropped her face into my armpit and mumbled into the bedclothes, "I was so scared, Thomas. I didn't realize how much you meant to me until I saw you lying there helpless. I've never seen anything so scary in my whole life. A bump on the head. They said somebody hit you with a blunt object. You hardly even had a lump." She wept while I ripped off the tape, cringed at the unexpected pain, and removed the intravenous line feeding my arm. I patted her head. Without warning, Kathy bobbed up and kissed me lightly on the lips.

"Bet I taste like tree bark under a birdnest," I said.

"Worse."

"Is this Providence?" She nodded. "Let's take a walk. I'll show you something."

"You crazy? You can't get out of bed until the doctor says. I won't let you."

"I'm stiff as hell. Gotta move."

"You can't."

"Watch me."

This time she couldn't hold me down, and she knew it. Even so, when I got upright and dangled my bare legs off the side of the bed, I was so woozy and thirsty I thought I'd pass out. When the insects and banjos and electric chain saws stopped cavorting inside my head, I gulped from a beaker of ice water on the table beside the bed. Kathy assisted me out of the hard hospital bed, wrapped her fur coat around my shoulders, and we shuffled down the hallway.

I tottered at first. The guy in the bed next to me appeared to be in a coma, skull swathed in bandages. Must be the brain ward. I touched my head to see if they'd scalped me. Nothing but hair and ears and the rest of what should be there, in approximately the same arrangement I'd last felt it. I deliberately led her to the

stairs at the south end of the building. It took a lot
longer than I had thought to navigate to the roof of the
building. On the way Kathy fretted about my well-being
and told me what had been going on during my nap.

"Horace gave a pretty fair description of the two
women on the motorcycle. He must have had his eye
on your place all night, ogling them through the windows. You're getting winded, Thomas." We were on
the stairs now. "You sure we should be doing this?"

"I'll be all right."

"Anyway, Smithers is almost over his cold now, and
he went and checked it out. Promised he'd be by later,
so I guess he'll tell you then. You remember what happened, Thomas?"

"I got out of your car on Fiftieth, and that's it."

"Horace said when you got home there were a couple
of real . . . robust women waiting for you. You went
inside, and all hell broke loose. The women made good
their escape on a motorcycle."

A motorcycle? Oh, no. I began to come to the full
realization of who must have been there. When we
reached the cramped hallway that opened onto the roof,
I propped the door open so we wouldn't get locked out,
and I showed her the city at night. Providence was set
one hill over from downtown, so it didn't command the
view of the bay that Harborview did. At one time the
roof of Providence Hospital had had a hothouse on it.
That was gone now, but there was a brick patio and a
view of the upper portion of the city's skyline and the
sun setting over the Olympics, and it all made me glad
I was awake, alive, standing beside this woman. Slowly,
as we braved the chill, Thursday night began to come
back.

"Desiree and some crazy dame named Queenie," I
said. Kathy turned away from the thick wall she'd been
leaning against and gave me a hurt look. Dizziness kept
me from getting too close to the edge—seven or eight
stories to the ground. "I called my answer machine at
the restaurant, and Desiree picked up the phone. They'd

broken into my house. I didn't tell you because you would have ribbed me.''

"Ah, Cisco. Me?''

"When I was trying to throw them out, somebody came in and popped me from behind.''

"Who?''

"From behind, I said.''

"Must have clobbered you with a Rolls-Royce. Smithers might know something when he gets here,'' said Kathy hopefully. She hugged my side, more to warm herself in the fur coat than to hug, I thought.

"Thomas?''

"Eh, Pancho.''

"You ever wonder why we never became lovers?''

Her face was pale in the light of the vanishing sunset. "Don't have to wonder. I know.''

"You do?'' She bit her lower lip pensively and looked up into my eyes. "Why?''

"Some other time. My head's starting to hurt.''

"The woman's supposed to have the headache.''

"Call me sissy-pants.''

"Sissy-pants.''

My thought processes weren't reacting properly yet, and I was afraid I'd say something I'd regret. And I didn't really know why we had never become lovers. What I knew was that at one time I had known. Right now I couldn't think of a good reason. Not a one. Two frantic nurses and a sulking doctor gave me hell when we got back to the room.

16

AFTER BROWBEATING ME FOR MY odyssey around the hospital, the intern poked, prodded, measured, squinted, listened, and then pricked, viciously, I thought. She asked me who the president was, what brand of automobile I drove, the month, my social security number, my school in sixth grade, and the name of my cat. "It's mud if he's scooped any more holes in my rose bed," I said. She harrumphed, pronounced me fit as a fiddle, and told me I'd have to stay another three or four days, for tests and observation.

"That's not my idea of fit as a fiddle, Doc."

"Tuesday at the earliest," she said sternly. "Apparently you don't realize how close we came to losing you. You still show some disturbing signs. In your condition another blow to the head could be fatal. I'm warning you. Another rap like the one you took Thursday night, and you might not ever wake up. From what your wife tells me, you have a knack for getting into trouble. Tuesday." She wielded the cautious authority that was symptomatic of young doctors. I didn't have the energy to quibble, and I resigned myself to that lack of vigor as an omen. Temporarily.

Shooing Kathy Birchfield away was harder than

shooing smoke. Because I had the feeling she had been sleeping in the hospital for two days, I made the effort. A tiny smile crept across her Madonna face, and she sat implacably in the corner, tucking her legs up beneath her on the chair. She wasn't going anywhere.

They brought dinner, and I dispatched it with calm efficiency. Before I was halfway done, my jaws grew fatigued from chewing. Kathy sat in the corner quietly, never taking her eyes off me. "Don't they miss you at work?"

"It's Saturday, remember?"

"You been here the whole time?"

"I ran some errands."

Beaming, Smithers came in as I polished off dessert. "Rip Van Winkle ariseth," he said. "They told me at the nurses' station. Does the world look appreciably different in the twentieth century, sire?"

"Who the hell whacked me?"

"God, it's good to see you awake and alive. You almost went tits up."

"I doubt it."

"One simple rap on the head. You'd be surprised how many people check out that way."

His belt and equipment jangling, he went over to the corner where Kathy was nestled and whispered something to her, handed her some keys, my keys, then stood beside my bed.

Pudgy, medium height, and tending toward the sloppy in his attire, Smithers hadn't changed a smidgeon since the day we'd mustered into the Seattle Police Department together. In uniform tonight, he had his Sam Browne belt slung so that the pistol was almost directly over his crotch. He almost always wore it there, as if by accident, and I often wondered what a psychiatrist would say about that. Under his blue uniform shirt he wore bulky body armor. I spotted a stringy speck of chewing gum stuck on the knee of his trousers.

"Using the vest these days?" I asked.

He nodded, absently. "Listen, Thomas, who dropped you?"

"Came from behind. Didn't see them. I'm just glad they didn't stomp me while I was down."

"Traced the name Desiree Nash. Real name is Juanita Nash. Lives in a biker pad out in South Park. But Senorita Nash is long gone. The dopeheads living there wouldn't give me the time of day. I'll take a spin out there again a couple of times this week, but don't hold your breath, pardner. We ain't got nothin'. And the department went over your place with a fine-tooth comb."

"Did they?"

"Doc said you might not pull out of it, Thomas. They were preparing for a murder investigation. Anyway, they found prints. This Juanita Nash. And another woman named Frieda Samms. In the trade they call her Queenie. She's been in the joint for manslaughter. What'd the two of them do to you anyway?"

"Way I remember it, absolutely nothing. Somebody came in behind."

"Found a bullet hole in your living room ceiling. Thirty-eight caliber."

"Thanks for poking around, Smitty."

"You would have done the same for me."

"Me?"

"Don't be coy, you big goofball," Kathy shouted from her chair.

"Wanta give me Nash's address in South Park?"

"You're not thinking of going out there? They're an ugly bunch, Thomas. Jolly Rogers. Belong to the national branch. Their idea of fun is turning out Girl Scouts. I had a back up when I stopped out there, and even then, I mighta wet my pants. Never know what those scumbags'll pull."

"Gimme the address. I want to send her a poinsettia next Christmas." Reluctantly he scrawled it on a scrap of paper. "You talk to the old man next door?"

"Quite a guy."

"He's got about a hundred birds in his house. Got feathers up his—"

"Thomas!" Kathy said.

"He saw two women running out?"

"Yep."

"Nobody else?"

"Not going in. Not coming out. Nothing missing in the house, really. Right, Kathy?" She nodded agreeably. We made small talk for a while; he told me about his most recent outrageous charge card balance—Smithers was a credit card junkie—then said, "I ran down the rest of those names you gave me."

"What names?"

Smithers pulled a notebook out of his shirt pocket and flicked it open. "Gunnar Rogers." He glanced over at Kathy. "Clean as a priest's . . . rosary. His kid, Dennis Rogers, has been in a heap of trouble, though. Vandalism. Drugs. Hotrodding. Several car wrecks. Veronica Rogers: clean. Fred Pugsley? Handled on suspicion of rape back in his college days. A date that got out of hand. Daryl Rittenhouse? Assault stemming from a minor traffic accident. Charges were dropped on all of 'em. That's more than I thought I'd come up with."

"Me, too." We made small talk, and Smithers left, hitching his Sam Browne belt up.

"Where'd they put my clothes?" Kathy got up resignedly and pulled them out of the closet, displaying the top hat and tails I'd worn Thursday night. I was going to have to sneak out into the February night in my hospital gown. "Cripes."

Without further ado, she brought out another set of togs: a pair of corduroy pants, loafers, a shirt, a maroon sweater, and a winter jacket.

"Thanks, kid. I might keep you after all."

"Thomas, don't leave the hospital tonight."

"I'll heal better if I'm up and moving around."

"What if you have a relapse?"

"What if an asteroid boinks me in the head?"

"Let me go with you."

"You're dead on your feet, little sister. I can manage." I stood and got dizzy, the edges of the room growing fuzzy. The ref was counting seven, eight, nine when I realized where I was. "Okay. Come with me. Be a pain in the behind."

We managed to bypass the nurses' station and get downstairs and outside into the cold evening without incident. The instant we went through the sliding doors, I began shivering. Smithers had ferried my truck across town and parked it on Twentieth Avenue, to the east of the mammoth red brick hospital.

"Mind getting behind the wheel?" I said weakly, tossing her the keys.

We checked eight service stations in the vicinity of Micro Darlings. Nobody remembered a blue Chevy van, and nobody regularly serviced such a vehicle. Two more were closed. I was grasping at straws, and I knew it. Long shots were for later. My head still hadn't cleared.

At Micro Darlings several cars dotted the parking lot, and oddly, lights were blazing on the top floor. I knew I was still feeling the effects of my hospitalization when the security guard began giving me some guff and I almost swung on him. He was pallid and officious, and I could have brought him down with one knotty sucker punch. Kathy interrupted our confrontation.

"We're investigating Fred Pugsley's death. We want to talk to whoever is working tonight."

"Oh," said the guard, scratching under his hat. "That? Surely, kiddo."

In the elevator I said, "Kiddo?"

Kathy said, "You all right?"

"Irritable."

"I believe the word is 'punchy.' "

"That, too."

It was an extraordinary scene, four of them in polo shirts and khakis huddled over a table, all behinds and elbows, as they constructed an elaborate graph on an eight-foot sheet of Mylar. Whizzes from the sales department. Daryl Rittenhouse was there too, overseeing, a modern crossbow in his hands.

When Rittenhouse saw us, he frowned, butted his heavy glasses up onto his nose, leveled the crossbow, aimed, and let fly at a dark figure across the room. The head exploded. The bolt shattered it, knocking a wrinkled fedora off. Kathy screamed, and everybody in the room turned toward her. Then she giggled. It was a dummy. Straw bales and sandbags. I noticed the blunt-tipped bolt had disappeared inside the bowels of the makeshift target range.

"You're up and around," said Daryl Rittenhouse. The huddled workers dived back into their charts. "Ashley stopped by Providence when he heard about it. Said you weren't looking too chipper. I was in for a week last year. Fell down a mountain. Aren't those enemas something?"

"Who told him I was in the hospital?"

Rittenhouse shrugged. "I'm surprised they released you. They wouldn't let me out until I produced nice stool."

"He escaped," said Kathy, giving me a motherly look.

"Head injuries can be tricky." Rittenhouse fitted another bolt into his crossbow, aimed, and fired. Thunking loudly, the blunt-tipped projectile buried itself out of sight in the sandbags. "Those head injuries . . . A guy's gotta be real careful. If I hadn't had an MSR on last year, I'd have cracked my skull open like a melon. You should be in the hospital. I wouldn't be surprised if you up and dropped dead on us."

"I'll keep it in mind. You come up here and shoot every Saturday night?"

"Hardly. I have a social life." He let his eyes roam over Kathy, who, even without makeup and ensconced in that long fur coat, managed to look slinky. "Thing is, these guys are brainstorming, and I thought I'd check in and see if I could help. We've been getting a lot of pressure from companies down South. If we plan things right, this could be our blast-out year.''

"Murdering your competition?" I asked.

A disarming grin on his face, Daryl Rittenhouse held the weapon aloft, and one of his eyes screwed down tighter than the other. "This? Just a toy. We do all our hunting with longbows. No sport to this thing. A crossbow is almost like a rifle. Aim and fire and then dig a hole to bury whatever you hit. I play with it. Hell, any hamburger can shoot a rifle can shoot one of these. Consequently, they're dangerous as hell.''

Sauntering over to a desk where he'd laid out his tools and gear, Rittenhouse snatched up a fancy quiver that had spacers built in. He withdrew a bolt and handed it to me: a three-way razor tip. I knew my judgment was off when I stuck my thumb on it and drew a bead of red. Kathy bit her lip sympathetically.

"I've seen those go through four-by-fours," said Rittenhouse. "No noise. Deadlier than hell. Watch."

"That's not really necessary." Kathy smiled wearily.

He led us into his office and proceeded to rick up volume after volume on top of his desk, including four telephone directories. Then he loaded the crossbow and knelt. "You don't have to do this," I said, watching as the razor tip caught a shaft of light and realizing for the first time that he'd been drinking. Was I slow? Ordinarily I would have picked up on an AOB the moment I saw him.

He let fly, and the bolt ripped through the tomes and buried itself in the wall behind the desk. It was gone, only a puckered hole remaining to show where to scrape and dig.

"These things are incredible," he exclaimed happily, a man impressed by kill power.

"When was the last time you saw Fred, Daryl? The very last time."

Rittenhouse stood up and thought about that. Menace laced his voice. His breath was spiced with garlic, booze, and cigarettes. "You really should be in a hospital bed."

"When?"

"Night before he bought it. Came by here. Ashley Phillips accompanied him. It was late. I don't remember what I was working on. Fred had picked up Ashley at the airport. He'd been at a meeting with one of our primo distributors in Southern Cal. Wasn't like Fred—picking somebody up at the airport—but I guess he did those things once in a while. Ashley's wife is pregnant and all that. They came by here, and Fred was his obnoxious self."

"Why come here? Pugsley must have been here all day. And he was coming in the next morning, right? Both of them. Why stop over?"

"Never thought about that. We all spend an inordinate amount of time in this bunker, so I didn't think it strange. Ashley might tell you. Supposed to be here any minute. Now that I think about it, Ashley might have been the last person to see Fred alive."

"Except for the killer," said Kathy.

As he fiddled with his crossbow, Rittenhouse turned to her and repeated, "Except for the killer. Maggie saw him."

"Think it's Maggie?" Kathy asked, challenging.

"Don't you?"

I turned to Kathy. "She been arrested yet?"

She shook her head, and her ponytail brushed the fur of her coat. I watched the motion entrance Rittenhouse, who always managed to look like a little boy his mother had just put into his Sunday best. His shirt was starched, his hair blow-dried and neat. He wasn't pretty, but he was groomed. "I spoke to Margaret this afternoon. She wants to talk to you, Thomas. Forgot to tell you earlier."

"We'll buzz over there later," I said, glancing at my wrist and realizing I had no idea where my watch was. "Daryl, I want to know more about five years ago."

"Still on that kick?"

"I was told Eric had some sort of burglar alarm on his house."

"Impregnable. I've got the same basic device on my place right now. Every possible entrance is monitored for movement. Even the rooms inside. Depending on the sensitivity setting, a cat could set it off. Mine calculates if there's enough commotion to be a person and sets off an alarm. If the housebreaker runs away, it shuts down. He stays, it automatically dials a security company. Nothing commercially available even comes close."

"Somebody said something about a code being required to get inside."

"On the front porch of my place there's a lighted box with nine digits. You have to punch in the right code, like a combination lock, or the thing goes off."

"And five years ago Eric's worked the same way?"

"Pretty much."

"Was it hooked to a security outfit?"

"Naw. Eric had a couple of old Navy aa–ooga horns hidden under the eaves of his roof. Would have scared the devil out of his jockstrap."

"Any possibility somebody beside Eric and Veronica knew the combination?"

"No way in hell. Eric himself bragged only he and his wife knew it."

"Maybe somebody cracked the code. You had a slug of crackerjack technicians working here."

"Not if Eric put it together. He was the best. And why the hell would somebody want to do something crazy like that? Eric didn't have anything of value in those days. Why burgle his place if they knew that? None of us had jack shit. And hey, he never denied those pictures were his if that's what you're getting at."

"Did Eric play around on Veronica? Was he going with anybody from the office? Anything like that?"

"Eric?" Rittenhouse's voice soared. "Are you kidding? Eric might have been a puke, but he kissed the ground she walked on."

Ashley Phillips trounced through the door, blurting. "You guys sound like a pair of fishwives hanging out laundry." He eyeballed each of us in turn.

"Dirt is my middle name," I said stupidly. Kathy rolled her eyes. Ashley frowned. Rittenhouse smirked. "All I'm trying to do is eliminate possibilities."

When Ashley Phillips noticed Kathy Birchfield, I introduced them and watched them exchange pleasantries. They had seen each other at the hospital. Ashley was dressed for the out-of-doors, and the building was cooking. He wore all black, shoes with soft uppers, trousers, clinging turtleneck sweater, coat, and leather driving gloves. A dew of perspiration speckled his upper lip.

"I understand Fred picked you up at the airport the night before he died. That would have been—"

"Tuesday," Ashley said, moving to Rittenhouse's desk and propping himself on the edge. He unbuttoned his coat, moving like a gazelle. Kathy watched his long, elegant fingers. He was good-looking, the pale, wintry skin contrasting with the black hair. "I had been in San Francisco, and Fred came out to the airport and got me. Our other car'd been in the shop all week. Brit wasn't feeling well that night. Fred's been like that, though. Always doing little things for people." Rittenhouse snorted loudly to register his disagreement, and Ashley added, "He was like that. He tried to keep it from everybody, but he was."

"Why'd you guys stop by here that night?"

"Had to pick up some materials for the project I've been working on."

When we got outside, I headed across the parking lot. A breeze cold enough to give nosebleeds kicked me in the face. "Where are you going?" Kathy shouted, running to catch me by the arm.

"Me?" I hadn't been going anywhere. I didn't know what I'd been doing. "Hong Kong?"

"Hong Kong can live without you tonight, Thomas. I can't. Come on. I'll drive you back to the hospital."

"Not a chance."

"Home?"

"Let's go see what Maggie has to say for herself. The drive'll revive me."

"You hate driving."

On the way Kathy said, "That Phillips, bet he's broken a lot of hearts."

"Seems happily married," I said. Phillips was one of those rare individuals who still cared about other people. I had been surprised, pleasantly so, to learn he'd visited me in the hospital.

"I forgot to tell you yesterday I phoned the agency that ran the polygraph checks for Micro five years ago. I wheedled and begged, and Marcia Henderson told me what there was to tell."

"On the phone? She nuts?"

"Leech, Bemis, and Ott has used them for a few things. Some industrial security last summer. She didn't really have anything to lose. She knows everybody at Micro wants Eric hung. So does she."

"What'd she say?"

"Sociopath. He thought he could flimflam the machine. She also said he had convinced himself that he was innocent so that when they all went, at his insistence, to his house, he actually expected the materials to be gone. Of course, they weren't. She said they've kept up on him over the years, but so far he's managed to keep his nose clean. They're waiting for a relapse. She hates him."

I flipped the sun visor down and saw a pair of crisscrossing Band-Aids on my right cheek. I'd fallen face-first into broken glass the other night. Or maybe my head had cracked one of the Heineken bottles.

"Let's go see what Mrs. Pugsley has to say about all this."

"Wouldn't it be better in the morning?"

"I have the feeling Maggie's ready to talk."

17

A STRANGER TO THE EAST SIDE, KATHY
soon was entrapped in the dark Belle-
vue streets and eventually conceded to the terrain,
chauffeuring me back across the lake via the Mercer
Island Floating Bridge instead of 520. Disoriented, head
pounding, I wasn't much help as a navigator. The long
chunks of the third floating bridge waiting to be assembled in the oily black waters just north of the first span
held me spellbound.

"Why not just pave the damn lake?" I growled. I
still wasn't coloring between all the lines. "Drain it and
build another parking lot."

"You're beginning to sound like your old grumpy
self. Feeling better?"

"Feel fine."

"You're not acting fine."

"Just drive, sister."

The truck radio cautioned against a light snowfall
later in the evening. When I checked the clouds, they
were black and puffy, but there were stars peeping
through, too. Over the water a gull flirted with the gusts.
Rolling the dial to another radio station, I found a news-
cast announcing that there still hadn't been any arrests

in the Laurelhurst murder. I had forgotten how many people were thinking about this case.

"Think it'll snow?" said Kathy, braving my ill humor.

"You talked to Maggie?"

"She called the office. When I returned the call, she said she'd been trying to get ahold of you. Wanted to discuss something."

"To confess?"

"Nary a hint of what it was about. We talked for a bit about whether or not she would be charged and why they were postponing a decision. I told her my feeling was that they weren't sure she was guilty."

"Cheer her up?"

"Couldn't say."

"You tell her about the picture under the body?"

"Afraid I did."

"Damn you. I would rather have been the one. And not on the phone." My voice was that of a lumberjack kicking a dog.

"Sorry."

Loyal, trustworthy Kathy Birchfield had kept a vigil at my bedside, and now I had been awake less than three hours and she was apologizing. Contemplating my insufferable rudeness all the way through town and then on NE Forty-fifth, I swallowed a load of gumption and didn't say beans. I wanted to tell her I was being a peabrain, but I couldn't say it. At one time I had been a brave man—seemed like only days ago—but now I was afraid to utter a kind word.

At Maggie's we found the BMW parked in the garage and every light in the house ablaze. Kathy wrinkled her nose at me and thumbed the chimes. I cracked my face into what I imagined was a smile, but she didn't see it. Three times she leaned against the chimes. No sign of movement inside the house. I rapped the door loudly, and it hurt my half-frozen knuckles. Breathing on my throbbing fist, I trotted around back.

At the rear of the house I banged on the kitchen door,

tested the knob, and discovered it was unlocked. Kathy cupped her hands around her mouth and yapped through the door. I cracked it open and let her turn it up to full volume. "Maggie?"

"Let's take a look around," I whispered, shocked at my stealth.

"What if she's in the shower?"

"What if she slipped on a bar of soap and hit her head on the potty?"

"I think she's in the shower. I'd better go in alone and see."

"We'll see together."

The house was hot. Clippings about the murder littered the kitchen table. The *P-I*. The *Times*. The *Journal-American*. She had cut out several copies of each article. We traipsed through the downstairs, still topsy-turvy from the police search, peeked into the basement, then tiptoed up the carpeted stairs to the bedrooms. In the bathroom at the end of the main hallway, an FM radio oozed soothing elevator music. "Maggie?" I knocked, pushed open the door which stood ajar, and saw no one. We checked the rooms one by one. Vacant, all.

Except for the master bedroom.

She was in there.

Alone.

Margaret Pugsley wore a skirt and blouse, the skirt pulled high, revealing wan thighs. She stood in an awkward crouch, back against the closet door. The emerald green blouse rode up around her white ribs, exposing a spongy belly. With her spine lined up along the edge of the closet door, her head was flopped to one side, eyes, face, and throat swollen and discolored.

"Oh, sweet Lord Jesus," said Kathy. "She hung herself."

I sprinted across the room and lifted her body, trying to unknot the two bathrobe belts that had been used. She was heavier than she had any right to be, and I couldn't keep the weight off her neck and untie the cloth belts at the same time. "Get a chair! Untie it. Or scissors. Cut it. Anything."

It took Kathy half a minute to get the belt undone while I held Pugsley's body up. We could both hear that she wasn't breathing. As Kathy worked, Maggie's head canted to one side, and her dry protruding tongue slowly pressed against my unshaven cheek. I suffered the sandpaper loving, hoping we'd discover a spark of life in her. When she was finally off the door, I laid her on the floor, none too gently, knocking her head. I was out of practice handling limp women.

"Christ," said Kathy. "Why us? Every time we come to this house we find something awful."

I laid fingers across her neck. Pressed my ear against her breastbone. Listened at her mouth. No pulse. No heartbeat. No breathing.

I ripped her shoe and one sock off and jabbed a finger into her dark skin. Lividity had set in. The blood had pooled. Resuscitation efforts weren't going to do her a bit of good.

Voice quivery, Kathy said, "Gonzo?"

"Gonzo."

I felt as if I'd been flayed, tarred, and ridden out of town in a truckload of duck feathers. Sprawled on the floor beneath me, one crippled leg twisted inward, one shoe and sock off, Maggie Pugsley looked like a doll used for some loathsome game.

Kathy settled down onto the bed.

"Why? We would have gotten her off the hook. Maybe . . . do you think she was guilty? Was that it? Maybe she killed Fred and felt so bad about it she—"

Knees popping in the silent room as I rose, I reconnoitered the arrangement on the closet door. Two silk belts had been knotted together, the first looped over the door near the jamb and wedged down the crack by the hinge, the other done in a figure eight arrangement so that it was firmly braced on the top of the door, terminating in a single loop which was still around Maggie's neck. Ingenious arrangement. Hard to believe

Maggie could have cooked it up. I whisked the bedspread off the bed and draped it across the corpse, poking the last snippet of emerald green blouse inside.

Kathy said, "How can somebody hang themselves
when their feet are touching the floor?"

"Cut off both carotids. Just a few seconds. Knocks
you out. Then you go limp, and your body weight does
the rest. The windpipe doesn't really need to be closed.
Clamping the carotids will kill you or give irreversible
brain damage. That's why they don't allow neck holds
in collegiate wrestling."

"Oh, Thomas. Why didn't she call somebody and
ask for help? I asked her if she was all right."

"It's not your fault. You were tied up."

I knelt and said good-bye to a woman I hardly knew.
I could still feel her desiccated tongue on my cheek.
Somehow it got mixed up with the kiss I'd felt when I
was in the coma. A kiss and a lick. I was having all the
luck with the ladies.

Three days ago Fred had answered a knocking at the
door, and a minute later there was a surprised new face
in hell. Now we had found Maggie dancing with a closet
door. Another ticket to hell.

"Perhaps they're together now," said Kathy, hiccuping on her tears. "Fred and Maggie."

"You think they went the same direction?" I began
rifling drawers.

"Thomas, what in heaven's name are you doing?
Looking for a suicide note?"

"Never even occurred to me."

"Then get out of her stuff."

"She wanted to talk. Maybe she had something to
show us. All the other rooms were still pretty much
trashed by the police search. Stands to reason if she
were saving something, it'd be in here. This and the
kitchen are the only places she's straightened up."

Perched on the bed, Kathy wasn't at all pleased with
me, breath whistling out her nostrils, cheeks stiff with
indignation and sorrow. She unbuttoned the fur coat

and reached across the bed to dial 911, her voice calm
and unruffled, her eyes teary. She was taking it well
now. It would hit her later.

I found them buried under a computer magazine on
the bureau next to the door. More crude Polaroids.
Child pornography. I didn't recognize either of the two
children. Or the settings. They were similar to the pictures I'd seen the first day but had been taken with a
newer type of camera and film.

"Maggie must have recovered enough of her senses
to begin looking around. She didn't recover these from
any obvious hiding place," I said. "Must have been
well hidden."

"What makes you think that?" Kathy's voice
cracked.

"If they'd been anywhere easy, the cops would have
confiscated them."

"Bet they gave her a real jolt."

"Unless she already knew about them."

"But why kill herself?"

I didn't want to field that one. I was woozy, and I
couldn't tell if it was from staring at the perversion in
my hands, from Maggie's tongue, or from signing out
of the hospital prematurely.

Ralph Crum took almost thirty minutes. Face flushed,
he bounded up the stairs and discovered just the five of
us in the room, two cops, Kathy, me, and Margaret.

"I thought you were dying," he said, catching his
breath and retrieving a dry pipe out of his overcoat to
suck. "Called Providence and the floor nurse said you
weren't looking real good."

"Thanks for the flowers." We both knew he hadn't
sent any. His grin was so huge his teeth separated.

Then he glanced down at the long lump on the floor,
leaned over, and took two fingers to lift the bedspread.
When he arched up at me, his grin had vanished. He
surveyed the closet door, glanced around the room, and
made loud clucking sounds on the pipe.

"Why'd she do it?" he asked, his pale blue eyes watery, but not from grief or conscience, mostly from being out in the frigid night and then coming into a heated room.

"What makes you think she did?" I said.

"You don't think it's suicide? Course it is. Somebody said something about a note."

"Haven't seen one."

"I must have misunderstood. Maybe they said they were looking for a note. What's that you've got?" I flashed him the pornography. "Oh, God. Not more of that." I showed him where I'd found it. "Well," he said, cradling the pipe in his palm, "must have been too much for her. The husband. The pictures. Worrying her noodle about jail time."

"I don't think she did it."

"You're nuts. Clear it. We are. Don't see any reason why not. We would have charged her Monday morning. It was airtight. She whacked out her old man and then did herself. Saved the city time and money."

"What if this was murder?"

"This?" Crum's singsong voice was dubious.

"You have your forensic boys go over the blood patterns on her arms from the other day?"

"Had her cold without that. Turns out that weapon had been stored at her friend's house, in the very bedroom where she slept the night before the murder. Her pals said she was awfully upset with him."

"Pals like that are hard to come by. I was in that bedroom, and the trunk where I think the tool would have been stored was covered with dust. She couldn't have gotten it out that morning."

"So she'd been saving it for a few days. How did you get in here?" Crum asked.

"Back door was open."

"We came on a lark," Kathy said. "He's supposed to be in the hospital, but he couldn't sit still two minutes."

"The case is over now," said Crum. "Funny, though. You two finding both of the bodies."

"Why did you wait so long to charge her? If you were so certain she iced her old man?"

"Footprints." Crum sucked on the pipestem. "Found a set of man's footprints in the backyard. Couldn't decide what to do with them. Didn't match anybody in the house. That and the missing Beretta. Pugsley was supposed to keep a Beretta. Wouldn't have answered the door without it. It's missing."

On the way down the stairs Kathy said desultorily, "Footprints?"

For the second time that night I headed off toward distant continents. Kathy grabbed my arm and steered me toward the truck. "You really think she was murdered?"

"I would have turned around. I was just thinking. She was pretty rocky last time we saw her. Could have done anything. It's just . . . women don't usually do it like that. JDLR."

"What's that?"

"Just didn't look right."

"I didn't even know you could do it like that. Hang yourself."

"That's what I mean. If she were going to kill herself, she would have done it in the garage, someplace where her feet were going to clear the ground."

"But she didn't look as if she had been fighting. Nobody could have gone in there and hung her without a fight, could they? Room didn't seem mussed."

"You'd be surprised what people can do."

"Why would anybody murder Maggie?"

"She told us she had something to say. Maybe she told somebody else, somebody who was in a position to panic at the news. Maybe she was getting in the way of a clean getaway for somebody."

"Well, if it was murder, I have a clue," Kathy announced grandly.

"What?"

"I smelled a man's cologne in the bedroom. Musk. I don't recognize the brand, but I smelled the same

thing when we were up there talking to Daryl Rittenhouse."

"Maybe it was Ralph Crum. Those homicide boys
all smell like French whores."

"Smelled it before Ralph showed up."

"Could be something. Could be nothing."

Kathy started the truck, and we wended through a
serene and complacent Laurelhurst. When I told her I
was famished, that my stomach had been growling since
I'd woken up, even though I'd eaten in the hospital, she
said she knew just the place. It was Saturday night, and
Pioneer Square was hopping. The sweaty Fat Tuesday
crowds jostled us. Music erupted explosively out of
dance joints. We elbowed our way into a Greek restaurant called Estoa. Only three of the patrons were in
costume, two of them wearing deer heads, the third a
gigantic fish head. Sleepy as she was, Kathy was in her
element in these wacky crowds. When we left, two
hours later, we passed three denizens of Pioneer Square,
dehorns, standing in the alley, huddled around a low
patch of steaming brickwork, each of them unzipped,
all three singing a Bruce Springsteen tune off-key.

Neither one of us had discussed Maggie. Or my injuries. Or the obvious fact that somebody somewhere
had tried to do me dirt, would likely try again. It was
possible the same individual had iced Fred, assaulted
me, and then iced Maggie. On the other hand, maybe
the person who'd smacked me was only a jealous biker.

On the trip back to Roosevelt I grew nauseated, then
dizzy. I was beginning to wonder just how badly I was
injured. We hadn't spoken about it, but we both knew
Kathy would stay over.

Five seconds after my face hit the pillow I was asleep.
The coma returned to wrap me in a velvet obscurity. I
wanted to roll over, but nothing happened. Vaguely I
was aware of Kathy's bumbling around the house, shutting off lights, locking doors, cleaning up. Later, in the
depths of the night, I felt someone gently kneel on the

mattress beside me. I recognized the fragrance. For the longest time a pair of soft lips molded themselves against my cheek.

18 IN THE MORNING IT FELT AS IF I hadn't stirred all night. I killed ten minutes lying flat, taking stock of the ceiling. I had been asleep ten hours. I rarely slept that long, never when on a case. The aroma of homemade biscuits and hot milk infiltrated the house, my bedroom, my nostrils. Somebody was singeing breakfast and singing songs. The house had been tidied.

Hair wet and full of dark ringlets from a recent shower, Kathy had snuggled into one of my terry-cloth bathrobes. She wore a pair of knee-high wool cycling socks from my stash, had tuned in a bebop station on my kitchen radio, and was singing in a whisper to a Little Richard melody.

"You're beautiful," I said.

She ceased crooning, turned, and said, "Always greet your guests in Jockey shorts?"

I felt like a transatlantic rat taking its first shaky steps across the wharf. I shuffled back to the bedroom.

When Kathy Birchfield attended the University of Washington, she'd lived downstairs in the basement apartment. Sunday mornings had evolved into a ritual with us. No matter how late we'd been gadding about the night before or whom we'd been dating—each other

184

only infrequently—we met in my kitchen for biscuits, jam, hot cocoa, and talk. We hadn't done it in a long while, and I could see from the flashing teeth that Kathy was disposed to resume our rite. "Chow time, you big ugly lug."

She brought out two pans of biscuits. Melted butter and honey. Strawberry jam from last June's crop. Orange juice. Hot cocoa capped with floating marshmallows. We grinned at each other, all gums and teeth.

After a while I noticed she was wolfing hers down, very unladylike. "Didn't you eat while you were waiting at Providence?"

"Of course I did."

"Liar. You haven't had anything but fingernails in your stomach for two days."

"Worried spitless about whether I was in your will."

"You're first in line for my gold teeth, towels, and all my aluminum cans."

"Pooey Phooey. I wanted the *Little Lulu* comics." I laughed. "You were sailing through outer space on a golden swan last night, Thomas."

She was right. And still I felt sleepy, a worrisome sign after a head injury. I should have been in the hospital under observation.

"The hospital is the place for you."

"Bullfeathers."

"Been thinking about last night?" she asked.

"If Mrs. P. didn't kill Fred, and neither of us thinks she did, it doesn't make a whole lot of sense for her to commit suicide. Seems as if she would have wanted to stick around, if only to find out who really murdered the guy."

"You're talking with your mouth full."

"Thanks, Mom. And who whacked me? Why? And where did that new porno come from? The stuff Maggie found. Was it Fred's? Was he the real pervert at Micro and not Eric? Or did Fred find it as a result of all his snooping?"

"Those pictures confuse me," said Kathy, sipping

chocolate from her old Winnie the Pooh mug, which
hadn't been used by anybody in almost ten months. A
dissolving marshmallow sketched a white line across
her upper lip. "Obviously Fred got new pictures from
somewhere."

"But where?"

I dialed an ex-cop I knew who had turned renegade
biker. On the force he had been a Jesus freak. Now he
had turned around 180 degrees, went on drinking sprees
three nights a week and whored five, earned groceries
as a welder for a truck repair outfit he swore was controlled by the mob. Chances were, he wouldn't be doing
a lot of two-wheeling in February. I'd done some investigating for him a couple of years ago and he'd never
paid the bill.

"Vetty? . . . Thomas Black here. Sorry to wake you.
How's it hanging? Still got that hog? . . . Eh? Is it running? . . . Great. You wanna clear that outstanding bill
you owe me? . . . Sure. Need to borrow it for an afternoon. Don't worry, I'll baby it. We'll be squares." Elbows planted on the table, face cupped in her hands,
Kathy winked at me. I could see she was already cruis-
ing around town on a big bad Harley, flashing those
violet heartbreakers at every slack-jawed schoolboy
we blew past. "Also, you know any of the Jolly Rogers? . . . Uh-huh. . . . By the way, what size are your
boots? . . . Uh-huh. . . . Bring 'em."

"What'd he say?"

"Drop it off here this morning. Before the Sonics
game."

"Smitty's got a Suzuki. Why don't you borrow that?"

"Harleys. You need Harleys for these people. They'd
laugh till next Sunday if we showed up on a foreign
bike."

" 'How's it hanging?' Do these ears deceive? Is that
'man' talk, or did I wander into the zoo? You sounded
like a couple of talking dogs."

"Cop stuff. It's code."

"Code?"

I dressed and took Kathy to her place, where she spent entirely too long in her bathroom. When she came out, she was a different woman—a cheap dame who bought her falsies mail order. Her hair, a wig, was mostly white, tinged orange along the crest. She'd fixed it using half a gallon of hair spray and the apparent help of two raccoon stylists, their paws dipped in contact glue. She looked wild and a whole lot different from anything I'd seen in a while. Ten years younger. Snotty. She chewed gum, wore a huge silver safety pin through her ear, and what looked like a piece of lost fishing tackle dangled from her nose, which wasn't pierced, so I don't know how she did it. I wasn't sure if she was biker or punk, but I didn't quibble. It would suffice.

Sidling up against my chest, she gave me a sassy wink. "You like?"

"You need a warning label."

"You blowin' brain cells awready? I just got here. How come you're not dressed?"

"Later."

"Warning label?" she said, feigning offense. "What do you mean later? You mean, we're not getting the Harley right away? What are we doing then? I can't go around looking—"

"Just fine," I said, grabbing her wrist and hauling her out to the truck.

"You should have told me. This is because of the tails and spats, isn't it?"

"Would I hold a grudge?"

First, we swung by Eric's place. I didn't expect any cooperation from the roach, but I was hoping to get some sort of reaction; maybe I could goad it out of him. But he wasn't there. The other tenants didn't know where he was.

I drove to the condo on Lake Washington where Ashley and Brit Phillips lived. I was bound to be first with the news, and I thought if I made the rounds soon enough, I might shake something loose. Besides, if Kathy had been correct about the scent last night, Rittenhouse, or somebody wearing Rittenhouse's cologne, might have been in the Pugsley house shortly before we got there. Who better to pump about Rittenhouse than his last remaining right-hand man, Ashley Phillips?

After Kathy had read the name on the mailbox aloud, she popped her gum and spoke in character, an octave above her normal voice, "Ooooh, the cute one."

"Keep your panties on, sister."

"What panties?"

I gave her a disgruntled look, and Brittany Phillips, still resembling a whippet, opened the door in time to observe it. Kathy snapped her chewing gum obnoxiously and said, "Oooh, when's it due, honey?"

"Anytime now."

"I admire a woman who knows what a man's for."

Brittany Phillips invited us in and told us Ashley was teaching a church youth group at their church's Lake Sammamish retreat, wouldn't be home until late that evening. "Ashley's giving a talk on drugs and prisons," she said. "He once worked in the King County jail, you know."

"Sorry we missed him. We wanted to ask a few questions."

She sat us down, eyeballed Kathy's outfit without seeming to reach a verdict, and slowly lowered herself onto the same hard-backed chair she'd used on my first visit. "Can't get off the couch without a winch."

"Daryl Rittenhouse have a girlfriend?"

"Daryl? Last few years he's kept his love life pretty much to himself. Ashley's always commenting on that. Daryl seems almost secretive about it. They used to confide in each other."

"I need to know where Eric Castle and Veronica lived at the time of the incident five years ago."

"On Lake Washington. Down on the other side. It was kind of a dump, really."

"Think you could find the address?"

She hummed, struggled to her feet, and lumbered off. I felt guilty making her stump around the house on errands. A few minutes later she waddled into the room, carrying a battered address book. I copied the street number. When she sat back down, she said, "That incident. Since Fred got killed and you were asking about Eric, I've been thinking it over. What a shock that was. Remember the day Kennedy got assassinated, how you can recall every detail? Same thing. I'll never forget it. I found the picture and I was all alone in the building and I had to call my boyfriend and tell him, just so I had somebody to talk to about it. You know? Same as JFK. For some reason you wanted to talk to people."

"We know," said Kathy, reaching over and patting Brit's knee. After she'd removed her hand, Brit examined the knee for tracks.

"Went over to see Maggie last night," I said without preamble.

Kathy gave me a warning look.

"How was she?"

"Dead."

"What? Are you kidding me? You're kidding. What?"

"She was strung up on a closet door by a couple of bathrobe belts knotted together."

"You're kidding. I know you are. But—"

"Police are calling it a suicide."

She began weeping silent tears, mumbling through them. Kathy was weeping, too. "No. This is not right. Ashley is going to feel so rotten. He said we should go over last night, but he had to drive out to Micro and do some work with Daryl instead. Oh, he's going to blame himself."

"When we found her," I said, "we also found more child pornography."

The tears stopped. "What?"

"Must have been remarkably similar to what you people found five years ago in Eric Castle's place."

"That's hard to believe." She mopped her eyes delicately against the back of one bony wrist. "But then, Fred's been on this crazy vendetta all these years.

Maybe he finally dug something up, some concrete proof that might put Eric into prison once and for all.''

"One last thing. Did Maggie call here during the past few days?''

"I wish she had.''

When we left, Kathy hugged my arm against her body. She looked easy as sin and twice as available, and she was bent on playing the part to the hilt. "She looks like Ashley. Dark trimmings. Fair skin. Going to be a nice little family.''

"Every time I go in there I'm afraid she'll go into labor before I can escape.''

"I'd like to have kids sometime,'' Kathy said wistfully. It was a line a blind man in a dark alley wouldn't touch with a stick.

In Lake City Sheila Balzac lived off an open balcony on the third floor of an apartment house. Some efficient soul had tarped the pool in the courtyard for winter.

The drapes were drawn, but Sheila opened the door promptly, looked us over, lingering on Kathy, then invited us into the warm, musty, cavelike apartment. Her hair was mussed, and she wore a tatty robe. A bookshelf was weighted down with scores of paperback romance novels. She had been working the Sunday *Times/P-I* crossword in front of a basketball game on a small-screen color TV. Her ratty pink slippers needed stitches. Her lopsided smile could have used some shoring up. Kathy's costume bothered her.

"Excuse me. I turn into a couch potato on Sundays. What can I do for you?'' She gestured for us to sit. Neither of us did.

"Fred's wife died last night,'' I said.

"Omigod.''

"Yes. What I want to know is, where was Fred snooping?''

"God! I can't believe it about Maggie. Fred snooping? You mean chasing women?''

"That, too. You were his secretary. With regard to

the Eric Castle incident. He was still looking into that, wasn't he?''

"I wasn't supposed to tell anybody, but you're the first one to ask really. We worked overtime the first of this week. He disappeared into Rittenhouse's office and stayed a long, long time. Technically we're not supposed to do that. There's memos out against it. Each person's office at Micro is supposedly inviolate.''

"Rittenhouse's?''

"Over an hour.''

"Where else?''

"Let me think. A lot of offices. Ashley Phillips's. Ashley was in California at the time. And then, of course, he went off to talk to Gunnar Rogers. Rogers called him on the phone last week. I didn't eavesdrop or anything, but they weren't simpatico. Fred yelled, and I could tell from his face, as he was listening, that Rogers was yelling, too.''

"You know Rogers?''

"Used to work at Micro. He's over there all the time for meetings. His company does the promotion. God, Margaret Pugsley's dead. I can't believe it. How on earth did it happen?''

I explained briefly. "You sure he was talking to Gunnar Rogers.''

"Fred hit on Veronica Rogers at a party. Whole office knew about it. I think Gunnar was calling to warn him off.'' I remembered Gunnar's threatening to break me in half if I went near his wife again. The imagination blossomed at what he would have done had I made salacious advances toward her.

"Why do you think that?''

"Because right after Fred spoke to Gunnar, he phoned Veronica. Fred was like that. Tempting fate was a hobby of his.''

"What?''

"It's just . . . Fred could be crude, but I thought he was funny, too. Know what he said to Veronica?'' I shook my head. Kathy inspected a pet fish drifting belly-up in a bowl. "He told her he had a throbbing blue veiner that glowed in the dark and it was harder than Chinese algebra. Sorry." She hung her head and looked ashamed. "I'm sorry. I shouldn't be repeating trash like that. I don't know why I do. Forgive me? I just thought that was funny. . . . " She winced. "In a bizarre sort of way. If Gunnar had heard it, I think he would have annihilated Fred." She thought about what she had said. "I guess I don't mean that."

"By the way, did you speak to Maggie in the last few days?"

"I haven't seen her in weeks. How can you do it on a door?"

Outside, Kathy took a long draw on the Seattle morning. "Fred must have been a real fun guy."

"Yeah."

"Where are we going now?"

"We have to spread more good cheer."

It was a ten-minute drive. The neighborhood hadn't changed. Across the street a ma and pa loaded a country wagon up with kids, locked the dog in the garage, and trundled off to church. I took a pair of ten-power binoculars out from behind the truck seat and fixed them on the blue van at the top of the drive. I couldn't tell diddly-squat. And strangely, I could no longer remember much about the van that had attacked Eric. My head injury had been like a nap in the middle of a chess match.

My assumption was the Rogers family didn't go to church, that they all were home, puttering around in pajamas and slippers and reading the morning paper, passing the funnies to the kids, and letting the cat out. Wrong. Veronica answered the door and immediately slammed it on my foot. I groaned at the pain. She was in her Sunday best.

"Maggie's dead."

She stopped wrestling with the door, my statement

slapping her into a mannered sobriety. "You're lying so you can talk to me."

"Swear on my dog's grave. Happened at her house last night. The police are calling it a suicide. Hanged from her closet door."

"Oh, dear," said green-eyed Veronica Castle Rogers, watching me carefully, letting go of the door, her pink tongue tracing the outer edges of her upper lip. It took her all of three seconds to regain her composure. "What do you want?"

"The cops think it's a suicide. I'm not so sure."

"I suppose you want to know where I was last night. Gunnar was working and I was at the *Ice Capades* with the family. Would you like to interview each of them?" As if on cue, Lucretia's red head appeared in the entranceway beyond her mother. The child smiled tentatively at me and then scuttled away. "Or would you rather just get out the rubber hose and knock me around?"

"Whatever gets you off." She looked over my shoulder down the hill at Kathy. In her garish wig Kathy looked just cheap and tawdry enough to confirm Veronica's estimation of me. "You had dealings with Fred the last few days before he bought it, didn't you?"

"What are you getting at?"

"Was Fred trying to make it with you, or was he trying to extract information about Eric?"

"I don't see what that has to do—"

"You've never come clean about this. Do you have some evidence on Eric that you haven't told anybody about?" She tightened her lips and sucked at me with those green vacuum-cleaner eyes. They beckoned the way great heights sometimes beckoned: Leap and die. "My point is, I don't think I've ever heard a definite statement from you about Eric. If you have some proof, tell me."

"The house is getting cold. I really have to go now."

"I have reason to believe you were angry with Fred."

"Fred came off the same assembly line you did."

''Just tell me this: Did Eric commit any illegal or immoral acts regarding your children?''

She gnawed her lower lip, then said, ''Somebody doesn't have to actually do something to be a threat.''

''Eric's never hurt or threatened to hurt your kids?''

''Not that I know of, but I'm certainly not about to give him the opportunity.''

''And your husband Gunnar fought with Fred shortly before his death?''

''Maggie killed Fred. Nobody else. Just Maggie. Now she's gone and it's over. Drop it.''

''Did Maggie call you recently?''

''Yesterday morning. She found something of Fred's.''

''Did you tell your husband about it?''

Veronica only bit her lip.

''There are witnesses that Gunnar fought with Fred.''

The door slammed, shutting me off from the tan, the blond hair, the eyes. Only the faintest trace of her perfume lingered to taunt. For an instant my eyes blotted over with black stars, and I thought I was going to pitch off the porch into the rhododendrons. I grabbed the wrought iron banister and squeezed, revved my blood pressure up, came to my senses, and focused on Kathy, staring up at me from the truck. She looked worried. Maybe tonight I'd see the doc again.

Before I switched on the ignition, little Lucy Rogers came bounding down the driveway, casting furtive looks over her shoulder. Her brother, Tad, stood looking on from the drive. Outfitted in her Sunday best, Lucy looked as fresh and saucy as her mother had. Her dress was so cute it required its own supply of oxygen. Cranking my window down, I said, ''Hiya, kiddo.''

''Do you really know my daddy?''

I nodded. I could see all the way to the moon in her patent leather shoes.

''Could you give him this? Please?'' She passed me a sheet of paper, then bit her lip until it turned white. It was a drawing of a house, a mother, father and three children standing outside. Beside the father was a bicycle. Decorated in red crayoned hearts, the caption read: "I Love You Daddy—Your frend, Lucy."

"I know he doesn't want me anymore, but if you could just give him this." She scampered off before I could think of a reply.

Kathy grabbed the drawing out of my hands and scanned it. "Pooey phooey "

"Life is a bitch, eh, sister?"

"Can't we do something about this?"

"Any suggestions?"

We drove for ten minutes before she asked, "What's next?"

"Next we find out who smacked me in the head Thursday night."

"Oh, boy."

"Bring your cosmetic kit. We might need a heavy weapon."

"What? You're not bringing your wit?"

19

VETTY HAD DELIVERED THE HAR-
ley. Horace was out in his backyard,
combing his grass with a rake, a regular rubbernecker,
alternating between Kathy and the hog, a lemon-lipped
sneer saddling his mouth. "Thanks for saving my life
the other night, Horace. I'll have to take you and the
missus out to dinner. How's Mexican sound?"

"That yours?" he asked, nodding at the Harley.

"Joining a club," I said while he checked out Kathy,
failing to recognize her. Horace was more than willing
to lampoon my life-style, to believe anything defama-
tory about me, had once gone completely off his nut
and seriously accused me of white-slaving out of my
garage. My ribald taunts didn't help. "They give you a
free woman with each new membership. How do you
like the one I got?"

"Not around here, you ain't. Them danged thinga-
majigs make too much noise. Scares my birds until they
crap all over."

"What? Women? She hardly makes any noise at all."

"Cycles! You deaf? They make the noise!"

"I'll have the free woman here knit some earmuffs
for your birds. You can use cotton balls and rubber
bands for diapers."

196

"You're sewer scum, Black. And you let that woman go free."

Kathy clung to my arm and cooed in a dumb-blonde voice, "But I love him."

Horace spat.

"Why antagonize him?" Kathy asked after we got inside.

"You helped, sister."

"Had to. But go easy. He's old enough to flop over and die without much warning."

From the rear of my closet I picked up a peculiar piece of merchandise, an imported cane I'd appropriated several years back from a limping pimp in Tacoma. It was stout enough to crack heads, and beside that, it had a gimmicky trigger mechanism on the handle that ejected a spring-loaded four-inch blade out the tip. One could use it as a sword almost. If one leaned on it and pressed the trigger, the blade tip would easily dig half an inch into a wooden floor. Pressed against a man's foot, it might produce a devilish squawk.

Vetty's boots were a size too large, but they would suffice. I found the oldest, grubbiest jeans in my closet, several layers of vests and ratty shirts, a leather jacket and topped it off with a fur-lined flying helmet and cracked WWII goggles. I hadn't shaved since before going to the hospital, and if I left the helmet on, combined with the beard and the Band-Aids and the goggles and my haggard Gila monster eyes, I might pass for a half-assed biker.

It took me a couple of blocks to get used to the shift pattern and the sloppy steering of the hog. When I thought I had it down, I circled back and picked up Kathy.

"Ooooh," she purred when she squeezed in behind me.

"Took the words right out of my mouth."

We made it to South Park on surface streets because the wind-chill factor on the freeway would have killed us. As it was, we couldn't stop shivering. Kathy wore jeans that fitted like primer, leg warmers from mid-thigh to her boots, a tatty and torn ski parka, and tight leather gloves decorated with chrome doodads across the knuckles.

Desiree's hutch, at least the house she'd lived in until two days ago, was near the back fence of a lumberyard. An anvil sat on the front porch. The place was shabbier than a Rat City doghouse.

From the yard we could hear the Sonics game, knew nobody would notice a doorbell over the racket, so we thundered across the wooden porch in our boots and banged on the door. When it swung open, three men and two women, all in T-shirts and jeans, were lounging around a console TV, sipping beer, cheering Sikma, and jeering the Lakers. The women I had never seen. One of the men had been at my place the afternoon Paddy threw me off the porch.

"Can I do for you?" asked the anemic woman who answered the door, a homemade tattoo of a snake head crudely imprinted on the triangle of skin between her thumb and index finger.

Kathy popped her chewing gum and said, "Man, I'm Desiree's cousin, ya know. She like said, ya know, to come down and motor with her when we reached the States, ya know."

"From B.C.," I said. "That's Canada."

"Desiree ain't livin' here no more. Humped out coupla nights ago."

"Oh, man," said Kathy, working her cold gum. "We come all this way. Oh, man." All the guys inside the house had stopped watching the game, were now watching Kathy. She showed her teeth, bobbed her head once at each word, and said, "You gen'men tell us where Desiree be staying'?"

They couldn't get it out fast enough.

"Eighth South. Up the hill. Five minutes from here. Coupla mean potholes on the way," one man said, while Kathy waggled and hitched at her jeans, trying on a cheesy smile for size. He gave us a house number, then marched to the door to watch Kathy straddle the hog. I stayed on the porch, cane at the ready, thinking he might try something funny. "Some old lady you got," he said flatly.

"She's a lawyer."

"Yeah?" He swigged from a beer can and belched. "My old lady used to work for the phone company."

"Small world."

Desiree's new abode, several miles out of the city on Eighth South, was even more dilapidated than the joint in South Park. Here there were no bikes, only ghetto cruisers. It was almost rural, a straight country road laced with mailboxes on crooked posts. We saw nobody until I'd tilted the hog on its kickstand and rapped the door with the knobby handle of my cane.

After a lengthy wait Queenie opened the door and surveyed us casually. She wore purple pants and a T-shirt that was so tight it must have been painful. I had kept my helmet on, goggles riding my brow, and she failed to recognize me.

"Desiree crashin' here?" I asked gruffly.

"Who needs her."

"Got her cousin here for a visit."

Blocking the doorway, Queenie shook her head and squeezed her eyes nearly shut. "Unh-unh. Desiree ain't got no cousin."

Kathy scratched a place well-bred ladies didn't scratch and said, "Ain't this Juanita's crib?"

"Well, maybe she does have a cousin," Queenie said, trying hurriedly to come up with another reason why Kathy would have known Desiree's real name. "I thought she was an orphan."

As I pushed past Queenie, I found Desiree just inside the door, curled up in an armchair that had been used as an ashtray, dozens of burn holes peppering it. Looking up sleepily from the Sonics/Lakers game, Desiree recognized me instantly, goggles and all, which I thought indicated love of a sort.

"Black, you ugly, nutless bastard."

Her words formed a lever, catapulting the two men into action. One of them was Paddy, shoeless, sockless, the long-haired biker who'd uprooted my porch railing a few days back. The other was a short, spindly creature who might have been called Bug Eyes. He went straight for Kathy, as did Queenie, as if she were the dangerous interloper and I were only a pest. I managed to make them hesitate a moment, holding my hands up, cane in my right fist.

"Whoa there, boys and girls. We're just here to ask a few simple questions. Somebody thumped me the other day, and I'd like to ask Desiree if she knows who. 'Kay? How's that sound? No trouble. Just questions."

After a minor hesitation they continued the rush. Paddy pushed me roughly against the wall and said, "Get the fuck out, cowboy. You been chasin' my woman too long."

"Hey, how about those Sonics?" I said, shaking my head, temples beginning to throb.

"Black, you're so ugly your mother fed you with a sling-shot."

After he reached down around his knee and made a fist, he tried to launch my head through the ceiling with it. I sideslipped it, feeling the breeze from his knuckles on my sweaty face. Desiree still had not moved out of the chair, had swung desultorily back to the basketball game. Queenie was maneuvering Kathy into some sort of armlock. Kathy was squealing.

"Thomas!" Kathy gasped, and I could tell from her yelp that in another second bones would snap.

I flipped the cane around, coldcocked Paddy across the side of the head. He stretched out at my feet, and I rapped him once more on the way down for good measure. Then I rapped Bug Eyes behind the ear. He went down like a sinking ship, but Paddy squirmed and twitched, merely stunned. He would be back for more.

Queenie jumped around and placed Kathy between my body and hers, tussling. She easily outweighed Kathy by eighty pounds. Gently I laid the end of the cane on top of Queenie's right shoulder, the tip safely in the air behind her ear, then squeezed the trigger. The blade flicked out, sinister and cold. She jumped, then stood very still as I raised it up under her ear.

"Okay, dude," she said, releasing Kathy and backing away, bloated white hands waving.

Kathy signaled me, and I turned to catch Paddy, head down, doing a lineman's charge at my midsection. My knee came up and connected noisily against his chin. There was a clacking sound that could have been shattered teeth; then he spiraled to my side, holding his face. I put another knot on the side of his skull with the cane. He collapsed in a heap on the floor beside Desiree's chair. Desiree lit a Camel, inhaled deeply, and raised her eyes. I set the sharp tip of the cane on Paddy's neck.

"All I want, Desiree, is to know who the hell came in behind me Thursday night?"

"We didn't have nothin' to do with it," said Queenie, suddenly bored with the proceedings. Paddy was making a leaky-faucet noise. Not tears. Not moans. It could have been choking, but it wasn't that either.

"He's dying, for chrissakes," said Desiree, reaching casually from the chair to stroke Paddy's head. A clod of ash from her Camel broke off onto his cheek.

"Just a bloody nose. He's inhaling the blood. Who was there that night?"

"Some old fart. Never saw him before. Looked like Methuselah."

Queenie added, "Had a big beard. Down to about here. Checked shirt. Smelled like steer shit just like my dad always did."

Desiree looked Kathy over and said, "I don't get you, Black. Seems like I offered you everything in the book and I still ain't got no counterofters. This your old lady? No wonder. Got steak at home, why send out for burgers?"

"What'd he hit me with? An ax handle?"

Bellowing a bully's laugh, Queenie said, "Alarm

clock. It was an alarm clock he got out of your kitchen. God almighty, you went down like a sack of shit. Your skull must be like an eggshell. We thought you were gonna sign off.''

"Cops said there was a gun fired that night."

"That was mine," Desiree said. Stroking Paddy's greasy head, she still hadn't moved out of her chair. "The old fart pulled out a heater. Was gonna waste you. Us too, maybe. So I fired a warning round into your ceiling. Hope you don't mind. You can put a cork in it." I noticed there were several corks in the ceiling of this room. "No shit. The motherfucker had it leveled at your ear. He would have done it."

Queenie confirmed, nodding, then said, "Why don't you two stick around, watch the rest of the game with us? Got some cola in the other room. Wanna line?"

"Thanks," said Kathy, stepping over bodies toward the front door, still ajar from our hasty entrance. "These clowns might be a little mad when they get up."

"Clowns," said Queenie. "They're going to love that."

"You see what this guy was driving?"

"The old man? Hell, no. We beat feet."

"Was he alone?"

"Near as we could tell."

"You ever watch cartoons?"

"Just the educational ones."

"Yosemite Sam?"

Snapping her fingers loudly, Desiree said, "That's it. That's exactly who he looked like. Kept chewing on his mustache. Yosemite Sam."

"Thanks."

"For what, man?"

"Saving my life."

Desiree didn't know how to take that. Queenie ignored me, mutant pinprick eyes on Kathy. She looked resentful over not being able to fracture Kathy's arm. I pulled out a wad of bills, peeled off a couple, and tossed

them into Desiree's lap. "Here's for your gas and bullets."

"Guess we did save your life. Tough guy. You went
down like a white boxer."

"Sissy-pants, they call him," said Kathy, stepping
out the door.

Outside, I kicked the machine into a dull roar. In
Burien we parked the hog at an all-day-all-night con-
venience store and phoned for a cab. Neither one of us
was up to shivering all the way back to the University
District. I called Vetty and told him where we were
leaving his pride and his boots, thanked him, and told
him it cleared the debt. In the cab Kathy said, "You
know who that old guy is, don't you? The guy who
slugged you?"

"He's not that old. Beard makes him look that way."

"So?"

"Name is Gregg Ghee. Lives over by Point No Point.
At one time he was Eric Castle's landlord. Right now
he's the landlord of a man named Aaron Barbour, who
must be the last hippie on earth."

"How does Barbour connect to any of this? Why
bring him up?"

"Eric's best friend in high school. And college, too,
I suppose. He was also Veronica Rogers's first boyfriend."

"Circles on circles," said Kathy.

"Somehow I have the feeling it's just started."

 THE CAB DEPOSITED US AT MY place, where I hurriedly changed out of my grubby duds and picked up the truck.

"What about me?" Kathy asked, pulling at her colorful fright wig.

"Don't have time to make your place. The ferry waits for no man."

"The spats and tails really bothered you, didn't they?"

"Be a four-star hit over on the peninsula."

We grabbed the two-twenty-five ferry, boarded, and leafed through real estate brochures on the ride over.

I knew private detectives who were never without their sidearms, but I considered that excessive and frightened behavior. On the other hand, there was a time to carry one, and this was definitely it. Only I couldn't.

I had mustered out of the Seattle Police Department because of a shooting. On the paperwork they had decreed the official reason a bum knee, and it still flared up from time to time. But the reality was that I had shot somebody dead, and it had left me both scared and scarred.

Since leaving the force, I had fired pistols a few

204

times, and at people. But so far I hadn't drawn blood and wasn't planning on it. Now I was a peeper, and those times when I should have had a gun, I simply didn't. Guns were for varmints. Paper targets. I knew from experience I was better off without one. It gave an illusion of safety, and each time I sighted down a barrel and choked, I was stunned anew.

It was Sunday afternoon, and when the ferry dumped us off, Kingston was almost totally devoid of westbound traffic, though cars were lined up four abreast for the weekend eastbound commute back into the city.

"Ghee?" said Kathy when I pulled alongside the mailbox, sloppy red lettering brushed on the rusted side. "Is that this guy's name?"

"G-h-e-e."

"Rings a bell. When you were laid up, I had one of the paralegals dig into Micro Darlings. All the piddly stuff. She brought a bunch of material up to the room, and I studied it Friday night. Ghee was the maiden name of Daryl Rittenhouse's mother. I'm sure of it."

"This bozo must be related."

"Don't go up, Thomas. There might be a bullet with your name on it."

"It's not the one with my name on it that worries me. It's the ones marked 'to whom it may concern.' He's probably not even home."

"That stupid cane you're carrying around isn't going to save you if he comes out with a Browning. Call the cops."

"And tell them what?" Kathy narrowed her eyes up through the brush in the direction of the farm, scanning. "That a biker mama who wouldn't piss on a cop if he was on fire told us a stranger matching this man's description sneaked up and almost killed me with an alarm clock? They'll get hernias laughing."

"Yeah, but don't you swap shoulder patches or dirty stories with a sheriff over here?"

"You know I don't collect patches. Wait here.'

"Like hell."

I dangled the keys in front of her face. "Hear shots or I don't come back in a reasonable length of time, drive up to the intersection and call the law."

"Oh, Thomas," Kathy said, anxiety nearly causing her to dance on the bench seat. "I didn't think about how dangerous this was going to be. You don't have any reflexes yet."

"Those bikers. Kicked their butts like a dog kicking fleas."

"Queenie would have broken us into tiny pieces if Desiree hadn't given her the high sign."

"Say that again, sister."

"Didn't you see Desiree warn that mother off? She was about to break that cane in half and shove it up your—"

"I brained the two guys!"

"Punks. Queenie would have hit you so hard your clothes would be out of style when you quit rolling."

I slid out of the truck and stepped into the mud, reached through the window, and bussed Kathy on the tip of her cold nose. "Pooey Phooey," I said.

A recent rainsquall had plastered down this side of the sound. As I hiked up the rutted road, a steady clunking reached my ears. When I got to the clearing where the house and barn were, I met Aaron Barbour splitting wood beside the main house. Despite the cold, he was sweating profusely, the Sonics game tattooing the afternoon from a portable radio.

"Afternoon."

Through his beard he gave me that sour-sweet almost evil grin and stopped to wipe his forehead against a checked shirt he'd hooked over a nail on the wall of the house. Rotating his head and body, he flicked his long, limp hair behind a shoulder. "You're back."

"Your landlord around?"

"Out back. Past the bullpen. Working on the well." Barbour gave me a disjointed squint and began whacking at a hunk of alder he'd balanced endways on a chop-

ping block. He wasn't very proficient, but what he
lacked in skill, he made up for in enthusiasm.

I glanced around the premises.

"Don't sweat old Aunt Mabel," Barbour said, chopping and grinning. "Greg said he shipped him back to
his brother's place in Redmond. Got sick of handling
him. 'Bout wrecked their truck."

It would be good to confront Greg Ghee out in the
open, in a place where he wouldn't have ready access
to moose guns, machetes, pitchforks, or alarm clocks.
Recalling his marshmallow gut and his age, I figured
even in my weakened condition I could handle him.
Besides, I had the cane and the secret inside it. I
tramped through the mud, but behind the barn Greg
Ghee was nowhere to be seen.

Beyond Aaron Barbour's shack, past a stand of trees,
I could hear the sound of a chain saw. Or perhaps it
was a recreational vehicle, a tinny two-cycle motorcycle
engine. Japanese dollars were making a racket in every
stand of woods in the state. Near the open gate, I surveyed Barbour's shack, the field, and the trees, trying
to calculate where the logical geographic location for a
well was.

Listening to the buzzing of motors in the distance and
realizing I didn't have a clue where to search, I stood
in the mud for a long while.

I was about to walk around Barbour's shack when I
heard the sound of running water. A garden hose. A
stream sluicing into the dirt, a whirring ripple of noise.
It was directly behind me near the barn. A drain hose?
Perhaps the well was inside the barn..

Pivoting around, I held my breath.

The cane, which I had been swinging against my leg,
froze in mid-stroke.

Not fifty feet away stood the largest bull I'd ever seen.
The garden-hose noise was issuing from Aunt Mabel.
Piss. Steaming, gurgling, puddling, lasting-forever piss.
The interminable rivulets flowed out from the pool un-
derneath his tank of a belly. Perhaps this was my

chance. Perhaps bulls didn't charge when they were uri-
nating. Then again, perhaps they did. His creamy hide
twitched in annoyance. Both wire fence gates between
us were open.

They might as well have stripped me naked, painted
me red, and dropped me into the corrida. Barbour had
lied. It was a setup. I'd clumped out here, a porker to
the slaughter.

Aunt Mabel stared. I stared.

Steam issued from his nostrils. I thought he looked
hostile, but I couldn't tell for certain. All I could do
was count heartbeats and watch his tail switch.

Neither of us budging, we paused a full minute, two
minutes, chess masters deliberating the next move. Run
the pawn? Gore the knight?

Aaron Barbour must have hustled around behind me
and freed the bull from the barn. The chopping had
ceased as soon as I left him, but I had taken little notice
of it. The barn door had been closed behind Aunt
Mabel. I thought I saw a shadowy movement in the slot
over the grain trough; then it was gone.

But perhaps I was being melodramatic. He was gigantic, but I had no reason, other than his look of malevolence, to think he was unreliable or dangerous.
Knees creaking, I started to move, but then the pissing
stopped. So did my heart.

Tendrils of steam curled up around Aunt Mabel's
hindquarters. Our eyes locked. I began to feel dizzy.
The closest shelter was Aaron Barbour's shack, but escape in that direction meant both the bull and I would
be moving in a straight line. In mere seconds the bull
would be tracking up my back.

I had about decided to disengage myself from the
staring and make a dash around the barn when I heard
the spitting. A pellet gun. The noise seemed to emanate
from the barn. Aunt Mabel's hindquarters hopped to
one side, and he flicked his tail wildly, snorting. He
was much more agile than any animal outweighing a
car had a right to be. Another spitting sound. To judge

from the twitching hide, this one had caught him amid-ships.

Some spook was provoking Aunt Mabel with a pellet gun. And Aunt Mabel was taking the bait. Lowering his head, Aunt Mabel whirled around in a complete circle until his horns were aimed at me again. It was clear there was nobody else in the vicinity, nobody to blame for his aggravation but the insignificant mite of a man in front.

Eyes inflamed, Aunt Mabel huffed and lowered his head. He pawed the ground. I was in trouble. A ton and a half of ugly.

Without warning, he shrugged his massive shoulders and stumped forward four or five charging steps, front legs almost straight, the hulk bouncing. The earth rumbled. It had been a test, and I had failed. He pawed. He snorted. I snorted, too, but I was choking on my own impending doom. I thought of running around toward the side of the barn, but that would have put me closer to him—granted, a fence between us, but a flimsy fence.

Another pphtt from the barn.

I heard the missile sting his hide.

Aunt Mabel leaped forward.

Hurriedly I tore off my coat. I whirled and sprinted at an angle, trying to keep some of the fence between the bull and my buttocks, hoping he would charge in a straight line. The earth shook. I slipped and scrambled in the muddy terrain. I heard a wrenching sound behind me, a stationary staccato of thumps. Cracking wood. Aunt Mabel had somehow gotten tangled up in the corner of the fence, wagging his head this way and that, shattering boards and balling up wire, enjoying his frenzy.

He knocked the corner post out as if it were a birth-day candle set in frosting. It flew across the yard, muddy concrete cap and all. I watched in awe as the muscu-lature under his hide rippled. He had about as much fat on him as your average squirrel.

Finished toying with the post, he turned his attention back to me.

There was nowhere to go.

I flapped my coat in front of myself, wondering how much bullfighting technique I had picked up from reading old Ernest. He didn't hold back, bounded right at me, three thousand pounds of blood and steaks and sudden death. I stood my ground, even as it trembled. The closer he got, the taller he looked. I couldn't see over his humped back. And the curved horns were sharper than I would have believed possible. He stopped six feet shy of me, and I chickened out, tossed my open coat at his head, and made a run to get past, back in the direction of the main house.

The coat entertained him long enough for me to get to his tail. He woofed and began rotating. I would never make it through the pens.

I grabbed his outflung tail, pulled on it, and went around with him, keeping his head 180 degrees away, straining desperately not to trip. Once I went down, that would be all she wrote.

The tail felt like a tree branch. His whistling snorts grew shorter, sharper, and fiercer. We went around three times like that, our momentum gathering. Slipping, careening in the mud, I knew it was only a matter of seconds before I'd stumble or he'd fling me off into Pierce County. He bellowed, and I let go, raced through his yard toward the barn. Instead of finishing his dance facing me, he ended up facing Barbour's shack, and it took him a moment to regain his bearings and sniff me out.

I scrabbled toward the barn door and got it open, flinging it too far on its sliding mechanism. It stuck. Aunt Mabel was already battering down a piece of the fence, charging full tilt. Quickly I backed out the doorway of the barn, concealing myself in the shadows as the barnyard rumbled.

Retreating another step, I backed into the belly of a man. Full beard, long hair, and baseball cap. I stepped three feet away, a move which allowed him to raise a pellet pistol at my face. It probably wouldn't have killed me, but a shot to the eyeball would have done some damage. And Aunt Mabel would do the rest. Before he could squeeze the trigger, I shielded my eyes with one hand and raised the cane to his shoulder. I shoved it against him and squeezed the blade ejection mechanism. The clicking sound was muffled by flesh; so was the blade, up to the hilt.

The scream wasn't muffled by a thing.

He dropped the pellet pistol into a mound of steer droppings and crouched, cupping his bloody shoulder against a dirty palm, yowling.

Aunt Mabel flew past us through the doorway and ricocheted against a blue Dodge van parked at the other end of the barn. The low vibrations, the rumbling earth, and the air movement all were too close. Aunt Mabel spotted us. I noticed a hook eight feet up, coiled my body, and leaped, grasped it, then snaked feetfirst high into the wood framing of a storage loft the way a crippled gymnast might.

I barely had time to get a stable grip on two pitch-coated rafters when Aunt Mabel collided with the man below me, the sound coming like a freight train.

The man wailed.

Waggling his head, the bull viciously stabbed a horn point into one side, then the other, then flung the now loose-jointed rag doll warrior against the wall of the barn. Producing an ugly cracking noise, the boards of the wall split and daylight shone through.

The bearded man wheezed air and grappled weakly with the horns a few seconds, then went limp under the relentless battering. The first horn tip had gone directly through his aorta. At most, he had sixty seconds, maybe ninety to think of a suitably quotable exit line. Aunt Mabel managed to shorten that by half a minute, tramping, sticking, battering. Ugly. Somehow, I couldn't tear my eyes off it.

The bull looked up, and all was silent. He was breathing like an iron lung, looking for me.

One forgets just how loud a .30-06 can be when one is standing on the muzzle side of the blast.

Shearing the afternoon in half, the first shot stunned Aunt Mabel, who gradually looked around, wobbled sideways a step, snorted, and pawed at the straw.

The wide-eyed figure in the doorway quickly chambered another shell and unloaded on the bull a second time, the recoil violently rocking his gun shoulder backward. Aunt Mabel shuddered and slowly, ever so slowly, toppled sideways—a small planet collapsing— sighed heavily twice, then dropped his stiff legs and was still. He just missed crushing the body.

Though I saw a gaping hole in his flank, I waited to be sure he wasn't playing possum, then dropped out of the rafters, startling the man with the rifle. I checked the bull's victim for signs of life. He was torn up and raw, done living this dream. I wiped off my hand—now covered with blood—on some gunnysacks, then draped them across the upper half of the warm corpse.

Watching his evil-shy halfway embarrassed grin, I turned to the figure in the doorway. "Nice shooting."

"Dead?"

"They're both dead, Aaron."

"Christ."

"Yeah."

"I don't understand. Ghee told me Aunt Mabel was gone. I bet he was planning to play some sort of weird practical joke on me again. That was his style."

Until the moment Ghee had aimed the pellet gun at my face, I had thought my tormentor was Barbour. Now I had to reevaluate things.

A moment later Ghee's wife mushroomed into the doorway. She gaped down at the dead bull, which, even on his side, stood almost as tall as she and easily twice as long as she could reach. Her gaze moved on to the pile of gunnysacks, to her husband's awkwardly twisted boots protruding from the burlap. She didn't weep, only scrutinized the corpse, stunned in disbelief, large dark sacs under her morose eyes. The three of us stood silently in a half circle, regarding the carnage. Before I knew it, Kathy appeared in the doorway also, inhaling and exhaling heavily from her run. For some reason her presence propelled me into explanations.

"Ghee sicked the bull onto me. Saw me out here and let the bull loose, then hit him a couple of times with the pellet gun to get him hot under the collar."

"What happened to Greg?" Barbour asked.

"I came in here trying to get away from Aunt Mabel. I didn't know where else to go. He got in the way." ·

"So brave," said Mrs. Ghee, her voice phlegmy and soft enough that we all had to strain. "My Gregory was always so brave. He stepped out to save your life and went down his own self. By the grace of God, it would have been you."

I had to think hard before I dispelled her delusions. "Mrs. Ghee, your husband sneaked into my house a couple of nights ago and almost killed me. I suppose, when he saw me coming up here, he figured it was him or me. He purposely set the bull out to gore me."

"No," she said, puzzled, shaking her head. "He saved your life. You don't have any right to say things like that now."

"That's how Greg would have figured it," said Aaron Barbour. "Greg goes after you. You go after him. His life philosophy was simple. Do unto the other guy before he does unto you. Christ. I was afraid he might try something on you after you were here. He went to your place? He was on a trip, man. After I told you he was at the well, I heard the bull. I honestly thought Greg had trucked him back to Redmond. Said he had. Even gave me some shucking and jiving about how much trouble they'd had loading him up. Must have been going to play some sort of prank."

"Played a little rough, didn't he?" Kathy asked.

"He was like that."

"But why?" said Mrs. Ghee, gawping at her husband's body.

"He was ticked off," said Aaron, more to me than to the bewildered Mrs. Ghee. "After you left the other day, he asked me all about you. He hated Eric Castle. Thought you were trying to get him off the hook."

Something inside the dead bull gurgled, and we all jumped, then exchanged glances.

"Just how much did he hate Eric?"

"Greg nutted out on us when Eric was staying here with me." Aaron Barbour smiled around the circle of listeners the way a man standing up to his chin in quicksand smiles when his feet finally touch something solid. "Punched Eric in the stomach and made him leave here in the middle of the night after he found out Eric was a pervert. It was a scene, man. Eric puked all over my rug. After that he was always after me to find out where Eric was crashing, you know? I never told him, but I had the feeling he snooped through my place when I was gone. Always talking about Eric getting same as he gave. You came here asking questions, he thought sure you were working for some slimy lawyer trying to clear Eric."

Kathy winced. I walked to the other side of the ramshackle barn and inspected the blue Dodge. Aunt Mabel had caved in a side panel, but other than that, there was no doubt in my mind, muddy license or not, it had to be the one that had almost flattened Eric Castle last week. It had been Ghee. Not Dennis Rogers. Not his father, Gunnar Rogers. Not somebody borrowing the Rogerses' van. Greg Ghee had been harassing Eric Castle, probably had stuck the snake in his bed.

"He's been on some sort of vendetta?" I asked.

Aaron Barbour shrugged, and it turned into a shiver. "Wouldn't surprise me. His favorite movies were the *Death Wish* series. He liked Charles Bronson so much he would have slept with him." Barbour turned to Ghee's flaccid-cheeked wife. "No offense."

"Had he been to eastern Washington in the past couple of weeks?"

"How'd you know?"

"Let me take you up to the house," said Kathy, dropping an arm across the older woman's hunched shoulders. When the older woman, eyes teary, looked at Kathy's weird getup and batted her arm away, Kathy said, unconvincingly, "It's okay. I'm an attorney." Ida Ghee batted her arm away again.

After they had removed themselves, one the height of overkill, the other the height of dishabille, Barbour asked, "That your old lady?"

"Sort of."

"Wild."

I began scouting around the barn.

Barbour refused to abandon the two dead things in the doorway. "Thought I'd come out and show you where the well was. I saw you and Aunt Mabel going at it. Nobody takes Aunt Mabel one-on-one. So I ran up to the house and borrowed Ghee's rifle. Got here just in time, eh?"

"Almost."

Poking through a toolbox, it didn't take me long to find a crescent wrench that had lost its bite, a lopsided star marring its side. I held it aloft. "Who belongs to this?" Maybe I was making a mistake. Still clutching the deer rifle, bolt open, Aaron Barbour walked forward bouncing on the balls of his feet.

"Damned if I know." I fingered the lopsided star and told him the significance of same. "Well, it could have been mine. Eric and I swapped tools more than once. He's still got a lug wrench of mine. And my stuff got mixed up with Ghee's all the time."

"Ghee related to Rittenhouse?"

Drying his crooked teeth, Barbour explained. "Uncle. That's how I found out about this place. Daryl told me his uncle was renting that shack, and I called up."

"Listen, Ghee was carrying on a campaign of harassment against Eric, wasn't he?"

'Thought it for a long time. Just never nad proof.''

"Eric ever talk to you about it?''

"Used to. But Eric thought Fred was after him. Eric was paranoid. He thought a lot of people were harassing him because of the molesting thing. I asked him to get counseling, you know. Get that sick head trip out of his system.'

''What'd he say?

''Nothin'. Just stared at me like he does and walked away. Stopped talking to me altogether. Eric should have been to a shrink a long time ago.''

"Or to a cell.''

21

As it turned out, the cops didn't keep us long.

I had something to mull over on the way home. Had a .45 been tucked under my belt in the barnyard, I could have slaughtered Aunt Mabel before he became a nuisance. Ghee would still be making carbon dioxide for the trees. And I might well have had a better answer to why he had mugged me.

It was dark before we headed back to town, and rather than cross at Kingston, we traveled down Bainbridge and hopped the Winslow ferry. As the rain-blurred skyline hove into view and the downtown lights skittered across Puget Sound, Kathy and I stood on the upper ferry deck inside the windows.

"I'm still not sure I understand Ghee's motives. Why did he go after you with the alarm clock the other night?"

"Wanted time on his side?"

"Seems awful risky sneaking into your house. Especially when you had company."

"I have the feeling Ghee went ahead and did whatever came to mind, risky or not. If he hated Eric enough to poison his life systematically with harassment, vandalism, the occasional potshot, he certainly wouldn't

217

have been fond of some fool he believed was trying to aid and abet Eric. He must have seen me that day training alongside Eric and decided I was in his camp.''

I visualized Ghee bending over my prone body, gun in hand, only the munificence of a pair of half-swacked pistol-packing floozies between me and teatime with the medical examiner. Bless their piston rings. If they hadn't shown up or if I had cut them loose sooner, I would be wearing a .38 slug in my ear.

The ferry disgorged us onto Alaskan Way amid a gaggle of tired tourists and weekenders returning to town. Kathy cut across the city the way a marmot bounded across a snowfield, missing all the arterials. The Sunday evening traffic was light, so it didn't matter, and I didn't bother to bruise her ego by mentioning it. She drove me to the south end of Capitol Hill near the hospital, and we picked up her car, which had languished unattended since Saturday night.

After she had followed me home, Kathy came inside to be sure nobody was waiting with an alarm clock. ''I'll get my stuff and come back.''

''I'll be all right.''

''You ran a stop sign and a light both. You drove over the curb at Broadway and John. Thomas, you're not one hundred percent. Not even eighty.''

''All I'm going to do is nuke a TV dinner, have a banana, and flop.''

Kathy looked at her watch. It wasn't seven-thirty yet. ''Okay, big boy, but I'll be over first thing in the morning.''

''You have to work tomorrow.''

''I'll call in some excuse.''

''They won't be pleased.''

''Let me handle that. Stay put till I get here. I don't want you going anywhere without me.'' She kissed my cheek, halted as if considering saying more, then left, hooking her wig on a chair as she exited. It took awhile for her aura to vaporize behind her.

It was nine before I got into bed. Kathy had changed

the sheets the night before, and they felt cool and smooth and tight. My head was spinning, but I sat listening to the radio, poring through the Sunday morning paper. Mrs. P.'s hanging had come too late to make the edition but there were several items about the Laurelhurst neighborhood being agitated over the murder, about the police investigation's being stalled, about an unsolved murder in Laurelhurst fifteen years ago, and so forth. Old stuff, all. Floating the newspapers onto the floor, I clicked the lamp off, reached over, and switched on the answer machine. I hadn't reviewed the tapes since before I'd gone to the hospital.

After the Desiree material there was only one message. I opened my eyes in the dark bedroom and listened to her raspy, overly polite tones, astonished that I hadn't thought to listen to these tapes earlier.

"Mr. Black. I spoke to you the other day, but I'm afraid I was holding back. There's a lot more to what Fred's been up to these past few weeks. I really should tell you. I know I'm in a bind . . ." She paused. "This is Margaret Pugsley. I've been asking around, and they say if anybody can help me, you can. So I'll have to trust you. I have something to tell you about Fred. For one thing, he slept with Veronica once, a long time ago. Call. Please."

It was haunting to sit there in the dark, alone, my head reeling, listening to a dead woman. I played the tape again, watching the scrawny shadows of a bush outside as they cavorted on my wall. And again. Fred and Veronica? It stymied the imagination. In the morning, when I played Margaret Pugsley's voice back again, it gave me another jolt, eerie and unexpected. I got out the pictures I'd taken of her the morning of the murder, half naked, covered in blood. I burned them in the fireplace and stirred the ashes.

Packing up several goofball hats, sunglasses, various coats, a change of shoes, I scrammed before Kathy arrived.

On Capitol Hill I spotted Eric Castle as he was leav-

ing his rooming house. It was bald-faced luck that I
caught him. I should have been there earlier. He
climbed into a shabby Toyota and drove across the lake.
I followed at a distance.

Bellevue was buzzing with school buses, country
wagons, swirling exhaust fumes, happy kids, and
grouchy housewives. I dallied until Eric almost spotted
me, then put on a hat and sunglasses. As far as I could
recall, he didn't know what kind of car I drove. He was
parked up the street from the Rogers homestead. In this
neighborhood he would have to keep on his toes, move
around frequently. Nobody was going to stand for a
snoop in a run-down Toyota. I waited down the street,
far down the street. From where I parked, I could barely
see the garage doors through my binoculars.

Veronica Rogers's two-tone Lincoln pulled out of her
driveway shortly after nine-thirty. When she wheeled
past, I scribbled her license number on my thumb in
case I lost her and had to spot-check Lincolns in parking lots.

Though she had two tails, she didn't waste any of her
life gazing into her rearview and, as far as I could tell,
didn't pick up either one of us. She ended up in the
parking garage outside Bellevue Square, a large, mul-
tilevel indoor shopping mall.

She had parked on the top level of the parking garage,
and as I arrived, I saw her blond head disappear across
the sky bridge into Nordstrom's. Eric followed her in,
and I followed Eric.

Nearly fifteen minutes later I bumped into him on the
main level outside a computer store. He didn't recognize me, in my backward baseball cap and sunglasses,
two Band-Aids pasted across my lip, didn't even glance
my way.

I cornered him and pushed him into a narrow hallway
that went east toward the parking lots. Knotting my fists
in his coat collar, I slammed him up against the wall.
Several pedestrians saw me do it, watched as they
walked, then, trekking out of sight, seemed to forget.

"What's new in the zoo?" I said.

Eric Castle blinked rapidly, eyes teary with the shock of confrontation, then recognized me under my half-baked disguise. "Black? What the hell are you doing here?"

"That's my question, peckerwood."

He tried a move on me, slipped my grasp and tried to box, threw two blows, and received two stinging slaps across his face for his efforts. His cheeks turned pink with my fingerprints. His bat eyes went ugly and simmered enough voodoo in them to kill a small animal. I had never seen him quite like that, not even when they were trying to run him down. "I'm just shopping. Mind your own business."

"Don't give me that jive. Nobody 'just shops' twenty yards behind his ex-wife. You're tailing her."

"Is Binnie here?"

I raised him up a peg, and the stitching in his collar snapped at us. "You know she is. What are you doing?"

He shook his head in small increments. "Don't have to tell you."

"Wrong. If I had any patience, you wouldn't have to tell me. I ran out of patience awhile back. Somebody tried to kill me Thursday. Sunday night they tried it again. Saturday night we found Maggie, Fred's wife, hanging from a closet door. And I found out about your hobby. How about if I whistle Binnie back here and we call a cop? We can have him make out a report, even if he doesn't arrest you. Then we can forward all this to her attorneys. You think that'll improve your chances of getting your kids back?"

All resistance oozed out of him as he slumped in my grip. I freed him. As close to the end of his rope as I was to mine, he whispered, "Black, you bastard."

"So they say. Talk."

"You lost me my job, asshole. Cops came 'round asking questions. You told them I killed Fred, didn't you?"

"I told them you were an interesting possibility."

"Well, they came, and they destroyed. I got fired after my boss asked me what it was all about."

"So what are you doing shadowing your ex?"

Head hanging, Eric Castle shrank against the wall, jammed both hands into his jeans pockets, and said, "I'm trying to get some ammo for my lawsuit. I want visitation rights back. I know they're going to say and do some pretty dirty things in court. Thought maybe if I had my own little bag of rocks, mine wouldn't be the only windows broken."

"What's old Binnie up to that we should know about?" Eric swiveled his dark eyes up at me, and they shone. "She selling dope to her cello instructor or what?" For a few seconds I thought he was going to take another poke at me. He was concealing something, but I had the feeling he'd never tell me about it. "You're not following her for the fun of it. You think she's into something, don't you?" He looked down, refusing to reply. "You called Barbour and warned him I was coming, didn't you?"

"I called him. So what? Mom said you were there asking about me, so I called him. What? I get the electric chair for a phone call?"

"Talk. I'll have the cops here in a second. Don't think I won't. What about Veronica? Why tail her?"

He only shook his head. On this point he was adamant. He would say no evil, hear no evil concerning his ex-wife. Maybe they were hiding something, together, the two of them. Perhaps Eric and Veronica were sharing a secret.

"Talk."

"I've learned about accusations, Black. I don't make them."

"I can't believe, psychopath or not, you were ever stupid enough to invite your whole office to search your house, knowing the evidence against you they would find. And everything else seems to hinge on that."

His voice was squeaky and weak. He looked up and

down the hallway for a moment. "You're the first person in five years to concede the possibility that I might be innocent."

"I didn't concede jack. I'm just saying, if nobody could get into your place, Eric, and you say you didn't put those pornographic pictures there—But you never did say you didn't put them there, did you?"

"Drop dead, Black."

"I just thought of something crazy. What if Binnie had those pictures, and not you?"

"I might have asked her about that, but I didn't."

"Why not?"

"It was so clear that she felt I was guilty, I saw no reason to wonder if she'd put the stuff there. She didn't, or she wouldn't have looked at me the way she did."

"And now you're telling me you didn't?"

"I'm not telling you shit."

"She ever show signs of mental instability?"

"The only person who's shown signs of mental instability around here is me."

"After the incident?"

"After. During. Before. I thought I was a freewheeling type of guy. I'm not so sure some of it might not have been disguised mental problems."

"Stop following Veronica. It can only get you into trouble. You can't even imagine what the cops would think if I told them."

"I don't have to listen to you."

Shaking him, I said, "And I don't have to leave you standing on two legs."

When I last saw him in the corridor, he was wiping his eyes on his sleeves. I had shaken him up good. In the main portion of the mall Veronica Rogers was long gone. I watched Eric abscond, certain he was hiding something. He knew something about her, and I wanted to find out what so I wandered the mall until I spotted her again. She was easy to tail—the ocelot on display.

Clad in jade green shoes, matching earrings, and a pastel affair that looked as if it'd come from the Middle

East, she shopped, and I watched. I saw her browse through a bookstore, poke around in a ladies' undergarment boutique, several department stores, and then settle into a jewelry shop. The raft of packages in her arms grew. She snacked at a small restaurant on the second level and met a well-heeled girlfriend I had never seen before. They dug into their sacks and compared assets. The lunch dragged on.

Shadowing a beautiful woman around town gave me a skittish feeling, somehow made my skin crawl. I was no different from some slime setting up a sex crime. Same notions. Same basic activity. Undoubtedly the same trills up my spine.

Veronica went back to her house and Eric didn't show his face again. A short while after two the older boy arrived home from school in his van. Twenty minutes later Veronica drove to an exercise club in downtown Bellevue. I parked across the street. It was dark when she flitted out of the aerobics studio and stopped at a grocery store. She wore a long coat over her exercise togs, her blond tresses matted with aried sweat.

I sat up the street while the Rogers household dined. Gunnar got home late, roaring up the drive and screeching to a halt inside the garage. Dennis came and went three times while I spied. I moved the truck four times. At ten, when it looked as if they were through for the night, I dragged myself home, cold, dirty, hungry, and exhausted. The more I thought about it, the more I thought Eric had a legitimate reason for following Veronica. I didn't know what it was, but it was there, somewhere.

Kathy ambushed me at my door. "Where have you been, you big, ugly snoop?"

"What?"

"You bastard."

"I didn't need any help." I tossed an assortment of hats and coats and sunglasses onto a chair. Angry as she was, Kathy, who couldn't resist any pile of clothing, sorted through them, possibly to see if there was something she could use in her outlandish wardrobe.

"You've been tailing someone. Who?"

"I'm bushed," I said, brushing past her. The brunette hair was coiled at the back of her neck. It seemed to pull her face tight and give her a slight Asian cast. She wore about a dozen layers of multicolored shirts and sweaters. I recognized one of the shirts. It was mine.

"Dinner's dried out. Fried chicken and mashed potatoes."

"I'll be out after a quick shower."

"Thomas?"

"What?"

"You look like hell."

"Thanks."

Under the shower I grew woozy and nearly fainted, had to grab the tile walls to keep my feet. I managed to get dried, dressed, and out to dinner in one piece. Kathy had waited, and we supped together, she strangely quiet after her opening tirade. "It was nice of you," I said. "Stopping by to fix a meal."

"How are you feeling?"

"Waves of nausea. Sometimes fine for five or six hours. Headaches off and on. A feeling of separateness."

"I want you to see a doctor."

"Not yet. I'm on to something."

"You've been tailing people. Who?"

"Give me another day or two, and we'll talk."

"I'm not going home tonight, Thomas. I don't trust you."

"I'm too tired for fun and games."

"Very funny. As if you would play anyway."

She had turned off the lights and lit candles for dinner. It was almost ten-thirty, and I was so exhausted I felt near death. Leaning close to one of the candles, the light flickering in her eyes, Kathy said, "Thomas?"

"Uh."

"The other day you told me you knew why we don't
. . . you know . . . why we never became lovers." I
nodded sleepily. "Why?"

"We love each other."

"Lovers!" She was exasperated. "We've never
screwed."

"Watch your language."

"Why do you think?"

"Some relationships are sacrosanct. Would you have
Howdy Doody screwing Clarabell? How do you think
that would look?"

"The truth."

I took a deep breath. "You're my best friend, Kathy,
the best friend I've ever had."

She nodded, and a tear crystallized in one violet eye.

"We start messing around, we'll lose that. I'm afraid
we will. And so are you. You know it. The end result
would not be exciting enough to risk it."

"Wanna bet?"

I winked at her and plodded into the bedroom, undressed, and dropped into bed.

Kathy canted against the doorway.

"Friends."

Quietly gliding across the darkened room, Kathy knelt
on the edge of my bed and created a lover's trough,
bent low, and whispered, "There was some excitement
at work today."

"Uh."

"They wanted to cancel you off the case."

"Every right," I murmured. "The client's dead.
Who's gonna pay?"

"That's what they said. I contested it."

"What happened? Your voice is funny."

"I got fired."

"What?"

She sobbed, laying her head on my pillow and crying. At first I thought she was pulling my leg. "Not
fired actually. Terminated. It was mutual, I guess. In
fact, I guess you could say I quit. It's a long, boring

story. I didn't like the way they were trying to talk
me out of criminal law all the time. And all I want to
do is criminal actions. And . . . Thomas? Are you
awake?''

I was and I wasn't. And then I was chasing the scant-
ily clad tooth fairy over the back fence.

In the morning I found her on the couch in the living
room, a warm lump wrapped in a quilt. I prepared a
breakfast of scrambled eggs and English muffins,
cleaned up the dinner mess, listened to the radio, and
was startled to see Kathy standing in the doorway in an
all-black outfit. It almost looked punk. The orange high-
top tennis shoes confirmed it. Her eyes were puffy. She
hadn't yet combed her hair into a rooster tail, but she
would.

"Sorry I conked out on you," I said.

"How're you feeling?"

"They really fired you?"

"I've been thinking about opening my own office
anyway."

"Want to tail somebody?"

"You feel so bad you really want me along?"

"In spurts."

"Sure thing, Cisco."

"Okay, Clarabell."

After a quick breakfast I gassed the truck up and
drove over to Bellevue. We were a tad late, but I figured
she probably wouldn't hit the road until the kiddies were
off to school. We parked and waited. Kathy didn't say
anything, although she knew who I was stalking. I got
her talking about her plans. She had a million of them.
Her aunt had left her a small stipend, enough, if she
opened her own office, to take her through a year of
lousy business, perhaps two. She had a small, but
growing, reputation. She would open her own law office. Start small. It was a dream she'd had for years.

As Kathy plotted her future, Veronica Castle Rogers's
two-tone Lincoln Continental coursed down the steep

drive, scraped a bumper musically on the street, and we were off like a herd of turtles.

She hit Bellevue Square first, then a men's haberdashery in Kirkland, then, to my surprise, headed into town. In Seattle she zipped straight up I-5 to the Northgate mall, and we almost lost her in the parking lot. In the end I had Kathy park the truck, and I tailed Rogers on foot.

I'd had the feeling things were going to break today. Fred's body had been released by the medical examiner's office at Harborview, and Micro had planned a huge event near Queen Anne Hill in his and his wife's honor; in lieu of funerals, a wake, of sorts.

Two hours later I headed outside in front of Mrs. Rogers. I found Kathy in the parking lot, sitting in my truck, basking in bubble gum music. The Lincoln was two rows away, partially obscured behind a terra-cotta van. "Hi."

"Who? I'm awake. No, she hasn't been back. How come you're here so early? Lose her?"

I slid behind the steering wheel, dropped a hand onto her knees, and said, "Hey, pal. Everybody gets fired."

"It's okay. I let all the boys grab my knees."

"It's only natural to be down for a while. Think about opening your own office."

Heaving a sigh, Kathy said, "I am. I'm scared."

I slipped an arm across her shoulders. "You'll knock 'em dead."

In smoke-colored sunglasses, white hose, high heels, a white dress, and a tawny jacket lined in fur, Veronica strode out, walking across the lot as if she owned it and most of the air I was breathing as well. She hugged two packages to her bosom. As we pulled out two cars behind her, Kathy said, "What is it with you and this lady? You investigating her for the case? Or you just following her around like a cat in heat?"

I was not amused.

We got trapped in traffic as she headed for I-5 but were able to make up time on the freeway. We followed

her to Pioneer Square, where she paid five bucks to park
under the viaduct. Kathy borrowed one of my hats, put
a surly look on her mug, and we leapfrogged behind
Veronica, first Kathy in the lead, then me, then Kathy.
Veronica browsed through the craft booths set up in
Occidental Park for Fat Tuesday. She went to the bank
and cashed a check. She sat in the restaurant in the
basement of Elliott Bay Books, crossed her legs, got
stared at by well-dressed men, and sipped espresso. She
bought a toy in a specialty shop, then a child's dress
and matching stockings across the street, then headed
back to her car.

My truck was parked two blocks farther north, so we
nad to scurry. As we jogged along, Kathy said, "She's
rushing. We spooked her."

"Baloney."

"She's moving faster than before. Either we spooked
her or she's late for an appointment."

"I'll buy an appointment."

22 A MIST HAD SETTLED OVER THE city, and the traffic plodded along in a glow of headlights. We tailed her north on Alaskan Way, fender to fender with the first angry echelons of the rush hour. She went up Broad like a butterfly on an updraft. She circled the south end of Lake Union on Eastlake, crossed I-5, found Roanoke, and from there took a circuitous route through one of the most exclusive neighborhoods in the city down to Portage Bay.

Portage Bay was a swollen tumor on the canal between Lake Union and Lake Washington. Boat traffic flowed through here on its way to the sound. On the northern shore one could see the Showboat Theater and several buildings that constituted the U of W Hospital. Boats of all shapes and sizes were moored helter-skelter.

After she had parked on Boyer Avenue East, she locked her car, looked around, and proceeded down a concrete walkway to the water and out onto a small private dock. The Queen City Yacht Club's massive sheltered docks lay to the south and east, jutting out into the tiny bay. I leaped out of the truck into the street, whispering loudly to Kathy, ''Park it.'' I sur-

veyed the vicinity for other cars I might recognize but
came up empty.

Before I had a chance to get close, she vanished below in a sailboat. From where I stood I couldn't see the
name on the escutcheon. I went back to where Kathy
had parked the truck and took out a tweed blazer, re-
placing the grimy jacket I'd been wearing, and switched
my grimy baseball cap for a houndstooth spy hat.
Snappy.

"Don't fall in the water, Sherlock."

It was a short wooden wharf. Twelve or thirteen boats
in a variety of lengths and configurations were moored
off it. The water was still and looked like black glass.
Gulls squawked in the distance. It was growing dark,
and across at the Queen City Yacht Club a cruiser
berthed, the low rumble of its diesel engines throbbing
in the dusk. Formless globules of exhaust hung over the
water. The two-masted sailboat she'd boarded was
sandwiched between a sloop and a squarish cabin
cruiser that appeared too top-heavy to be seaworthy.
They could call it the *Desiree*.

Hands in pockets, I shambled along, taking in the
boat, the dock, and glancing back up the road. I took
out a small notebook and penned the name of the sailboat, *The Glass Slipper*, then the address I'd seen on a
set of mailboxes at the end of the wharf.

I stepped off the wooden planks and boarded the vacant sloop moored next to the boat Veronica had disappeared into, trying not to jiggle the small craft as I
made my way alongside the slick hull of the *The Glass
Slipper*, inspecting it porthole by porthole. It wasn't
until I was midship that I found a sliver of light. From
my precarious position I could see just a slice of the
cabin through the curtain. Music was playing. Classical
music. Strauss.

A man's legs protruded into the pencil of light. He
was sitting very low and very relaxed in some sort of
plush custom easy chair that was decked out in purple
corduroy. He tapped bare feet to the music, and he wore

either shorts or nothing at all, at least nothing that I could see. In the shadows his bare arms dangled limply over the purple arms of the chair. I couldn't make out who it was. All I could see was a backpack he'd been working on and an ice ax for mountain climbing. And a pair of eyeglasses on the arm of the chair. Veronica sauntered casually past his chair and set a drink on the arm. He sipped from it, and in the murk I still couldn't see who it was. She was out of her jacket now, wore heels and her dress.

I glanced around the area. Nobody on the wharf. Kathy was parked out of sight behind the shrubs on the parking strip. She'd toot a warning if a squadron of police cars swooped down onto the waterfront. Somebody from the Queen City Yacht Club looked over, and I pretended to fumble with the tarpaulin on the sloop. Dusk was descending, and the nightly traffic spotter planes were already zigzagging over the 520 bridge nearby, advising people of the fastest route to their beer and slippers.

The sloop bobbed rhythmically, so my view through the knife blade of light wasn't perfect. She came back wearing only a slip. I had never seen her so relaxed. The man remained lounging, knees high, his feet going tap-tap, but Veronica walked around, tidying. It wasn't Gunnar. He wasn't heavy enough. It wasn't anybody I could recognize in the shadows, not from his knees and hands. She kicked off her shoes, finally, then stripped off the slip. Her loose hair drooped across her face à la Marilyn Monroe. It hadn't occurred to me before, but Veronica was an icy version of the sin queen. Had she been a rose, they would have named her American Ice.

They talked as she moved around the tight quarters. I couldn't make out any of it. I wanted to be a bad boy and bang on the window and hoot and holler, but I kept still and watched. I was seven feet away from the woman I'd been tailing for two days, and she had finally done something of note.

And she was good.

From time to time she wafted out of sight, as the tapping foot tapped faster; then she wafted back into view, wearing less each trip. She moved slowly and sinuously.

Riveted to the porthole, head swimming, I stayed until she wore next to nothing, panties, a skimpy brassiere she spilled out of, and a smile that would have made a dead man sit up and salute.

A secret lover. Tuesday afternoons lollygagging on the sailboat. I watched, and my stomach twisted like burning wire.

"What do you think you're doing, clown?"

A man only a smidgen smaller than a motor home stood on the wharf, heavy legs splayed for action, arms hanging at his sides like a gorilla. He wore a uniform that would have impressed a Boy Scout and a frown that would have cracked glass. I was hoping the music and the general mood inside *The Glass Slipper* would drown out our chitchat.

"Talkin' to you, clown!"

He was ferocious, his face beet red, nose bridged with tiny spiders where booze had gotten the better of his capillaries, a drinking man who hadn't had nearly enough this afternoon. I made my way from the sloop to the wharf. I had already tugged the houndstooth hat low, disguising the shape of my head and scrunching the top part of my face. He was some sort of security guard. No gun. He didn't need a gun. His arms looked like cannon snouts.

Stepping up onto the wharf away from him, I said, "Halbert said I could look this little sloop over. Thinking of makin' an offer on it. What do you guess it's worth?"

"Dan Zeigal owns that boat, and you're fulla crap. You're a fuckin' peepin' Tom."

"Halbert doesn't own it? Why, that liar."

His thick hands reached out to grab my jacket, but I tapped his kneecap with the toe of my shoe and slipped

his grasp. It all happened hastily wordlessly, not a
sound between us.

I was halfway down the wharf, walking in a high
scoot, when I felt the boards rumbling. I cast a look
over my shoulder, and he looked like the Incredible
Hulk limping after me, arms reaching, though I wasn't
close enough to snag yet. Then I took a shortcut. The
dock jogged twenty yards to the left, but I knew I could
make the short gap. It would save half a minute. I
leaped from the wharf to the shore.

The black water sucked me down until I was thigh-
deep in the sound, splashing and grabbing the concrete
abutment to keep from going all the way under. I pulled
myself onto a concrete sidewalk and sloshed up the
walk, losing twenty, almost thirty seconds. I felt as if
I'd been quick-frozen from the thighs down. The Hulk
was right behind me now.

I sprinted past the hood of my pickup truck, both
shoes sloshing, slacks pasted to my shins. Inside the
truck I could hear laughter. When I twisted my head, I
spotted Kathy, mouth wide to air her fillings, howling.
The Hulk didn't want to arrest me. He wanted to mas-
sage my face with his knuckles, break my elbows backward, tap-dance on my brain.

Darting across Boyer, I dodged a pair of freewheeling
cyclists and headed up a steep hill on Edgar. The Hulk
managed to get halfway up the hill before he relin-
quished the race, huffing, hands on knees, polishing the
kneecap I'd kicked. Another block or two, and he'd put
his lunch on the parking strip. From the top of the hill
I could hear him panting. He waved an arm disgustedly
and turned back down the hill.

When I gazed down at the wharf, all was quiet. Apparently the pair in the sailboat had remained oblivious
of our melodrama. This was the second time I'd gotten
all wet because of Veronica Rogers. But this time was
worth it.

I headed south at a fast trot, still uphill. A few moments later my pickup truck sped up the street and she

hit me in the face with a brilliant beam from the spot-
light I stowed under the dash.

"Hey, sailor, wanna good time?"

"Didn't your mother tell you anything about
strangers?" I climbed in, and Kathy headed up the hill,
cackling as loudly as she could, took Roanoke to Harvard Avenue, and drove to my place on surface streets.
She would chuckle, stifle it for a moment, then erupt
again, riding the crest of hilarity for half a minute, then
stifle it and go into the routine again. I thought she was
going to succumb. I thought we were going to crash. If
anybody ever had a case of terminal laughter, this was
it.

"Don't wet your pants," I said, and the quip set her
off again. I wanted to circle back and find out who was
about to bed Veronica Rogers, but the security guard
would be alert for hours. "The wake for Fred begins
at eight. You want dinner first?"

"This a date, sailor?"

"Whatever."

"Then what? After dinner."

"We go to the wake."

"And what are you going to do? Let's talk about this,
Thomas. I hear something sneaky in your voice. What
was going on inside that boat?"

"Let's go. I've got calls to make."

At home I called the King County assessor's office,
where a nasal-voiced lady complained about its being
quitting time before giving me the name of the owner
of the mailbox off Boyer. He lived in Maple Valley, and
I dialed but got no answer. I showered until I was warm
again and then used the phone. I dressed in a suit, the
only one I owned, drove Kathy to her place where she
showered and dressed.

While I waited, I used her phone. It was just after
six when I reached the owner of the mailbox, presumably also the owner of the wharf. He sounded about a
hundred and two years old, voice phlegmy and full of

vibrato. If he wasn't wearing a pacemaker in his chest, I was no judge of character.

"Edward Haskell here. I tried to rouse somebody last night out at your dock, but there didn't seem to be anybody around. That is your dock in Portage Bay?"

"Got a couple of 'em," he said.

"Got one with a sailboat called *The Glass Slipper* moored to it?"

"The big un. Yep."

"Nicked the hull last night coming into berth across the way. My son-in-law had a few too many, and it was entirely my fault. The long and short of it is, I owe some money for repairs to whoever owns *The Glass Slipper*. Left a note last night, but I haven't heard. Mind telling me the owner's name, so I can contact him? Taking the Lear down to the Bahamas here in two days; otherwise I'd drop him another note."

"Ghee."

"Pardon?"

"G-h-e-e."

"You got a first name to go with that?"

"Judith. Judith Ghee. Young kid in her late fifties."

"Thanks a heap." All I could figure was that Judith Ghee was a sister or sister-in-law of the late Greg Ghee. His wife had been named Ida, not Judith.

Hair pulled into a knot at the nape of her neck, she wore a black hat with a black veil, black heels, hose, and a black sheath dress. It was the sort of getup that had total strangers asking her to marry them.

"You're going to steal the show."

"Not hardly. We'll have two dead people, the rich and famous, and a few beautiful ladies to steal the show. Plus I have a feeling you're going to pull something."

"Me?"

"I couldn't help noticing you've got a miniature tape recorder in your coat. What's that for?"

I adjusted the flap of my pocket. "Nothing."

"What was going on inside that sailboat? Who was she meeting?"

"Didn't see his face."

"His?"

"His."

"You're looking a lot better, Thomas. But something smells fishy."

"Tag along. It'll be fun."

23 TWENTY-FIVE MINUTES LATER WE were parked in front of the house near the south end of Lake Washington. "What's this place?" Kathy asked.

"Five years ago Eric and Veronica Castle lived here."

"What do you think you'll find?"

"Ancient history."

But I expected more. I had been thinking about the events over on the peninsula. Aunt Mabel. Greg Ghee. Aaron conveniently showing up with the rifle at the last moment. Aaron had had access to that van just as Ghee had. And Aaron's explanation of why he had left Micro Darlings five years ago after Eric did smacked of fable. Desiree and Queenie could have given me a bum description of my assailant. Perhaps it hadn't been Ghee who had clobbered me with the alarm clock. Maybe I was flying off on a tangent, but I wondered if I'd been hoodwinked. Something else, too. The owner of *The Glass Slipper*, Judith Ghee. I wondered how that tied in. Some cases were like a pot of cooking rice: Remove the lid too soon, and you ruin it.

Tenants, who undoubtedly knew little or nothing of the hapless history of the house, had settled in for the

238

night. The narcotic strobe light from a television pattered against the curtains. It was a small house with a narrow covered porch leading to a front door. An untended yard stretched all the way down to a ramshackle dock on the water. A tricycle lay on its nose in the grass beside the porch. Shabby or not, it must have seemed like heaven to a young family without much money.

Across the street I found a retired bachelor, wine globlet in hand. He didn't recall what he'd had for dinner, much less the neighbors five years ago. In the next house a widow in her mid-forties talked my nut off. She remembered the Castles, didn't recall that they had children.

The best bet stood almost directly across the street. From the stoop a body would be able to take note of anything that happened at the Castles'. Cars. Visitors. Packages. Perversions. Situated on a slight rise, it had a view downward into the Castles' living room window.

Earlene Wilson refused to admit me until I hollered that I had come to gossip about ex-neighbors. Salesmen were one thing. Gossip was an entirely different matter. Prior to unbolting the door, she examined my ID through the tiny swinging peep door, then toddled across the room and phoned her son-in-law to tell him she was letting a stranger into her place and to call back in a few minutes to be sure she wasn't being raped. Watching through the still-open peephole, I noted a certain sense of adventure in her words. I thought her cautions excessive, but then, I wasn't prancing around in orthopedic shoes.

She was thin as a rake, with arms like toilet paper tubes. Her dark brown eyes had eighty-five years' worth of fizz in them. Modeling a worn dress that had been minted fifty years ago, a corset, clunky heels, and stockings, Mrs. Wilson felt me out before she started in on the dirty jokes (not filthy-dirty, just cute-dirty), bestowing coy, twinkly looks after each one. I noted that the chair she naturally gravitated to, aside from being smack in front of a soundless black-and-white

RCA, also sat smack in front of the window overlooking the street. I gabbed, gradually bringing the subject
to a boil. In every neighborhood there's one old biddy
who knows more about what's going on than the people
doing the going-on. I had the feeling I had struck the
nerve center of this enclave.

The first ribald joke was about nuns having sex in
heaven. The second was about a woman who demanded
her lovers have a minimum-length instrument. The
woman in the joke picked up a man in a bar, made her
demand, and was shocked when he stomped off, reply-
ing that he wasn't folding his in half for "no woman."
The old lady grinned. Her son-in-law phoned back, and
she told him everything was swell, hanging up abruptly
so we could get back to the hanky-panky.

When she had wiped the tears of mirth out of her
eyes, she went through the relative bit, a tale to go with
every picture on her piano. Her husband had passed on
thirty years ago, buried with an "I like Ike" button in
his lapel.

"You remember the Castles?"

"Two of the sweetest kids you ever did see. How he
doted on those children."

"You know about what happened then?"

"Mrs. Blumberg trotted over here that morning and
filled me in. The wife always asked Mrs. Blumberg to
watch the kids."

"How long had they lived here?"

"Oh, couldn't have been more than two, three
years."

"You see much of them?"

"From my window I could see everything. Such a
sweet young couple. The whole neighborhood was upset when they found out. People drove by and tossed
rocks through their windows. Set fire to their mailbox.
It burned mine, too. Almost lost a social security
check."

"The way I understood it, the wife stayed home, and

he went to work. She have much company while he was away?''

Mrs. Wilson gave me a coquettish, puckered smile and said, ''My, my, you know about that, do you?''

I shrugged.

''You know all that commotion over there, all that fandango with the police going over and all the people from his work that day, nobody ever come over here and asked me. I'd have told them. I'll tell you. Earlene knows. But nobody ever asked me.''

''Okay, Earlene,'' I said, squatting on the edge of a little-used sofa. I hadn't settled in before because I was afraid she'd never stop chattering, but her place was fifteen degrees too hot and the air six feet up was getting thin. ''Tell me what old Earlene knows.''

She let the suspense build, her face alive with naughtiness. ''Why, she was seeing a fella. Seeing him all along. Twice a week, getting serviced just like clockwork. She took her two young-uns over to Mrs. Blumberg's and ran back home. Not ten minutes later he'd show up. Must have gone on for a year.''

''The last year?''

''She done nothing in the beginning.''

''You remember what this visitor looked like?''

''Does a chicken have lips?'' She almost purred, so delighted she was that someone important had finally come to let her bask in her glory. ''He was an athlete. Heavy glasses.'' She winked. ''Nice caboose, as my friend Thelma always likes to say.''

''You sure about the heavy glasses?''

''Does a chicken—''

''Tell me all about him.'' I was growing confused. I made her give me a full description, then pumped her for more details, pumped her until I had a firm physical description that could match only one person I'd met on this case. Still, it didn't necessarily mean anything. So Veronica had been having an affair. So what?

''This is very important, Mrs. Wilson. How did this gentleman caller get into their house?''

"Why . . ." My simple query flustered her.
"Through the front door. He didn't climb in no window
or nothing. All happened in the middle of the day.
Tuesday and Thursday afternoons around two, two-
thirty."

"What I meant was, did he ring the bell? Did he have
a key? Did she wait out front for him so they could
drive away? What?"

She had to think about this. Finally she raised an
alabaster tube of an arm, pointed across the street, and
said, "Why, he punched that thingamajig they had on
their wall. Had this here box. Never did figure out what
it was all about. Thought maybe it was a call box. Next
folks moved in, they just yanked it."

"You're sure he punched it?"

"Oh, honey, the frame's worn out, but the engine
works just fine."

I got her phone number in case I had more questions,
left my card, then fumbled my way out through the dark
yard to Kathy in the truck.

"What'd you find out?" Kathy asked.

My theories were beginning to bisect reality, and it
was all I could do to keep from blurting it out. "Nothing."

The razzmatazz of Fat Tuesday had every café, tea-
room, and chophouse within walking distance of Pioneer Square jammed, the crowds packed so tightly
everybody involved wanted to pee. After fifteen minutes we found seats at the Iron Horse, a quaint little
place on the outskirts of Pioneer Square where the
booths are constructed from old train diners and your
food chugs around the outer wall on an electric train.
It was good for toddlers and cheering up people who
had just got the ax from the most prestigious law firm
in town. We were hideously overdressed.

Though I was fairly confident I knew who had done
what, I was also confident obtaining a confession was
not going to be easy.

The Fat Tuesday celebration was winding up tonight,

idling cars, besotted pedestrians, and roaring fire engines making the streets uninhabitable, and it was all
so appalling and teeming with miscreants that Kathy
asked me to bring her back after the wake. Even though
I knew a trip back would become a tiresome dot-to-dot
around all the watering holes and dance joints, I acqui-
esced. There would be fireworks and shouting and police whistles and pissing in the alleys and maybe even
a riot. New Orleans had the Mardi Gras. Seattle had
Fat Tuesday. She wouldn't miss the last night for the
world. This case had already ruined most of the week
for her, had started last Wednesday, and she hoped it
would end tonight on Fat Tuesday.

A week of celebration coinciding with a week of
murder.

We drove to the base of Queen Anne under the
shadow of the Space Needle and found parking half a
block from the church. The edifice was almost directly
across the street from the western perimeter of the Seattle Center, which had been the grounds of the Seattle
World's Fair back in the early sixties. Elvis had made a
movie here. Assorted clumps of people stood outside
the church, murmuring and rubber-necking at other
clumps.

Kathy said, "You be careful, Cisco. I smell beeeg
trouble here."

"Got some quarters to call the cops?"

"Always carry quarters when I'm out with you."

It was an informal, almost impromptu affair: trays of
food and bottles of booze stacked on long tables in a
room off the chapel; nattering, snacking, gossiping, no
official ceremonies, just Fred and Maggie wedged into
matching caskets; the people; the memories. It was what
I would have wanted, though I couldn't imagine a troupe
this big squatting around my grave.

We hadn't been inside five minutes when Veronica
Rogers abandoned her two starched youngsters and
strutted across the foyer toward us. Lucy and Tad were
holding hands tightly as if they'd been commanded to

do so, Lucy wearing the dress we'd watched her mother purchase that afternoon. I winked at the girl, but she only clenched her teeth and smiled through the desperation.

Veronica gave me such a smoky look I thought she was going to lay a kiss on my cheek. "What are you doing here?"

"Evening, Binnie. This is Katherine Birchfield. She was Fred's attorney."

Veronica appraised Kathy and said something she obviously didn't mean. "Nice to meet you."

Swaddled in black, just the merest hint of a tanned swelling breast under the V neck, Veronica was attired far more sedately than Kathy's slinky résumé. I couldn't help thinking how Mrs. Rogers had looked this afternoon in the boat. Nor could I help recalling all the rest of what I'd recently learned about her: Fred; the lover at the lake. She wasn't what she seemed.

"I made it clear I never wanted to see you again," Veronica said, eyes glinting.

"It's a big world out there, Binnie. Good friends like you and I are bound to bump into each other occasionally." I slapped my forehead with a palm. "Fact, didn't I see you this afternoon? Southcenter? No. Portage Bay, wasn't it?"

Her voice dropped. Her mouth twisted as if an invisible hand were kneading it. "Get out of here! This affair was designed for friends and relatives."

"Haven't tasted the dip yet."

"Then I'll leave."

"Oh, come on. Stick around, Binnie. You're going to find this amusing. Perhaps the most amusing night of your life."

She didn't betray herself, just spun on a sharp heel and vanished.

"I can smell the chemistry between you two," said Kathy. "Sulfur and rotten eggs."

Veronica Rogers, despite her threat, did not exit the church.

Largely ignored except by some children in stiff clothing, Fred and Maggie reposed in closed coffins in front of the chapel, surrounded by a beard of flowers. Somebody had written an epitaph to them on computer paper and tacked it on an easel beside the bier. When we got close, it proved to be the handiwork of Ashley Phillips. Kathy perused it while I contemplated the crowd. Poor Maggie. Poor Fred.

The half of Seattle that wasn't at the Fat Tuesday celebration was jammed into the room off the chapel, spilling into the aisles and foyer, the overflow making do in the pews. Sprinkled among the faces I didn't recognize were several that I did. Aaron Barbour, in jeans and a jacket, laughing outrageously so that people around him were visibly uneasy. Sheila Balzac, looking prettier than I had ever seen her, speaking to a heavyset man in a yarmulke. Daryl Rittenhouse. Ashley and Brit Phillips. The Rogers clan. Fred Pugsley's mother and father. Some friends or relatives we couldn't identify. Dozens and dozens of grim faces from Micro Darlings, including the security guard who'd let us in Saturday night, along with his jowly wife. The neighbor from across the alley in Laurelhurst was there, her hoary-headed husband beside her. Off in a corner, nobody heeding them, I saw Eric Castle and his son Schuyler. It had taken balls for him to show up, and I noticed Veronica piloted Tad and Lucy around so as to avoid them. Eric did the same thing with Schuyler. They were like magnets with like poles repelling each other. Schuyler's grandparents were at the punch bowls, re-filling timorously, their drab Sunday-go-to-meeting clothes thirty years out of date.

Kathy turned away from the computer printout, eyes glistening. "Ashley must have loved them very much. Read it."

"Later."

Daryl Rittenhouse drifted over and, drinking Kathy in, said, "This isn't the woman you had with you the other night, is it?"

I said flatly, "Maggie didn't do Fred."

"Oh?"

"And she didn't kill herself. I know who killed them both."

Rittenhouse screwed up his face. "Who, for chrissakes?"

"A loving mourner in this very room. Tell me something. Was Aaron Barbour working for Micro Darlings five years ago?"

"Uh, yeah." Rittenhouse gazed across the room at Barbour's laughing form. Barbour had bits of cheese on his lip and Wheat Thin tracks in his beard. "Yeah, I think he was."

"And he rents a little house from your uncle?"

For some reason that shook Rittenhouse. "You've been there?"

"Uh-huh. And seen it. And your uncle. And the bull. You got another relative named Judith Ghee?"

Face flushed, Rittenhouse darted a look at Kathy, bumped his heavy glasses up onto his nose with the knuckle of a thumb, rode his weight up onto his toes, and said, "Say, Black, what the hell have you been doing?"

I shrugged. "Looking for the boogeyman."

"You know what happens to people who put their noses where they don't belong?"

"Suppose you tell me."

"They get burned. It can get very painful."

"That your aunt's boat down off Boyer? Judith Ghee?"

"My mother's. What about it?"

"You live on it or what?"

"Sometimes. I've got a condo in Kirkland. What's it to ya?"

Unhappy with my line of inquiry, he looked up, eyes glazed, then left us, traversing the room. He ended up next to Gunnar Rogers and his son Dennis, both of whom had been watching me since I arrived. When Sheila Balzac meandered over, I told her that Fred had not been murdered by Maggie and that the evildoer was here at the wake. Inside fifteen minutes the congregation was abuzz.

Kathy whispered, "You know what you're doing, Thomas? You know what slander is?"

"Hey, sister, slander is my middle name."

"Not funny." She wore a look of reprimand as she began making small talk with a stooped man she had known in law school. I found a peaceful alcove not far from where Eric and Schuyler were standing and situated myself in a corner, spine to the wall, the way an old-time gunfighter would set up.

They drifted into the alcove by ones and twos, as if to discuss a private deal. Sheila Balzac and Daryl Rittenhouse were first. Next, Ashley and Brit Phillips sidled into the alcove, Brit to chat with Sheila, Ashley to fidget in his trousers' pockets. He wore a swank black suit. He could have been on Broadway. He winked at me. I winked back. Aaron Barbour, clumsy hands laden with free food and drink, gravitated to the alcove also. He was accompanied by the widow Ghee. Eric Castle loitered around the corner, within listening range. Gunnar and his son, Dennis, were the last. Except for Veronica, who stood behind a pillar—close to Eric, though in the crush of mourners she probably didn't realize it.

Rittenhouse glanced around at the flock I'd piped in and spoke loudly, "Okay, Black, what is this horseshit about one of us being the murderer?"

"You people all were willing to get together and decide who was a child molester five years ago," I said. "How about a murderer? You want to find that out?"

"You know something?" Ashley Phillips asked. His spouse, Brittany, molded herself against his long, elegant backside as well as she was able, given her condition. "For godsakes, if you know something, tell us. The police said Maggie did it."

Aaron Barbour's grin went sour. "Hey, what is this? I thought this was supposed to be a wake. We all were going to have fun and get smashed."

'Fred was killed with a tool that used to belong to
Eric Castle,'' I said. ''Almost anybody here had access
to Eric's tools at one time or another. Barbour. Veronica. Gunnar. Rittenhouse. Ashley. Brit. All of you, I'd
bet.''

Brittany Phillips spoke in a voice that lacked courage.
''Me?''

Her husband frowned. ''What are you implying,
Black? That my wife might have had something to do
with Fred's death? I'm not normally a contentious person, but you're getting into sticky territory.''

Kathy barreled around the corner, squeezed through
the crowd, and whispered, ''Thomas, have you flipped?
I thought you were just trying to stir things up. You're
really going to accuse someone?''

''Five years ago Brittany Phillips arrived at work early
one morning and found a picture that disturbed her very
much. Disturbed everyone, since it was a photo that
involved indecent liberties with a minor and only a few
months earlier there had been just such an incident on
the premises Micro Darlings leased. In fact, it involved
her niece. She had a right to be upset. I was led to
believe that nobody was told, that Brit waited until Rittenhouse showed up, and that one by one, as the rest
of you made your appearances, you were escorted into
a conference room, where you were isolated until Rittenhouse confronted you for the first time with what
happened. True?'' Several people nodded their heads.

''Is that true, Gunnar?'' I asked. Peering around un-
comfortably, Gunnar Rogers nodded.

''So you ran the polygraph, and even though you
should have known polygraphs are only eighty-five to
ninety percent accurate, you all proceeded out to the
house of the first person who ran a negative on the test,
correct?'' More nods. People, noting Eric's proximity,
glowered, and I could almost feel the waves of radiating
hatred. ''The way I understood it, everybody wasn't
tested. The crux of the case hinged on, among other

things, the fact that Eric Castle's house was supposedly burglarproof.''

''It was burglarproof,'' said Gunnar Rogers, almost in a shout. ''What are you implying?''

''I'll accept that it was burglarproof. So Eric could get inside. And Veronica could get inside. And supposedly nobody else.''

''The case hinged,'' said Rittenhouse patronizingly, ''on what we found at Eric's place. At Eric's invitation. What's this all got to do with Fred's death? And what do you mean, 'supposedly nobody else' could get in?''

''I'm getting to that. You assumed the stuff couldn't have been somebody else's because nobody else had access to the house. Correct?'' Rittenhouse nodded reluctantly. ''Now, how many of you ever thought, no matter how perverse, that Eric was stupid enough to invite you to search a house he knew was riddled with pornographic pictures?'' Silence. ''Guilty or not, Eric was no moron. Had he been the guilty party, he would never have invited you out there, especially if he had put the pictures there himself.''

''He is the guilty party,'' said Gunnar. ''Nobody else could have put them there. How do you explain that paradox?''

Veronica Rogers stepped around the pillar and blinded me with her hot icy green. I was glad she didn't have a gun, for to judge by the look on her face, she certainly would have emptied it into my major organs. ''Just what the hell are you hinting at, Black?''

''If Eric wasn't stupid, that meant he didn't put those pictures up there in the attic. Only one other person could have.''

Sheila Balzac blurted softly, ''Veronica,'' and the alcove suddenly took on a stunned silence. All eyes turned to Veronica Rogers, who braved it like the hardy lass she was.

''Veronica,'' I said. ''Or somebody Veronica had given the combination to.''

''That's absurd,'' said Veronica, distorting her lower

lip with her teeth, smearing lipstick across her precision incisors. "Nobody knew how to get into that house except myself and my ex-husband. To suggest otherwise is just plain . . . asinine."

"Besides," added Gunnar, rushing to his wife's rescue, "what if somebody else could get into the house? So what? Eric flunked the lie detector. Eric said all those incriminating things. We know he did it."

I said, "If the villain knew in advance there was going to be an uproar at Micro that morning, he might take all the dirty materials he had been hoarding and dump them, right? Maybe in a Dumpster. Maybe someplace else. Perhaps in the home of another possible suspect."

"Yeah, but Eric didn't move them. This is crazy," said Rittenhouse. "I never told anybody about that photo. We just put people into that room one by one. Nobody had a chance to call out. There wasn't even a phone. We made sure."

"You never told anybody," I said. "You sure?"

Glancing around nervously, he said, "Yeah."

"And you didn't leave the building yourself? Or make a call?"

"No."

Brit confirmed this, nodding.

"But you weren't the first to find the photo." All eyes turned to Brittany Phillips. "Brit told me. It was understandable. She was shook up, so she telephoned her boyfriend, and he consoled her. He was good at consoling, wasn't he, Brit?"

"What are you trying to imply? That I lied?"

"You told me yourself the first thing you did was to phone your boyfriend."

"I called him. So what? It didn't hurt anything."

Kathy Birchfield cleared her throat. "Who was your boyfriend five years ago, Brit?"

A tear dribbled out of her eye and crawled down her face. "He told me everything was going to be all right.

I'm glad I called him. Ashley understood me, even then.''

"What are you driving at?" asked Gunnar Rogers. "They caught the bastard. They just never figured out how to get him in the clink.''

"Did they catch him? Until a moment ago there were only two people who could have placed that particular pornography in that particular attic. Nobody had advance notice that the molester had been found out. The stuff had to be Eric's. Or Veronica's. And nobody figured this for a woman's perversion. Up until a moment ago Eric Castle was locked into this. No way out. Now a crack in the scheme appears.''

Gunnar said, "So how would Ashley get into Eric's house? Nobody could get in.''

"Maybe Ashley called somebody else," I said.

"Of course I didn't. You're being perfectly silly," said Ashley Phillips, stroking his temple with the palm of one hand. He moved like a cat licking himself. Shiny black hair; winter clear skin. Kathy couldn't look away. Neither could Sheila. Nor Veronica, whose eyes were getting jittery. "You're stretching a bubble of conjecture way past the bursting point. I'm not even sure I'm following all this.''

"How about if I spell it out for you?" I said. "You go home from work one night, and on your way out a piece of filth falls out of your briefcase or pocket or what have you. The next morning Brit finds it, calls you in tears, and you realize pandemonium is just around the corner. You take any other materials you may have at your disposal and hightail it over to Eric's house, punch in the combination on his burglar alarm, and dump them in the attic. Maybe you're planning to ditch a few more of the little buggers in Eric's office just to make the frame take. Maybe not. Eric falls right in with your plans. He's so upset about the whole thing that he fails the polygraph, which you cleverly decided you would take last. Even more upset now, he invites the entire clan to come out to the old homestead and search to their heart's content. *Voilà*. Instant devastation for Eric. And you're in the clear.''

"We don't have to listen to this claptrap," said Brit Phillips, grasping her husband's lean arm and pulling him toward the vestibule of the church.

"No," said Ashley Phillips. "This is sort of funny. I want to hear him out. Just how do you claim I broke into a burglarproof house, Black? And what the hell does all this have to do with Fred Pugsley's death? And why would anybody set Eric up instead of just dumping the stuff? What was the motive?''

"Veronica can tell us how you broke in," I said. When all heads had turned her way, her face became flushed.

"No.''

I let silence settle onto the little group, then broke it deliberately. "Binnie was having a little fling, weren't you?" She didn't reply, just stared at Gunnar, who looked alternately dubious, angered, and chagrined.

Features chiseled and hard, Eric appeared around the corner behind his ex-wife. She jumped when he shouted, "She wouldn't do that!"

"Tuesday and Thursday afternoons. He knew the combination, didn't he, Binnie? You'd take your kids to the neighbor lady, slide into the shower, pretty yourself up, put *Bolero* on, and wait for the tall, handsome man to punch himself in, so to speak. Tacky, tacky.''

"That's absurd," protested Gunnar Rogers.

Brit Phillips said, "You're dirt, Black. You're implying that Binnie was having an affair with the man who was my boyfriend. And that my boyfriend—now my husband—is a pervert. We all know who the pervert is.''

"Absurd? Veronica has had lots of affairs. She's having one right now, aren't you? Isn't that right, Daryl? This afternoon in Portage Bay. I know. I followed you. I watched. It was touching. I would have stayed to the end, but I wanted some exercise, and I was beginning

to gag. You borrow that sailboat a couple of times a
week, don't you, Daryl?''

"Yeah, so what? People do these things. It doesn't
mean a whole lot. What does this have to do with Fred?
Maybe we should look into this Eric thing, but what
does this all have to do with Fred?''

Sniffling and gasping for air, Brittany Phillips did a
crawl stroke out of the group and disappeared into the
church. Ashley wanted to follow, but I had him on a
string, hooked through the gills.

"Fred was investigating this Eric thing. He never gave
up on it. Even busted into your offices and searched
them when you weren't around, right, Sheila?'' Balzac
nodded woodenly. "Then he picked up Ashley at the
airport Tuesday night. Ashley said he was always doing
nice things like that. That was a lie. Fred never did a
nice thing in his life. Fred had found something of
yours, hadn't he, Ashley? Something you didn't want
anybody else to see. He confronted you with it on that
drive home from the airport Tuesday night. You waited
until the next morning to murder him. He had the goods
on you. He had to be disposed of. The neighbors didn't
hear a car because you jogged up to the house. Nice
touch. Even then you were trying to frame Eric; used
his bike tool. You and Brit were over at the Rogers'
from time to time. You could have picked it up. Maybe
one of the kids was showing you Eric's trophies in the
trunk.

"But it didn't quite work out. Maggie stumbled in
after you had left and hugged Fred, thinking she could
bring him back or whatever. Her clothes got so wet with
blood, she had to take them off. The cops saw her and
tried to pin it on her, and your plan to finish off Eric
by framing him for Fred's murder flew out the window.
You thought you'd picked up all those photos, but you
hadn't. There was one underneath Fred. The cops do a
little work, they might be able to trace it to you. There
were two more upstairs. One of them might even have
your fingerprints on it. And Maggie. She must have let

the word out that she'd found something. You decided
to get it from her and silence her forever. If she com-
mitted suicide, the investigations would cease and you'd
be in the clear.''

''Black, you're psychotic,'' said Ashley Phillips, but
my linking the photos to the police had put a rodent
trill into his throat. ''I feel sorry for you.''

''What if I said Sheila saw those pictures? That Fred
found them in your office and showed them to Sheila?''
It was a long reach, and I was about to fall off my
ladder. Ashley stared daggers at Sheila Balzac, who,
mouth quivering, nearly fainted but eventually held. I
owed her one. She instinctively knew what I was doing
and kept her mouth shut. It took a long time for him to
speak. The room seemed to get heavier, and nobody
was breathing. Outside the alcove the suppressed hub-
bub of the wake continued without us.

''So I had some photos,'' Ashley said, shrugging.
''They were Eric's. I found them in Eric's stuff after the
incident and didn't know what to do with them. Fred
and I talked about it, nothing to it. He didn't accuse me
of anything. He knew Eric was the deviant. I just had
a couple of photos. They were Eric's. It makes more
sense that Fred phoned Eric about them than that he
got upset with me. Fred was like that. He would have
called Eric. The logical person here, if we assume
Maggie didn't do it—and I don't know that we dare
make that assumption—is that Eric did it. Far be it from
me to accuse anyone, though.''

We all sat on that statement a moment.

I said, ''*You* had access to the house. Five years ago
it was you having the affair with Veronica. I have witnesses. You had photos last week, and you had them
five years ago. You were in a position to benefit if Eric
left the company. You each owned a share, and when
somebody left, your share grew. Bet you didn't particularly feel bad about Eric's leaving his wife either. But
that part didn't work out, did it? Perhaps she felt too
guilty to marry you.''

Veronica spoke, eyes transfixed on a spot of lint floating in the air between her nose and mine. Five years before she'd known the culprit in the molestations had to be one of the men she regularly made love to. Nobody else could have gotten into the house. She'd made her choice, and now she had to justify it, publicly. "Black, a man who molests small children is not—"

"Doesn't like women? Doesn't make love like an angel? Is that how you decided? You knew three people had access to that attic. You, Eric, and Ashley. And you decided Eric was the one. How did you choose? You could have saved Eric five years ago, but you kept your mouth shut and watched him go down the toilet while you were building a cushy life for yourself out in the suburbs." For the briefest moment I thought I saw a crack in the facade, thought the granite memorial would split right down the middle; but in the end she didn't flinch or even bat a lash. "Or did you have some other reason to feel Eric had been molesting kids? Speak up. It may be your last chance."

"All the evidence pointed to him, the lie detector test, all of it. Everyone agreed."

"I'll have my lawyers look into this, Black," said Ashley Phillips. "I'm not certain, but I think I've got you by the short hairs. You've accused me of some heinous crimes in front of people. Retribution will be forthcoming."

"Amen. Looking forward to it," I said, drying my teeth for the troops. "Love to get you into court. In fact, I've been planning on it."

If he was guilty, the last thing he wanted was to hash this out in open court, but it hadn't occurred to him until I mentioned it. Ashley turned and walked away from me. So did Gunnar Rogers. The others dispersed, casting looks at each other, all except Eric and a grinning Schuyler. I reached into my pocket, pulled a child's drawing out, and handed it to Eric. He stared at it, the paper twittering in his hands. He gazed across the room, looking for Lucy, but she wasn't in sight.

"You didn't do it, did you?'

"Nobody would believe me. '

"I think they might now."

"After a while I gave up trying to convince them."

"It's over now."

"Like hell. Wait until your wife looks at you the way mine did. Wait until all your old friends are hauling you into court, phoning you up in the middle of the night and asking what you've done to their children. It'll never be over."

"People expect the innocent to assert their innocence. Why didn't you say anything to me when you knew I was investigating this?"

"Listen, man, if one cat's howling on the fence, you throw a shoe at it. A thousand cats? You put a pillow over your ears and go back to sleep. You were just another cat."

"I think I almost understand that."

"Was Binnie really playing around on me when we were married?"

I nodded and watched his eyes squeeze down to shut off the pain. He still loved her.

"And Ashley whacked out Fred?"

"That's the way I read it. Proving it's another matter. Anyway, things might start looking up for you."

"It's hard to believe about Ashley. I knew I didn't do those things, but it's hard to believe Ashley did. He's always been such a swell person. And Fred? I can't believe he killed Fred. I can't."

"People will do a lot of things when they're about to be found out."

When we were finally alone, Kathy grabbed me by the ears—the ears—and said, "Thomas, if you're not right, you're the biggest boob I've ever seen. You just put everything you own or ever will own on the line so he'd confess, and he didn't say diddly-squat. What are you going to do now?"

Removing her hands from my ears, I said, "Calm down, sister. He'll be back."

"I thought you were dead wrong until I saw him glare at Sheila Balzac when you said she knew about the pictures. She didn't, did she?"

"Very astute of you."

"But he didn't know that. That look he gave her was scary. Somebody gave me a look like that, I'd turn and run."

"Sheila almost did."

We mixed for a while, keeping our eyes on the players. Veronica had grabbed the kids and gone off to lick her wounds. Gunnar was speaking to Rittenhouse, possibly about Tuesday and Thursday afternoons, the veins on his neck straining against his starched collar. Ashley Phillips was consoling his tearful wife in a room off the foyer.

Aaron Barbour bustled through the crush and smiled, a fine mash of Velveeta and Wheat Thins in his teeth. "Gotta admire you, Black. You like to put it all on the line, where anybody coming along with a sharp blade can chop it off."

"Some people rappel off tall buildings. I bait people. Bulls and people."

"You're about as fucked up as a soup sandwich. Ashley isn't a child molester. I've known him for years. Anyway, come out anytime. Got about twenty pounds of Aunt Mabel in a meat locker with your name on it."

"Thanks."

After ambling outside, I stood under the portico beside Kathy Birchfield, waiting, watching. Nothing happened. On the center grounds the Space Needle was lit up like an aluminum Christmas tree with a short circuit.

"Think you blew it, Thomas," said Kathy, giving me a gentle squeeze on the biceps to show her support.

"One more turn at bat," I said, watching Ashley Phillips leave the church through a side exit, walk across the street and half a block down to a new Chevy Blazer, which belonged to Rittenhouse. He opened the back and proceeded to sort through some materials, removing some and placing them in his Audi. He moved more like a ballet dancer than the vain record-keeping jogger I suspected him to be.

He looked up at me, as if only just discovering that I was up the street. His breath made fuzzy balloons, and his shouted words carried clearly in the crisp, cold air. "I want you to know, Black. No hard feelings. You're mixed up. You've been in the hospital. I'm not even mad."

"Go snitch free crackers or cloth napkins or something," I said to Kathy.

"Not on your life. I'm with you."

"He won't talk if you're there. I'll get it on tape. Now move."

"Be careful."

"Me?"

24 As I approached the Blazer, my footsteps sounded off like the tick-tock of a wooden heart. Ashley Phillips stopped what he was doing and faced me. It occurred to me that we were a long way from help should anything go awry.

There were just the two of us and a couple of derelicts fifty yards away casting about for a parking meter to jimmy. Beneath the streetlights his skin was flushed and purplish. His suit didn't have a wrinkle. The Italian shoes were spotless. We two, a couple of purple baboons playing out the last inning in a game nobody could win.

"I'm told you checked out of the hospital before the staff was ready to let you. Foolhardy."

"That's me, taking all of life's corners on two wheels."

"I feel sorry for you. I just want you to know, I don't bear any ill will. People make mistakes."

"Who are you trying to kid? There's nobody listening. Just you and me. I know you did it. I've got people who can identify you as having gone repeatedly to the Castle house by the lake. They saw you punching the electronic box on the front of the house. You wore glasses five years ago, didn't you? That threw me off

259

because you switched to contacts. In glasses you fit the description to a T. You had access. The neighbors know it. Veronica knows it. Your big mistake was in confessing you had some sicko pictures for Fred to find.''

"I never make mistakes, Black. You're just flapping your lips."

"People are going to start thinking about it. Your wife is going to have her doubts. She didn't know you had pictures, did she? She's going to wonder. Veronica is the one to be worried about. Think I turned her around. She knew it was either you or Eric. I turned her around. I talk to her another time or two, we might hatch something together. One more thing."

"What's that?" Phillips was sounding deader and deader, stewing in a funk of hopelessness.

"Those were Eric's pictures? From five years ago?"

"That's what I said. So what."

"The Polaroid camera those pictures were taken with wasn't manufactured until two years ago, which in itself will hang you." I'd scored a bull's-eye. I could see it in the way his bony shoulders stiffened, the way the intelligence behind his eyes shut off, the pilot light of his civility snuffed. "I can get the cops stirred up about Fred, too. One of the reasons they didn't charge Margaret was that they found footprints in the yard. Yours? I wouldn't doubt if we found Fred's missing Beretta at your house. And Margaret. You killed her, too, didn't you? That Saturday night at Micro you came in dressed in black and all sweaty. Kathy smelled the same cologne in Maggie's bedroom she'd smelled at Micro. That was you she was smelling. Maggie let out that she'd found some more evidence of Fred's, and you decided to put an end to it. I'll nail you if it takes the rest of my life."

"Black, your imagination would be good in our industry. You could program spy games." He calmly reached inside the back of the Blazer and lifted out a box of manuscripts, carried them to his car, and loaded them in the back seat. I followed, stood behind warily, as if he might lash out with a leg as he bent over.

"In a day or two," I said, "everybody at Micro is going to know those photos came from a camera that wasn't around five years ago. Fun times in the old lunchroom, eh? Wait until the executive john clears out when you unzip."

He returned to the rear of the Blazer.

"You worked in a jail. No woman in the world would hang herself where her feet were still touching the floor. But an ex-jailer would know how effective that could be. Meanwhile, you're going to get a dose of what Eric's been choking down for the past five years. Whispering, funny looks, midnight phone calls, a wife who's not quite sure that glint in your eye is meant for her or the children next door. Live with it. Maybe I can't build a case in court, but I can sure gum up your life. And you can't sue me because you know it's all true. You wouldn't dare drag this into open court."

Folding his long, angular arms across his chest, Ashley leaned against the Blazer, glanced around to be sure nobody was eavesdropping, and looked me over the way a nurse looks over a lesion.

"Sheila didn't even see that picture. You admitted it for nothing, clown. She's one more person who's going to know you did it. And you'll get trapped in more lies."

"Smart guy. Okay, I played with a few kids. So what? What am I supposed to do? Kill myself? I didn't hurt anybody. And Fred? That was self-defense. He wanted to ruin my life. After all we've meant to each other, he couldn't just forget what he found. I had to kill him. What did it matter if I put the blame on Eric? His life was already wrecked. Fred or me. Can you imagine that stubborn bastard wouldn't give me a break?"

"What about Maggie?"

"Hey, I really hated doing that. I really did."

"It's all over. Everyone's going to know what you are when I get finished with you."

Air whistled out his nostrils, and his face slowly grew into one similar to the mask he'd used on Sheila Balzac. "If you were to go bughouse, the people who heard you tonight wouldn't give what you said much credence, would they?"

"The only one nutting out is you."

"That's where you're wrong," Ashley Phillips said, reaching a long arm into the back of the Blazer. He came out with Rittenhouse's crossbow and a quiver of bolts, each bolt tipped with three-way razors for pushing through flesh and meat and stone columns. When I began to move forward, he aimed it at my belly button. It was armed, a bolt in place. He must have prepared it before my arrival. I backpedaled, slowly, so as not to precipitate anything.

"You should be doing loop-the-loops in a rubber room, Ashley. You'll never get away with something like this."

Pulling an index finger delicately along the razor edge of the bolt, Phillips said, "You're the crazy one. You came at me. I was forced to defend myself."

"It won't work."

He clucked his tongue. "When these tragic things happen, there's so much confusion. People don't know what they're seeing. I should know. I've been through several of these events lately. People get so confused. I'm the only one who's going to remember this properly." He was spilling his guts only because he thought he was talking to a corpse.

We were on the sidewalk, and I knew an entrance to the Seattle Center was only a few yards away. He had one easy shot, and if that didn't turn the trick, I had a slim chance: somewhere in that gap between slim and forget it. I wondered if he could reload on the run. No, he would have to stop each time to cock that thing.

Attempting to be stealthy, Ashley Phillips fired from the hip.

He fired before I was ready, before he was even ready, the weapon braced at his waist. He leveled it and let fly. I was already moving toward a tree. The move saved my life. Overcompensating for my jog to the right, he kept sweeping. He fired into the bole of the tree, about fifteen inches in diameter. Had the bolt gone into anything softer, it would still be on its way to Bellingham.

I wheeled and ran.

The smart thing might have been to rush him before he could load up another bolt; but he had, among other things, a handful of razor-tipped bolts, and in my frenzy to keep plasma inside my skin and steel outside it, I ran.

Down the sidewalk, up some concrete stairs and into the Seattle Center, into the dark. Casting a look over my shoulder, I could see that he was giving chase, loading the crossbow and giving chase. Another hurried shot whizzed past my ear so fast I didn't see it until it plowed into a garbage can chained to a light standard. It thonked through both sides of the can and disappeared in the turf.

I tried to recall the layout of the center grounds. The Science Center was to my right, and I didn't want to go in there. It was filled with open spaces and pools lined with pennies, and all the doors would be locked at this time of night.

When I calculated he had his third bolt ready, I began zigzagging, batting away at the bushes as I ran alongside the far right side of the path, heading straight toward the Needle, a miniature golf building to my left, closed down for the winter. He was fleet, quicker than I on the level, as I had somewhat expected, since he jogged and I cycled.

At the open space where the closed amusement section started, I took a hard right, intending to circle around one of the vacant refreshment stands, which were maybe eighteen feet long and about ten wide.

Three grinning Hispanic males watched me running, tourists. I blew through the trio like a moped through a library, upsetting the paper plates they were snacking from, scattering Mongolian rice. One of the men thought we were waltzing, got his feet tangled in mine, and we went down hard.

I heard a thwack and a slow moan, which quickly mutated into a mawkish shriek that ripped the evening in half.

Scrambling to my feet, the sight didn't entirely register until I got behind the food shack. Phillips had fired as I was falling, had missed me, and sent a bolt through one of the men's arms, tacking him to a tattered Grateful Dead poster on the shack. Bone splinters and bits of flesh entertained the wounded man and his slack-jawed friends. I peeked past the back side of the shack. Phillips was circling, his intention to come at me from the path behind.

Timing it so that he was west of the shack, probably up the embankment and in the shrubbery, I moved out onto the tarmac. I needed to be sure he hadn't doubled back. He wasn't likely to botch another shot.

The men were frantic, had no idea how to unhitch their partially ·crucified compatriot. The missile had drilled into the wall and through his arm so that only about a bloody inch of bolt was showing.

Long before I should have, I heard his footsteps behind me. He must have found a hobo path through the shrubbery. Keeping the shack between us as well as I could, I ran back into the macadam path, searching madly for someplace to hide. Phillips was quick.

A shallow duck pond lay at the western side of the Space Needle, between the base of the Needle and the kiddie amusement section, a metal fence and an eight-foot drop the only barrier. Inside the pool in the open spaces away from the drooping willow trees stood a sculpture rising thirty feet, enormous orange metal tubes rising from the water at various angles.

Without hesitating a beat, I let myself down over the wall and sloshed through the water. After I had passed the first steel tube, I tried to place it between my back and my attacker. For thirty splashing feet he didn't get

another shot off. The rocks under my shoes were slimy
and slick, and I went down to a three-point stance twice.

Two women pushing strollers loitered on the far bank.
I was afraid for them, afraid Phillips would airmail one
of those steel-tipped missiles into a baby buggy or a
mother's breast. One of the infants clapped and giggled
at my plight.

I waded out to the right, exposing myself yet moving
the target over so the background was dirt and sidewalk
instead of mothers and buggies. Hands high in the air
for balance, I didn't even realize I'd been hit until the
bolt ricocheted off a rock and dropped into the dirt in
front of me, in front of the lighted gift shop under the
Needle. I knew my coat was torn, but I didn't have time
to think of much else. Smithers hunted deer with a bow.
He claimed those razor-tipped arrows were so clean that
frequently a buck would run long past where he'd been
hit, unaware that he was maimed. It was only loss of
blood that dropped them. The two handsome mommies
gawked, realizing suddenly they were seeing something
more than a goofy drunk frolicking in a pond.

I plowed on and forged into the lobby beside the elevators. A mixture of moony young people gussied up
for dates and oldsters who ate here regularly, the crowd
got a kick out of my trousers, wet to the knees, and my
squishing shoes. When I looked outside the windows,
all I could see were reflections from the lobby. I ducked
into the gift shop among the browsers, cards, Seattle
pennants, souvenirs, and bric-a-brac.

"Listen," I gasped, addressing a button-nosed young
woman in a smock who stood behind the cash register
in a pose that dared people to ask for assistance, "call
the cops. There's a man out there trying to kill me. And
send a medic unit over to kiddieland while you're at
it."

Her cheeks crinkled into a dubious smile, and she
said, "You're kidding."

"Call 'em."

I looked outside. Nothing but reflections and a pair

of old duffers peering in at the merchandise. When I
turned back to the cashier, she was dialing 911, a wary
eye on me. I had turned from an eccentric customer to
a big bad booger before she could say, "You forgot your
change, sir."

"Where are the stairs?" I asked.

She pointed, her fingers arched oddly, still leery.
"But you can't go in there, sir. They're locked."

The shop curved around the base of the Needle as if
it had been fitted inside a giant beveled doughnut, and
I heard something drop and break behind me. Knickknacks. Tinkling glass. Ashley's milky tones carried
through the shop. He was so debonair and carefree I
almost puked. "Excuse me, young lady," he said.
"There's a man chasing me with a gun."

Even now he was setting me up. I felt under my
jacket, my fingers coming out wet and warm and very
red. It didn't feel deep, but it stung when I touched it,
a laceration beneath my armpit. Blood trickled down
my ribs.

I spotted his reflection in one of the beveled windows, the crossbow and quiver held low at his side,
camouflaged under a raincoat he'd picked up somewhere. I was sweating, dripping with it, and the dignity
he maintained, even now, irked me. Yet the one with
the waders and pole in his hand was always bound to
have more pizzazz than the squiggly one with the hook
in his lip. He smoothed his hair. He was staring into
the darkened windows the same way I was. He was
staring at me.

I scrabbled past a crowd of Nikon-carrying Japanese
tourists, and then yelled at them, "Burt Reynolds. Au-
tographs. Burt Reynolds." It worked. They smiled and
pointed, politely stampeding toward Ashley in small,
shuffling steps.

It looked like a broom closet, set into the base of the
wall, shelving on either side. I tried the knob. Foreign
chatter filled the shop behind me. The cashier was

wrong. It wasn't locked. It was cool and airy, and I got up a flight and a half before I even thought about it.

Up. I could go up. He could outrun me on the level, but I could wear him out on a run up. Cyclists ran stairs in the wintertime. Thousands of stairs. If he found me, I would run him, him and his skinny runners' quadriceps. I would run him until he was tripping over his tongue.

The door burst open below me, my last chance for a clean exit blown.

"Black!"

We were alone in the stairway, the night air wafting through open grates along the walls, machinery from the elevators alongside the stairs. I had never been inside the Space Needle stairs before, and as far as I knew, they went uninterrupted to the upper restaurant, approximately six hundred feet. Sixty stories. Several years ago, much to the dismay of the purists, another saucerlike restaurant had been installed about a third of the way up. I had no idea whether that structure obstructed the stairs or not. Or, if it did, whether the doors would be unlocked.

Propelling myself with one hand on the railing, I began ascending. I sprinted the first five or six flights, taking the steps two at a time, bounding gloriously, listening for the sounds of his footsteps as the wind rushed my ears. The sucker didn't have a prayer of keeping my pace. Yet all he had to do was get within one flight, and he'd have a clear shot at my backside. I did a hesitation move on the sixth flight to get a quiet spot to listen and was stunned to see his hand on the rail below.

The bastard was gaining!

I tore up the stairs, gasping, heart thumping in my gut. He had only another couple of steps to make up, and he'd be able to lance me. Even my slight hesitation to listen might have been enough.

Taking the corners hard, I held my hand on the rail and used centrifugal force to help keep from losing speed. Had he not been carrying a crossbow, he probably would have had me already.

On fifteen or sixteen and near collapse, I realized I had forced myself to take the first flights far too rapidly, depleting my oxygen reserves. I felt as if the insides of my lungs were being peeled off a layer at a time. My legs ached, heavy and trembling. I was moving more and more slowly. Any minute he'd pierce my backside. I wanted to stop, but I didn't. I couldn't allow myself to rest.

Now I was taking the steps one at a time instead of two, laboring, moving slowly enough to listen again. I had gained. Thank God.

Still moving, I hesitated for a moment to peek over the railing. His hand grabbed the banister two flights, no, three flights down. It encouraged me. If I managed to slip into some sort of rhythm, I'd be able to clean his clock. I'd go all the way to the top and get there with plenty of time to call the cops and take the elevator down and maybe scan the cartoons in a *New Yorker*. Sixty stories. We had maybe forty left. I sailed right past the lower restaurant. Four flights later I listened. He had bypassed it also. He was going for broke.

When I got the stitch, I was within twenty floors of the top, the lights of downtown Seattle attracting my gaze out the wire mesh. I knew I was losing concentration. The pain knifed into my side. I eased my pace a bit and listened, startled to find that he had gained since my last check. Two flights behind. He didn't sound good, but then, neither did I.

The stitch grew worse, and I clutched my side, hoping the external pressure would alleviate it.

No luck.

In another flight or two it would force me to stop, doubled over in pain unless I could run through it. I forced my breathing, trying to move beyond the pain. But it grew worse, turned to agony.

One more flight.

I staggered; then I stopped, huffed, and pivoted

around to face him. When I braced my hands on my
knees and leaned over to catch my breath, I saw tiny
wisps of steam curlicue off my trousers, damp from the
pond. This was it. Do or die. I couldn't manage another
flight.

 **25** I WAITED AROUND A CORNER, TRY-
ing to quiet my breathing, evalu-
ating the pain in my side, which didn't lessen. Must
have been the hospital stay. I hadn't had a stitch in
months. I could feel my thighs and calves twittering.

His head and shoulders appeared first. He wasn't
looking up, was slogging, winded—he had stamina for
a jogger—the crossbow dragging down his outside arm.
It was cocked and armed, the bolt ready to warm itself
in my gut.

Waiting until the very last instant, until he would see
me if I waited another second, I swung around the railing and leaped. He held the crossbow low, head bowed.
He didn't see me; not at all. Not in time to aim and
fire, not in time to duck. Knees first, I crashed into his
chest, and we both tumbled down to the next landing,
clattering and thumping. I got the best of it, riding atop
his cartwheeling torso, punching him in the jaw once
when I thought of it. Before he could extricate himself,
I had my fingers at his eyes, ready to gouge.

It didn't bother him. He was hurting in other places.
Slowly I untangled myself, got to my hands and knees
without removing my hand from his face, and carefully
surveyed the situation.

270

The quiver that had been across his back had spilled open, and a razor-tipped bolt had pierced him high in the shoulder blade, the bolt pointed toward the outside of his shoulder. The crossbow had gone off, the projectile long gone. I tossed the bow up to the next landing. We both were breathing as hard as two men could breathe. It took awhile before we could get anything out, and then it was in gasps, long takes between each sentence.

"I woulda caught you," he said.

"Doubtful."

"Woulda. I was gaining. That gizmo was damn heavy."

We glared at each other for a while after the exchange. He managed to wiggle up so that he was leaning against the wall, a leg propped on the stairs of the next lower flight. He winced with pain. My stitch was disappearing, and so was my sympathy. The arrow tip had gone in about an inch and three-quarters, looked as if it had snagged on bone.

"Black, you're the luckiest bastard who ever lived. But you still don't have a thing on me."

"We'll see."

He huffed and laid his head back against the wall. "We had a tiff. Your word against mine. You shot that fellow down there, not me."

When I looked down at him, his grin was wide enough to put my foot into. I said, "You took his job. You took his kids. You took his wife. Were you sleeping with her all along?"

"Quit after everybody thought my pictures were Eric's. Vivacious woman, Black. Eric couldn't handle her. Fred did her first." He stopped and breathed hard for a while.

"What did you say?"

"Fred had her. He used to pester her when Eric wasn't around, and one day she relented, more to see what it would be like than anything, I suppose. She never did like Fred, but I guess he had a reliableness and an availability about him that made it seem safe. Too much for Eric to handle. She always was."

"You were going with Brit then."

"So what?"

"And Maggie? Fred I could understand. But Maggie?"

"She called Veronica, and Veronica called Brit. She had some stuff of Fred's. Said she was going to turn it over to the detective. You."

"So you killed her?"

"I put that belt around her neck and just pulled."

I reached into my pocket and brought the recorder out, displaying it for Phillips. He shook his head as the realization of what was happening slowly began to sink in. Holding it down in front of his face, I turned it and aimed it toward him. The wheels inside the machine were still revolving. "No. Black, you bastard. No."

"Everybody you know is going to hear this tape."

"It's faked obviously," said Phillips. "Very clever but clearly a fake. I really don't hold anything against you, Black. You're just mixed up."

As he spoke he shifted, presumably to ease the pain in his shoulder. It took me a second to realize he'd reached into a jacket pocket. By the time I saw the small automatic, he'd flicked off the safety. Damn, he had a gun.

I feinted, kicked, missed. He swung around, and the Beretta barked. Sharp, loud, and ugly. He missed but was already squeezing off another round.

I punted his head toward San Francisco. I didn't make California; but I connected solidly, and he tumbled down another flight of stairs like a wooden puppet. He was very still at the bottom. The pistol was six steps up. He was looking up at me, cognizant, but he didn't even twitch. The crossbow bolt had gone clear through his back and come out his shoulder. I picked up the Beretta. It had to be Fred's.

Collecting the quiver, bolts, and my wet shoe which had flown off at the contact, I stopped and stared out

the mesh at the lighted buildings of downtown Seattle.
"Nice view."

"I need help, Black." Already the side of his face
was beginning to swell. And he hadn't moved an inch.

"You always have."

"That's not my voice on the tape."

"You never give up, do you? Ever hear of voice-
prints? Look at that ferry. Sure is pretty at night."

"You going to get me help or what?"

"I'm thinking about it."

"You'll do the right thing, Black. Won't you?"

I dipped Fred's Beretta into my pocket. "Some of us
try to do the right thing."

We'd been biking on the Marymoor track: Kathy and
myself, Eric and his three youngsters. Now, in Bellevue, we were parked in front of the Rogers homestead.
Eric was inside, turning his kids back over to his wife
after his weekend with them. He came ambling out and
walked over to the truck window. Kathy rolled it down.
He looked at us both for a minute before he spoke. "I
haven't said it yet, but I really don't know how to thank
you, Black."

I shrugged. I'd run out of silver bullets to pass out.

"Actually you should thank Fred. He's the one who
spent five years investigating because he wasn't satisfied. Fred's the one who cleared you and sent Ashley
on his way to prison. And he got killed for his trouble."

"And I hated him. I thought he was harassing me.
Thought he hated me. It's ironic. Everybody's been so
correct with me," said Eric. "If you hadn't played that
tape at Micro, I don't know . . . I never did want the
job back, but I figured . . . Anyway, I've sold my new
series of programs and I'm starting a new company on
my own. I've got Schuyler living with me in Walling-
ford. Maybe I'll get the other kids, too. Someday."

"That what you want?"

He shrugged. "Gunnar loves them, but he wants to
be fair. We're talking joint custody. At least Gunnar and

I are. Binnie hasn't spoken. Hasn't said a word to me since the wake. Gunnar apologized all over the place. Offered to invest in my work, interest-free loans, whatever I needed. He feels awful about the whole thing.''

"I don't understand, Eric,'' said Kathy. "You didn't stick up for yourself very much. Not even at first.''

"If somebody wanted to believe a whispering campaign, I couldn't stop them. I wanted people to accept me for what they saw. Not what people told them. Too goddamn idealistic. I always was. Course, it didn't work out. I ended up with no friends and looking like a sexual psychopath to boot.''

I thought about his ulcer and wondered if his health would recover. He hadn't looked particularly chipper at the track. I had a suspicion it might take several years of hard work before his body repaired itself.

Eric said, "Why did Ashley try to frame me for Fred? I still don't understand that.''

"He was afraid somebody would track down what Fred had been doing and find some of the porno. He figured if they did, pinning it on you would seem logical to a lot of people.''

"I used to think he was the nicest guy in the world.''

"Veronica hasn't said anything?'' Kathy asked.

"Not a word.''

"Perhaps after a while.''

I looked up the hill and saw her watching us from the doorway, stolid, voluptuous, a body built for slow dancing, green gut-wrenching eyes. Despite her beauty, her heart was a cybernetic miracle. She was the type of woman you wanted to kiss or slap, couldn't make up your mind. I was tempted to feed him every last dirty detail about her and Fred, her and Ashley, all those trysts at the house on the lake and in *The Glass Slipper* with Daryl. Their life together had been about as meaningful as the kiss of a whore. I kept my mouth shut.

As we drove away, we spotted Schuyler in the backyard, high in the arms of a mountain ash, perched contentedly. Tad and Lucy stood under the tree gazing up wistfully, neither daring to climb up and dirty their clothes. Slowing, we watched them. "You didn't get much of a Fat Tuesday this year, did you?" I said.

"There's always next year. Will you come?"

"If there're no murders, rattlers, or biker mamas. Come on. Let's go paint your new office."

In the Rogers backyard Eric dashed under the tree, playfully scooped Lucy up in his arms, and fell to his knees in the grass. Lucy wrestled with him while Tad whooped and tackled him from behind. They tumbled in a heap of hugs and laughter, and even from the street we could hear the children's high-pitched giggles. Mom would be upset. Grass stains all around. Schuyler scuttled busily down the tree to join the fray, a grin on his face wide enough to slide a 747 into.

Look for

THE MILLION-DOLLAR TATTOO

a new novel by Earl Emerson
in stores now!
for a glimpse of this new novel,
please read on . . .

I WAS WORKING MY WAY THROUGH A RECURRENT DREAM about a women's softball team when the phone woke me. The voice on the other end of the line was all too familiar and slurred, though not with sleep.

"What time is it, Thomas?" Kathy asked, pushing her pillow over her face.

"Four o'clock."

"Are we waking up from a nooner?"

"It's four in the morning, Sister," I said, peeved at being awakened from the softball dream.

"Good grief. Who is that on the phone? Snake Slezak?"

"Listen," I said into the receiver. "You're drunk. Get some sleep and I'll come over on my way to work."

"It *is* Snake." Kathy slammed her head into the pillow.

His voice sounding slightly metallic and raspy, Snake

said, "There's a woman in my bed. What am I supposed to do, Thomas?"

"There's a woman in my bed, too. If I have to tell you what to do, you've got a problem."

"But she's dead."

"What? Are you sure?"

"Her eyes froze up and she stopped breathin'. She won't leave. I *think* she's dead. Thomas, we gotta get her out of here before she stiffens up."

"How long has she been dead?" Kathy sat up and knuckled the sleep out of her eyes, her dark hair huge from having slept on it.

"I don't know."

"A couple hours? A couple days? Give me a ballpark figure."

"A couple hours, I suppose."

If rigor mortis hadn't set in, she probably hadn't been dead more than two hours, for it generally took two to three hours for the process to begin. It took even longer for it to become complete, maybe eight to twelve hours. The clock across the room said 3:51 A.M. If Snake was telling the truth, she'd died around one or two, perhaps earlier.

"Look, Snake. Hang up and call the medics."

"I ain't callin' no medics. They'll bring the police, and if the police come, I'm afraid I'll shoot one of 'em. Besides, she's long gone."

"Okay. Don't touch anything. Stay where you are and I'll come over."

"Right. But there's something else you should know."

"What's that?"

"She's an alien."

"What? Mexican?"

"I'm a little too drunk to explain now."

"Drunk might be the best way, Snake."

"Damn it, man. She's from another galaxy."

Kathy was watching me in the dark. "Are you okay, Snake?" I said.

"You think I don't know it sounds crazy? Come over and look at her. She don't even look American. She's from outer space." The line was silent for almost thirty seconds.

Snake Slezak was in the habit of playing gags on his friends, at times elaborate gags, and I had to admit a dead woman from outer space was the sort of stunt he might pull, yet his voice was strained, his words halting and tremulous, and this didn't sound like a joke.

"Thomas? You there?"

"I'll be right over. Sit tight."

"Promise you won't tell Kathy."

"Kathy's right here. She already heard."

"And when you come, bring a jumbo freezer bag, okay?"

"Say again?"

"We'll stuff her in your freezer until we can make a deal with a museum. You got one of those big chest freezers, right? She'll fit in there perfect."

"You at your new apartment?"

He grunted.

"Ten minutes." I hung up. He'd been flush lately, rolling in dough, had a new apartment, a new Cadillac, lots of new girlfriends, as well as several new teeth.

"You're not going somewhere, are you?" Kathy's voice was slurred with sleep.

"You want to come?" I asked.

"Come where? What's going on?"

"Snake thinks he has a dead woman in his bed. He says she's from outer space."

Kathy sat up and dropped her legs over the edge of the bed. "Oh, boy."

"He's soused and he sounds confused."

"I wouldn't miss this for the world." Kathy gave a

short sigh and walked across the hall to the bathroom. "You know, Snake should have a psychiatrist on call. Like those daredevil car-jumpers on motorcycles who have an ambulance standing by. Snake should have a psychiatrist and a bunch of guys in white coats and crew-cuts following him around. This was bound to happen."

Kathy came back into the bedroom wearing a pair of jeans and nothing else, turned on the light, began bending over the opposite side of the unmade bed searching through the bedding for her nightshirt, an oversized football jersey. "Why aren't you getting dressed?" she asked.

"Wanted to make sure you found whatever you were looking for."

Kathy gave me a tiny smile and continued digging through the bedclothes. "Quit grinning. You look like a cat in a shrimp factory. And put your pants on."

I removed a pair of jeans from a chair back, sat on the edge of the bed, and began tugging them on. "How did Snake sound?" she asked.

"Quite reasonable, considering. A little swacked, but quite reasonable."

She found the football jersey and let it drift down over her outstretched arms. "Snake has always believed in little people from outer space, hasn't he?"

"I wouldn't get too revved up. This is probably a gag."

THE MILLION-DOLLAR TATTOO
by Earl Emerson

Published in hardcover by Ballantine Books
Available in your local bookstore.